Rajesh Parameswaran

I AM AN

EXECUTIONER

RAJESH PARAMESWARAN's stories have appeared in *McSweeney's*, *Granta*, *Zoetrope: All-Story*, *Five Chapters*, and *Fiction*. "The Strange Career of Dr. Raju Gopalarajan" was one of three stories for which *McSweeney's* earned a National Magazine Award in 2007, and it was reprinted in *The Best American Magazine Writing*. He lives in New York City.

I AM AN EXECUTIONER

◆ *Love Stories* ◆

Rajesh Parameswaran

B L O O M S B U R Y

LONDON · NEW DELHI · NEW YORK · SYDNEY

First published in Great Britain 2012
This paperback edition published 2013

Copyright © 2012 by Rajesh R. Parameswaran

Selected stories in this work were originally published in the following:
'Elephants in Captivity' in *Five Chapters*; 'The Infamous Bengal Ming' in
Granta; 'The Strange Career of Dr Raju Gopalarajan' in *McSweeney's*;
and 'Demons' in *Zoetrope: All Story*.

The moral right of the author has been asserted

Bloomsbury Publishing, London, New Delhi, New York and Sydney

50 Bedford Square, London WC1B 3DP

A CIP catalogue record for this book is available from the British Library

ISBN 978 1 4088 3114 4

10 9 8 7 6 5 4 3 2 1

Printed and bound by CPI Group (UK) Ltd, Croydon CR0 4YY

www.bloomsbury.com/rajeshparameswaran

*For my parents and
my brother*

✦ CONTENTS ✦

I AM AN
EXECUTIONER

THE INFAMOUS
BENGAL MING

THE ONE CLEAR THING I CAN say about Wednesday, the worst and most amazing day of my life, is this: it started out beautifully. I woke up with the summer dawn, when the sky goes indigo-gray, and the air's empty coolness begins to fill with a tacky, enveloping warmth. I could hear Saskia and Maharaj purring to each other at the far end of my compound. I'd had to listen to their cooing and screeching sex noises all night, but it didn't bother me. I didn't know why yet, but I realized: I was over it. Saskia could sleep with every tiger in the world but me, and I wouldn't mind.

I stretched and smacked my mouth and licked my lips, tasting the familiar odors of the day. Already, I somehow sensed that this morning would be different from all the other mornings of my life. On the far side of the wall, hippos mucked and splashed, and off in the distance the monkeys and birds who had been up since predawn darkness started their morning chorus in earnest, their caws and kee-kees and caroo-caroo-caroos echoing out over the breadth of our little kingdom. These were the same sounds I heard morning after morning, but this morning, it was all more beautiful than ever; yes, this morning was different. It took me a little while to puzzle out the reason, but once I did, it was unmistakable:

I was in love.

It wasn't with one of the tigers in my compound—no, I had exhausted the possibilities of our small society long ago, and other than Saskia, there hadn't been any new arrivals in years. In fact, the object of my love wasn't another tiger at all. I was in love with my keeper, Kitch.

I know it sounds strange. It kind of caught me by surprise, too, but there really wasn't any avoiding the conclusion.

And it was all the stranger because I had known Kitch for years. When I was a cub, he had been something like an assistant to my first keepers. He had thick hair then, and he was skinny and nervous. It was amusing to see him struggle to keep a clear path between himself and the compound door, in case he needed to make a quick escape. It's true what they say about us: we can smell fear, and that's why I noticed him. I was nervous around people then, too, and his manner piqued my particular interest.

Over the years, other keepers came and went, tigers disappeared and new ones arrived, but Kitch was always there. He grew a moustache. His cheeks got round and his belly filled out. His hair went thinner and thinner every time he took off his cap. He shaved his moustache. He lost the wariness that I had once found so intriguing.

His manner changed, his appearance changed, but he was always the same sweet Kitch. And that Wednesday I had woken up and realized: Kitch. Kitch! I love Kitch. Realizing I loved Kitch was like realizing that a bone you have enjoyed chewing for months is actually the bone of your worst enemy. The bone hasn't changed, nor your enjoyment of it, but suddenly things are seen with a whole new perspective. Actually, that's a very negative example, but the point is this: I had just discovered a deep and endless love for the best friend I had ever had in my life.

I should probably clarify. This wasn't the sort of love like when you see a hot new cat and can't keep your claws off her.

I didn't love Kitch like I had loved Saskia, not with the same, shall we say, roaring passion. This love wasn't as agitating.

This was a different love. Every morning, when the big metal doors opened in the fiberglass rock, and pound after pound of cow meat and fresh organs came slithering down the passageway, whose face was there in the dark distance, shovel in hand? Kitch's. When Maharaj growled and got restless and came looking for a fight, who was the first to hear his shrieky howls, to fire a water hose and scare him off me? Kitch. I was inexhaustibly interesting to him, and he was an inexhaustible curiosity and a comfort and joy to me.

I think I'd call that love.

And once I realized I loved Kitch, everything else in the world seemed to make so much perfect indescribable nonsensical sense. Saskia rejecting me; fiberglass walls; lonely, zoo-wandering old ladies; little children eating caramel corn; cockatoos and monkeys; and everything under the sun, so funny and strange, and I just loved it all. I had food and water and friends and Kitch. I really didn't need much more than this, did I?

It's a little embarrassing even to think back on it. That was Wednesday morning.

It didn't take long for things to take a turn for the worse. The first sign was when I walked to the fiberglass rock down which my food usually came slithering, leaving a trail of red, wet glisten. This morning I walked to the rock, looked up, and waited. Nothing came. I sniffed and I waited. I closed my eyes and opened them.

No food.

I waited some more. And I waited and I waited. I started to play a game: I would shut my eyes for a few moments at a time, and while my eyes were closed I would convince myself that as soon as I opened them, the food would be there. I kept them closed for longer periods each time, but the food never arrived.

Now I was very hungry, and when I'm hungry my head hurts.

In fact, it pounds. I shut my eyes firmly and tried to sleep it away, but the sun was quickly becoming unbearably hot—this was the middle of August—and I didn't want to go in search of shade lest I miss the food when it finally came, and Maharaj, finished with his own meal but greedy still, would come and pilfer it.

So I lay down right there, under the sun, and tried to quiet the pounding in my head. By this time the people had started to arrive—not just a few early morning walkers, but thick hordes of people, huge summer-vacation swarms, three or four deep, five or six herds of summer campers alone, plus tourists and regulars.

Normally, I don't mind the people who visit the zoo. They have their business, I have mine. They come, watch for a few minutes, point and stare, talk about me, eat their ice creams, whatever, I don't care. But today there were so many of them, and they were so loud, and I was so hungry. My head was pounding and I was just trying to relax, to stay calm and wait for my food, but they kept talking; and some little kid started to scream, "Wake up! Wake up, tiger! Wake up!" And then a whole chorus of kids joined him. "Wake up, tiger! Wake up!"

I might have been able eventually to block them out and fall asleep, but right then I smelled Saskia, and that smell made me perk up. She was walking directly toward me, with that little sashay, that little walk of hers. I loved to contemplate the fluffy patch of white fur right beneath her tail, and the way her tail brushed over it lightly as she swayed from side to side to side. As I said, I was over her. I was totally fine with the idea of her together with Maharaj, fucking Maharaj. But that didn't mean I had to stop appreciating her walk, that didn't mean I was prohibited from inhaling a deep whiff of her gorgeous aroma as she ambled toward me.

I purred to her, very casually. Just a "Hello there, Saskia" kind of purr. I waited for her to return the greeting, but she didn't even look at me. She walked past me like I wasn't even there.

Now, this annoyed me. It's one thing for her to sleep with

Maharaj. That's her business and her prerogative. But to ignore me like that, as if we were no one to each other—that was too much. I felt a little stupid for having let myself get carried away with admiring her walk and everything, and just to show her that she had put me out of sorts, I snarled. It was a small snarl, accompanied by a little swat of my paw: a warning swat. There was no way I could have made contact. But when she saw me lift my paw, she jumped around and roared so loudly that I swear to God I almost pissed right where I stood. All right, I actually did piss. Then she walked away as cool as could be.

I could hear the schoolkids laughing at me now, but I ignored them and curled around and lay down again. Then I heard a familiar noise in the bushes, and I started to get nervous because it was the sound of Maharaj. Maharaj is a massive beast of a cat. He has almost three times my bulk, so he makes a lot of noise when he moves. He must have heard Saskia's growl and was coming to check out the situation.

Maharaj took his time, moving real slow, hefting his huge body through the brush, and I could smell him now—it was definitely Maharaj, so the fear and the pressure were kind of building up inside me. I was debating: Should I try to get away, and risk attracting his attention; or should I sit still and stay as quiet as possible and hope he'd ignore me?

I decided to make a move for it, but this turned out to be the wrong decision. As soon as I got up and started to walk, I heard Maharaj break into a run, and in three quick bounds—boom, boom, boom—his heavy body was on top of mine and his claws were in my back and his teeth were sunk deep into my ass.

I screamed and writhed, but he kept me pinned down for thirty seconds or a minute, during which time I heard him fart, casual, loud and stinky, as if to demonstrate how relaxed he was, how little effort it took him to keep me locked down and in pain. Finally, he released me, as calmly as you please. He got up and started to walk away. (He didn't even look at me—just like Saskia.) He paused in front of the metal door in the fiberglass rock where I usually got my food. He crouched down and sent out a fat stream of piss. That smell would stick to that rock for days, and he knew it.

At this point I was thinking: Kitch. I just want Kitch. I just want him to show up and salvage this day and restore it to its original promise. I want Kitch to bring me my food and wash my rock. I want Kitch to hang around for a few minutes and keep Maharaj away from me. I want to hear Kitch's voice flattering me and telling me what a good cat I was, and telling me what to do. Actually, it would have been fine if Kitch didn't do any of these things. He could have forgotten the food and said not a word to me, for all I cared. I just wanted him to be there. I just wanted to see his face for a few seconds, just to look at him. In fact, even thinking about Kitch's pink face made me feel better, gave me a feeling of hope and calm, and made the throbbing in my ass and my head fade a little. He would be here soon, I knew it.

I settled down again and closed my eyes. The noise of the crowd also settled, finally, into a distant hum and chatter like it usually did, like a sonic blanket over the world, and in a little while I managed to fall asleep.

When I woke up it was gray and cool, a bank of clouds having moved in over the sun. My headache was better, but now my whole torso ached from hunger. I sniffed around the metal door, but there was still nothing there but the odor of Maharaj's catpiss.

Kitch still hadn't arrived. I couldn't believe it.

At that moment, I heard a familiar noise wafting over the moat that separated me from the visitors:

The river is chilly and the river is cold, Hallelujah
Michael, row the boat ashore, Hallelujah.

Oh, God, I thought. Not the "row-your-boat" lady, not today of all days. She sat down on the bench, sweatered and stinking, hair astray, grinning with her broken teeth. I could smell her from where I sat!

I roared at her instinctively, but she didn't shut up. In fact, she let out a whoop and a holler and sang all the louder.

The river is deep and the river is wide, Hallelujah
Milk and honey on the other side, Hallelujah.

I got up and paced back and forth, pausing every now and again to glare, but she wasn't intimidated in the least. She sang and she sang and she sang. After maybe half an hour, the singing faded into soft, incoherent chatter, until finally she slumped low on the bench and started to snore.

Still, the day dragged on, and the sun had barely even crested in the sky. I felt a painful knock! knock! knock! in my head, and looked up to see the teenage zoo attendant banging his litter stick against the bench, trying to rouse the row-your-boat lady. Finally, she woke up and walked quietly away.

Kitch, I kept thinking. Kitch Kitch Kitch Kitch Kitch.

And just then, I saw Maharaj rising over the hill again, moving steady and fast, fairly bristling for another confrontation. What had I done this time? I kept repeating Kitch's name like a mantra. My head was about to explode into a million pieces. It hurt so bad I could barely move it from one side to the other, and Maharaj was moving in for the kill, ready to carve up my rump and shit on my lair for good measure. And just at that moment, just as the pressure in my head was reaching the point where my brains felt like they would liquefy and boil and shoot from my ears in jets of steam, just as Maharaj crouched down for the pounce, just as all these things were about to happen, the people door creaked open and who was there but Kitch!

It was really him, his red face aglow in the sunlight, and I almost jumped into the air with delight. Maharaj turned and galloped away to hide. The pain in my head melted into some pink, loving bliss. Where was my hunger? Where was all the gloom and trouble of the day? It was all gone. Kitch was here!

I paced back and forth and meowed, like a lovesick lynx. I ran around in a circle and bit my tail. I peed in a long, hot stream, with a big grin on my face. I paced up and down and up and down again, then I rolled on my back and let my tongue loll out. And then I popped upright and roared. It was Kitch! Yes, Kitch was here! And I loved him! And he was here!

Little did I know, the most horrible thing was yet to happen.

Kitch was still standing near the door. In fact, he seemed, for some reason, unnaturally cautious. He hadn't advanced toward me at all, nor had he called out to return my greetings, and that's when I realized there was someone with him—an older man with thick glasses, and wearing white rubber gloves on his hands. Kitch began, finally, to walk to one side of me, slowly, while trying to shield this other, nervous, man from my view.

Well, I had no time for this nonsense. Kitch was here, and I had something to tell him. I loved him, and my love couldn't contain itself, and I wanted to make Kitch feel it, too. I pranced right up to Kitch, to just about three feet away from him, as close as I had ever been.

I'm here, Kitch, I meant to say; and I love you.

When I jumped forward like this, the man with glasses behind Kitch gripped Kitch's shoulder hard and said something I couldn't quite hear, and Kitch yelled at me sharply. And then Kitch did something I couldn't believe. He had a long stick in his hand—he always carried it, but I'd never seen him use it before. Now he raised this long stick high above his head and brought it down hard on my nose.

I yowled and backed away, stunned. I couldn't at first understand what had happened. There was a sharp, reverberating pain between my eyes; the world before me seemed to split into two or three identical sharp-edged versions of itself, then everything became clouded in hazy splotches of red.

Slowly, my senses returned to me. I began to realize what had happened, that Kitch had actually hit me, that he had hit me hard in front of this new person. But why? What had I done? I had only been trying to show how much I loved him.

Now I began to feel very bad—not just the pain in my nose,

but a different, difficult kind of anguish. Why would Kitch do a thing like that? Didn't he appreciate me? After I had wanted nothing more all day than to see that beautiful fat face and to love him, even though he had ignored me since yesterday, even though he had left me all alone and hadn't bothered even to feed me? All that love he could have had for the taking, but instead he'd gone and done a thing like this: he'd hit me! I was embarrassed and ashamed, and my ears began to run hot with blood. And then I began to feel angry.

And all at once the anger welled up inside me so sharp and fast, filling me like a hot liquid, and before I knew what was happening, I took a huge leap and tackled Kitch. We fell down with a hard bang to the ground, my claws holding him fast—and in a way, it felt good to hold him like that, a powerful kind of feeling. And then I bit him, just once, hard and quick.

It happened so fast, and it wasn't at all intentional. At least I don't think it was intentional. It didn't feel intentional, but to be honest, it didn't quite feel accidental either. It was somewhere in between. I was on him and I bit him—just once—and then I stepped away, all in the blink of an eye.

The old man behind him screamed and retreated behind the people door; and then I blinked and looked down at where Kitch was lying.

I had bitten him on the neck, and I saw there were two round, black holes where my teeth had entered him. And now two thick streams of blood began to spout out of those two holes. Kitch was staring at me with a concerned look, his mouth was moving up and down, and now blood was coming out of his mouth as well.

I couldn't quite believe what I was seeing. Just a few seconds ago Kitch was standing up and healthy and I had been so happy to see him, and now he was lying on the ground with blood spilling out of his mouth because of something I had done. This hadn't happened. This couldn't be happening. I had never hurt anyone in all my life. I didn't even know I had the power to take a man down so deftly. The blood was spreading black and wet around him.

Now, I knew I had to put a stop to this. I had to reverse whatever this was that had happened. I ran up to Kitch, and I saw that he was scared of me now. I licked his neck from where the blood was coming and tried to make the blood stop. Kitch feebly pushed and tried to kick at me, but I ignored him and kept licking. I licked and I licked, but the blood kept pouring out, and so I licked faster.

And as I licked for what seemed like minutes, I slowly became conscious of the fact that there was no way my licking was going to stop this blood from pouring out. And yet I couldn't stop licking. I didn't want to stop licking, because another surprising realization was forming in the back of my mind, something that had never even remotely occurred to me before, a realization that made me want to lick and lick faster, and keep licking forever. The realization was:

Kitch's blood was delicious.

As soon as this thought formed itself in my mind, I jumped back in horror. This was Kitch's blood I was drinking—Kitch, whom I loved! What was I doing?

I turned around to look for help. Saskia and Maharaj were standing at a distance, staring with eager curiosity, but neither of them made the slightest move to help me. I knew they were too cautious to get involved, and I couldn't be bothered to convince them.

I looked then to the other side of the moat, where dozens and dozens of people were staring at us and talking and pointing in alarm. One of these people could surely help Kitch, I thought. I ran up and down and roared, and tried to get their attention, but none of them made the first effort to cross the moat and help us. In fact, some of them started to throw things at me—paper cups full of soda, little rocks—and to yell. To hell with them, I thought. When I turned back around to check on Kitch, I saw that the old man with glasses had crouched down and was trying to do something to my friend. Was the old man helping? Was someone helping at last? I ran back to check, but as soon as I did so, the old man fell backward and scrambled hurriedly out of the people door, leaving that door swinging wildly behind him.

Poor Kitch! Nobody would help him. His eyes were open and he was pale. The blood from his neck had slowed to a trickle and the ground around him was soggy like a three-day rain. His lips were moving so slightly, and then they stopped moving, and his eyes just stared up. I licked his sweet face, but he didn't respond. Oh, Kitch! What had I done? I had to find help for him, if it was the last thing I did. I turned and ran out of the people door—I had never been outside the people door before, but I didn't even think twice about running out of it.

There were hundreds of people outside—literally hundreds—but why wouldn't any of them stop to help me? They all ran away, as if terribly frightened of something, everywhere I looked. What mysterious terror could have overtaken the zoo's entire human population, on this day of all days? What could be so horrible that it would keep them from helping Kitch? Had an elephant escaped?

The situation finally became clear to me: I was Kitch's only hope. I ran back to the door of my compound, but as soon as I got there, I saw a bright flash and heard a blast. When the smoke cleared and my ears stopped ringing, I saw that a tall, thin man had kneeled down very quietly behind the popcorn stand across from my compound. He held a long gun in his hands. He had been waiting for me, apparently, and now he fired again.

I crouched down and stayed very still. He fired a third time, and I heard a loud crash behind me. I tried to lunge toward him, but then he fired once more, and the blast came so close that my face burned with its heat, and I had no choice but to turn around and run.

I ran and I ran, and the people around me screamed and ran,

too, and I ran behind these people, and then I ran alongside them, having nowhere else to go; and finally I ran away from them. I kept running until I had no idea where I was anymore. There were no animals and no people: just a long ribbon of black, with objects rushing by, things on wheels that groaned and squawked and growled. Every few minutes I heard—or thought I heard—the crash and fire of the tall man's rifle that had almost burned me moments earlier, and then I ran even harder. I ran alongside those fast-rolling things, and they swerved and smashed and croaked and honked. I kept running and running, not sure where I was headed, just desperate to get away from the madness at the zoo, the madness that was my life, and hoping still to find some help, somehow, for Kitch.

I ran until I could barely pick up my legs any longer, and each breath raked my lungs with sharpened claws. I slowed down and looked around me and saw that the rolling objects had grown, finally, sparse and distant. I saw wide grassy expanses, with small houses set back nicely on the neat grass. Everywhere I looked: houses and grass, nicely spaced, as far as the eye could see. And this vista, the longest vista I could remember ever having seen, stirred me with a strange exhilaration. I could run as long and as far as I wanted here, with no wall to stop me! And I did run. As tired as I was, something in my heart stirred me to run again, in great leaping strides. It was a strange feeling—to be on the run; to be worried about Kitch, whom I had hurt; to be away from the only home I had known; and yet to feel this strange and almost terrifying euphoria. On one of these great lawns, behind a small house, I was gratified to see a huge ice-blue pool of water. I stopped here and drank as much as I could hold. Then I put my very head into the pool and lifted it out, sopping and cool. And now the pull of sleep was overwhelming, so I sank down where I was and closed my eyes.

But the sleep was brief and fitful. On the backs of my eyelids, I saw again the image of Kitch bleeding and struggling on the ground; I saw the man with thick glasses and rubber gloves, reaching those gloved hands toward me. I saw Maharaj and Saskia, staring at all this with strange glee on their faces. Finally, I heard the soft steps of the man with the rifle, and heard the sharp lightning of his gun, and I woke up with a start.

Was he really nearby, or had that been part of the dream? The wide, open vista which a few moments before had brought me a feeling of elation now seemed fraught with danger. I was too exposed here. That quiet man with his long gun was probably this moment lining me up in his sights.

The pool where I had drunk sat right behind a small house or building. I crept up to it and sniffed for any danger. It was hard to smell anything in this place, but an odor of humans seemed to linger in the air, like it did at the zoo, wafting from a distance; and this smell reminded me of the comfort of my home. I pushed and shoved at the glassy doors of the building until I found an access that gave at my pressure, and quietly, I stepped inside.

The house was shadowy and silent, and walking on the soft, furry floors, I came to a cavelike room, dark and quiet and cool, and here, for the first time, I fell asleep and slept so that I forgot myself, for a short time at least.

I woke up well rested, and eager to resume searching out some help for Kitch. But when I opened my eyes, I saw that the room was brightly lit, not dark, as it had been earlier. There were colored pictures on the wall: red-nosed clowns carrying motley balloons, just like I had seen some days in the zoo. On one side of the room was an open-topped cage raised on small stilts, and from inside the cage came the strangely calming sounds of a murmuring human cub—again, another sound I was well used to hearing in my home.

But before I noticed any of these things, of course, I noticed the woman standing across the room from me. She was a full-grown human, with brown curly hair and pink skin, like Kitch's skin. Her back was against the wall and she was inching toward the cub's cage with small sideways steps.

I lifted my head from my paws, my nose quivering with

excitement, my ears and the hair on my back rigid with attention. When she saw me perk up, the woman paused where she was standing, and took a sharp breath inward. Her arms were spread behind her, and her fingers were splayed backward with their tips resting against the wall. She seemed to force herself to breathe again, with great, trembling deliberation. Finally, she released the wall and began to walk once more, slowly, toward the cage.

A cat has an instinct for such situations, and my instinct quickly told me: this woman was mother to the crying cub. Normally, I would have thought that she'd be a threat to me only insofar as she would try to protect her young, but my recent experiences had warned me that humans were dangerously unpredictable, and I had better be careful of her regardless.

I rose and stepped, very slowly, in a direction opposite to the direction that the woman was walking—that is, I walked away from the cub's cage—and the woman stalked carefully toward her cub, and like that we circled the room warily.

The baby human was murmuring in the softest, most innocent way, and in fact I wanted this mother to take it and care for it. Like most cats in the zoo, I considered myself an orphan. Where I came from, who my mother was, I have no recollection. But as I walked that strange duet with this cautious human mother, I had a brief and visceral flash of an older female tiger, a warm and orange-colored softness, a light and muscular embrace. I felt my legs quiver beneath me, and then I had another brief flash of memory: a strong blow to the face, like the blow that Kitch had given me; a fast run through the brush, a panic of voices.

Now I felt dizzy with strange emotion. And that human woman must have sensed my unsteadiness. She took the opportunity to move quickly toward her own cub, and with arms shaking terribly, she reached inside and pulled out the gurgling thing.

Her sudden movement brought me back to my senses. I turned swiftly, to keep a track on her actions; and when she saw me move like that, the woman let out a terrifying shriek; and in her panic she allowed her little one to slip right from out of her hands.

What happened next happened so quickly I can barely describe it. I saw the fleshy child tumble toward the ground, and in one instinctive surge I lunged toward it.

The next thing I knew, the tiny human dangled, upside down and crying, from my mouth; I held it only by the crinkled piece of cloth it wore around its bottom.

The mother stood a few feet away from me, and she cried out now even more uncontrollably than her cub did, and her cheeks were flushed bright red. I had never seen a human so upset before; I had no idea how she would behave now.

I started to move forward, thinking I would return her offspring to her, but as soon as I lifted my paw to move, she yelled and quivered more alarmingly than before, so I stepped back again.

Now I really didn't know what to do. I couldn't move in any direction without sending the woman into further hysterics. I just stood there blankly.

When it began to seem that our terrible, nervous stalemate might last forever, this woman ended it in a totally surprising way. She slowly bent down and picked up a couple of wooden blocks, baby's toys. She got up and flung them at me hard.

The blocks hit me sharply on the flank, and I backed off into a crouch. The woman seemed to gain her courage back when she saw me cower. She started to pick up anything she could get her hands on—plastic things on wheels, blocks of many colors, soft and furry shapes resembling bears and lions and people—and she rained these objects on me in a continuous, angry hail.

As soon as I got over my surprise, I began to realize that as hard as she threw these objects, they didn't really hurt me. And more often than not, they hit wide of their mark, anyway. Frankly, I was more concerned that, with her wild arm, she would hit her own cub—and in fact this happened: even as I tried to curl around and protect it, a high-flying train flew over my head and bounced off the piss-wet leg of the little one.

Now I was thoroughly annoyed. I let the cub drop onto the pillowy floor and turned around and roared at the mother with all the might of my hot and humid lungs. Then I stepped toward her and roared again as loud as I was able to.

As I said, humans are so unpredictable. As soon as I roared like this, the curly-haired lady collapsed as instantly and softly as a pile of feathers from a startled bird. She fell to the ground in a dead faint.

After a few seconds, I gathered the courage to approach her inert body. I bent down, sniffed her, licked her face, but she didn't wake up.

Now what was I to do? The cub had begun roaring, wailing and crying, rolling this way and that on the floor. It didn't seem right to leave it there so helpless, with its mother lying unconscious. I went back to the little one and sniffed it. I had thought that Maharaj was an ugly-smelling beast, but this human cub smelled terrible. I licked its pudgy, salty face, but this had no comforting effect. Finally, I picked it up again by its soiled cloth. I pushed my way back out the door through which I had entered the house. I went to the ice-blue pool where I had enjoyed such a refreshing drink a few hours previously, and I held the baby human's face to the cool water, thinking perhaps it was thirsty.

But it didn't reach for the water—in fact, it seemed a little frightened of it. So I took the liberty of dipping its face into the liquid, ever so gently. But now the little thing coughed and spat, and began crying all the louder.

With this loud crying, my pounding headache from earlier that morning began to creep back. I also worried that the loud noise would draw the attention of people in the neighboring buildings, or of the man with the rifle, who I was sure, even then, was stalking me. I thought to leave the little one there and run away, but I couldn't bear the thought of this helpless, unde-fended, motherless cub in the open. Really, something had to be done, and quickly, to quiet this confounding little human. I admit I don't have the instincts of a mother, and for a long time I had no idea what to do.

Then I had a stroke of inspiration. I laid the cub down softly on the grassy lawn. I opened my mouth wide and took its whole head, gently, inside my own mouth, and in this way I picked it up again.

There! The sound of the cub's crying was considerably muf-fled. My mouth also provided a kind of warm and comforting womb for it. And soon, in fact, the flailing arms and legs of the little one stopped moving, the cries in my mouth softened into comforted whimpers, then finally into silence as it drifted to sleep.

Only when I released the cub's head, and laid him gently out on the grass again did I realize what I had done. Yes, the baby human had stopped crying, but it had stopped breathing, too! I had stupidly, inadvertently, recklessly suffocated it. Oh, God. I picked it up and shook it left and right. I dropped it down and roared at it and then picked it up and swung it about some more, hoping somehow to wake it.

By the time I finished, the cub was no more alive than it had been when I started, but its body was considerably worse for wear, with little rips here and there, dislocated joints, bruises spreading like lakes, and puncture marks everywhere, most upsettingly (for me) in its right eye, which dribbled a colorful syrup.

I felt sick to my stomach. How did I keep doing this, time after time—killing people unintentionally? What was wrong with me? Was I evil?

I picked the human up again by its filthy cloth, this limp little human whose head I had crushed, and carried it away with me, dangling from my teeth. Now I had two people to fix, and at least I was comforted by this notion: If I could find someone to help me fix this cub (who was light, and easy to carry), then I would know there was hope for Kitch.

(And yes, I couldn't help but taste the blood of this human; it tasted even sweeter than Kitch's blood. But even though I had eaten nothing for a full day, the thought never crossed my mind to eat this child. To be precise, it crossed my mind once, but I quickly put the sick notion out of my head.)

I walked through the streets of that place, dangling that dead, dripping human baby before me like the night watchman in the zoo carried a lamp in the dark, and I saw no other creature. There was no one who could help.

I must have walked another quarter day until I reached a vast sea of resting vehicles, and a large building that was thronged with people. I walked toward this throng—and again, people screamed and ran away from me—but I was so inured by now to this reaction that I simply ignored it. I was looking for that one person who would see me, and stop, and know what to do—that person who would know how to help this cub and to help me and to help my friend—my love—Kitch.

I pushed my way into the building and people yelled and ran away from me in every direction, but I calmly walked forward. People carried bags of clothes, of toys, of devices and things, and they dropped and flung these bags everywhere as they saw me, but I simply and calmly walked.

When I reached the other end of the building, I stepped outside again into the sunlight. No one had helped me, and I wondered, really, did nobody care for a dead baby? Was there nobody in this world who cared?

By this point, the sun was sinking low in the sky, and I was depressed. I just wanted to lie down and forget everything, I wanted to unwind this day and let it disappear into nothing.

I found my way across another avenue—the vehicles screeched and crashed and almost hit me, but I didn't care—and I found a quiet corner beneath a large bridge or overpass. Above me I could hear those fast rolling things, but down here it was dark and cool and quiet. I set the human cub carefully down, and I lay down beside it. Far in the distance, I heard those wild howling sirens. The objects whooshed and whooshed overhead, and the bridge shivered and clanked with their weight. From somewhere in the sky came the cluttered drone of objects flying, and every sound in this world seemed ugly and new. In the distance, I thought I heard the loud report of a rifle, and I knew that the orange fire of that gun was near in my future. I wanted nothing else but to be back in my enclosure, and for the baby to be alive, and for Kitch to be okay again. But I knew it would never happen. I had been kidding myself—nothing in the world could bring Kitch back to life. Certain things can never be reversed. It would simply never happen.

I thought of Kitch's pudgy face as it was a few days ago, bright and pink beneath his khaki cap, and a smile settled on my face. I remembered the cooing noises of the row-your-boat lady singing her sad song. It had annoyed me so, but now that noise seemed so lovely:

My brothers and sisters are all aboard, Hallelujah
Michael, row the boat ashore, Hallelujah.

And the noise was so close and so real that I thought she could have been there right beside me, singing, and when I looked up, she was. It would have surprised me to see her there on any other day, but this day nothing surprised me anymore. She was sitting beneath the same bridge as I was, amid a nest of bags and garbage. She looked at me and sang, smiling through her broken teeth.

Then she got up and walked right up to me. "You came all the way here to see me, tiger?" she asked me.

I was too tired to get up, but I raised my head slightly. I was so happy to see her that tears were streaming from my eyes.

She saw the human baby lying next to me, and she shook her head. "Oh, tiger," she said. "Oh, that's a shame." She bent down and stroked the top of the cub's head. "Ming the merciless!" she whooped, and then she started to chuckle to herself, and that laugh was the strangest, sweetest sound I think I had ever heard.

I closed my eyes and saw the zoo and its miniature red-green forest, and it was full of tigers, just like me. And Saskia and Maharaj were there, and I had forgiven them and I ran and I played with them. And the baby's curly-haired mother stood nearby, but she was my mother, too—she had been my mother all along. And in my dream, I had my own kids, baby tigers, playful little cubs, as small as I had been once, just as small as the human baby I had killed. The tiger babies tumbled over each other clumsily, so cute. I tried to lick them and play with them, but I saw that my tongue and my paws were rough and too powerful, and the slightest touch would have damaged those babies, so I stopped playing, and instead I stood guard and watched over them.

On the other side of the moat, Kitch and great hordes of humans watched and admired; and then, one by one they started to climb over the wall, and wade through the moat—so eager were they to reach us. Soon, great armies of people were crossing over into the tiger compound, and they came running up my hill. There were so many of them that I couldn't protect my delicate babies from their heavy feet. They trampled right over my cubs, mashing them down in their oblivious rush, and the strange old man with thick glasses and rubber gloves came around and picked up my dead babies and dropped them into a plastic bag, and I was distraught. But then Kitch came to me. He stopped and patted me on the head, and scratched me behind the ear. He told me it was okay. He said the tiger babies were gone, and it was okay, and he was gone, and that was okay too. And I realized that as he petted me, he was beginning to crush my head, like wet sludge in his hand. His fingers were deep in my brain, and he was massaging it into a pulp, and it felt good, in a way, but it terrified me also, because I knew I would soon be lost in oblivion.

When I woke up, it was dark. I had the aching hunger that stretched my ribs. The droning noise from the sky was harder and closer, and I knew soon I would have to get up and keep moving, to stay out of the reach of the rifles. But at that second, this thought didn't bother me. I had that morning feeling again, that feeling I had when I first realized that I loved Kitch, and the world had made a brief and wonderful kind of sense.

Everything seemed so clear again, everything that was horrible was sensible, and everything was good, and I understood it all. I looked down and saw that the row-your-boat lady had fallen asleep with her head resting on top of me. She was curled into a ball, with her head nestled right up against my haunches, as peaceful as could be, and I thought, She is a wonderful person. I love you, row-your-boat lady, I said to myself, as I opened my mouth wide and worked my teeth into her soft stomach and pulled up her viscera.

She gasped just once, without even opening her eyes—sharp and sudden like she had just had a wonderful surprise. And then she stopped, never exhaling.

It felt so right, killing her like that. It moved me. I didn't do it from anger or from hunger; nor was it an act of recklessness, like with that poor little human baby. A word that comes to mind is *instinct;* and yet I know I *chose* to kill her. I chose to kill her, and it felt inevitable, and it made me sad and happy all at once. I set myself to my work, and when I had ripped out and eaten every organ and every sweet strip of flesh that I could peel from the row-your-boat lady, when I had sucked down even the soft rounds of meat in the cheeks of her face, when she was just a shiny hub of bone and muscle, I turned around and picked up the human cub. It took me just two bites to crunch and pop and slurp and swallow the whole thing, and I was crying as I did so. I had never felt so much love in all my life.

THE STRANGE CAREER OF DR. RAJU GOPALARAJAN

NONE OF US WERE SURPRISED WHEN we heard Gopi Kumar had been fired from his job at CompUSA. We imagine he came home and bragged to his wife that at any minute his manager would realize what a mistake she'd made and beg him to take his job back. Manju would have breathed out hard and told him, "Go to the unemployment office anyway and fill out the forms" (as Gopi eventually did). But what Manju didn't know—what none of us understood—was that Gopi had already decided to make his living by impersonating a doctor.

In fact, within three weeks of that day, Gopi had signed the lease on a small office in Manvel, a good hour and a half from where he lived, a place where he hoped none of us would run into him. He told his wife he was looking for a job, and later he said he had found one, as a television salesman. But he would come home those days carrying as many books about medicine and surgery as the Doakum County Public Library System possessed. Every evening he pored through them, making margin marks with his pencil, consulting the Internet for clarification on difficult points; and Manju would have stood in the doorway and watched, in her weary way.

"You're not supposed to write in library books," she would

say. Manju was a secretary in an insurance agency, and it seemed to us she was shy in public, a little insecure—the sort of woman who always wore saris, and who would respond in Tamil when you spoke to her in English. But we also noticed she had grown to be bold at home with him, because when you are married to a man like Gopi, a man who is always going to be a bit oblivious to those around him, you can be a little loud and say what you think and still not risk offending.

"Why not? My taxes pay for them," Gopi might reply.

"As if you pay all your taxes. What are you reading, anyway?"

And then he would turn to her and say, "Mind your own business," or, "Don't you have enough work to do that you don't have to stand there and bother me?" or, "You should try reading yourself one day, you might learn something."

"And you're such a genius yourself," Manju would answer. Or she might instead hold her tongue, deciding it wasn't important enough to continue provoking him.

Of course, when Gopi went to sleep or stepped into the bathroom, Manju would peep into the books herself to see what was engrossing her husband, and this is why some people say that she must have known and chosen not to stop him—that she was just as responsible as he was for all that happened later. After all, Manju herself told the story of the day in India when Gopi had gotten so fed up with the traffic outside their house that he had assembled a police uniform using his father's old air force khakis and gone out into the road. He had issued homemade tickets, ripping them up in exchange for boisterously negotiated bribes, stopping only after Manju pretended to call and report *him* to the police. Obviously, they say, Manju knew her husband had a history as a charlatan, and when she looked in those library books, she should have reached the logical conclusion.

But the people who say this don't understand that there was more than one logical conclusion. During their twenty-one years of marriage, as everybody knows, Manju had been unable to have a child, and seeing the books her husband brought home, with their graphic photographs of women's parts, of glistening uteruses and palsied vaginas, of dead, blue-green fetuses and rash-covered nipples, she might just as well have thought her husband was feeling the loneliness of being childless and almost old, and was seeking again a cure for a problem they had long ago decided would have to be left to the whims and the graces of God.

We liked Manju so much, and we miss her. She had a beautiful voice, and always we asked her to sing at our functions. She would sit down with crossed legs and clear her throat and the room would quiet and parents would hush their children. Then the voice would come out of her, low and quavering and full of awe and sadness, singing of beautiful, dark-skinned young Krishna and how she loved him and longed for him, how she lay alone and burned for him but never could be with him. And when she sang like that we would notice a hollow space in our own chests, and we would feel that space filled with a sweet longing we couldn't understand, and our eyes would grow hot and wet. When people talk about Manju and her husband and what they did and what happened to them, they should try to remember that people have depths.

The office space Gopi rented with his and Manju's small savings had previously housed a veterinary clinic, and Gopi would have liked it because it seemed to require little work to convert to a proper medical office. It was a small storefront in a low-rent strip mall on a quiet country highway, separated from other businesses by a grassy field where a dozen long-dead oil pumps stood like big-beaked birds, a field where in the summer grazed cheaply fed hamburger cows.

It was the sort of place where in the mornings young men

wearing baseball caps and Stetsons gathered in the parking lot and stood there until the sun grew hot, then moved into the thin shade that rimmed the building. Gopi would have seen them when he arrived in the mornings to clean and prepare, their hats bobbing outside his office window as they waited for the pickup trucks that arrived by ones or twos, and for the men inside the trucks to point out the ones they wanted.

One day, Gopi offered one of these waiting men thirty dollars to help clear trash out of the closets and wash the walls. The man seemed happy to do it. His name, as everyone knows by now, was Vicente, and he had a big smile and looked to be about twenty-three. Gopi asked him where he was from, and Vicente answered, "Puebla, Mexico. You?"

"Madras, India," said Gopi.

We picture Gopi and young Vicente sweeping the little poops and pet foods that lay scattered on the floor. They tossed out the rusty small-animal cages stacked here and there and scrubbed the strange stains on the small metal examining table that stuck out from one wall. They followed without luck in the walls and dark closet corners the knocks and noises that Gopi was convinced were the scamperings and squeals of someone's lost and forgotten pet; and when they were finished, the place still smelled stubbornly of urine, but Gopi was pleased.

To make the office seem complete, Gopi ordered over the Internet a phone, a scalpel, forceps, scissors, gauze and cotton, rubbing alcohol, bandages of various sizes, rubber gloves, a microwave oven, and, from a friend who worked in a hospital in India, a small supply of prescription drugs.

After two weeks of preparation, Gopi was open for business. At a copy store he had made a small sign advertising the alias he had decided on: DR. RAJU GOPALARAJAN, MD; WOMEN'S DIFFICULTIES AND ALL OTHER MATTERS. Now he would have taped this sign in his window. We imagine he wore a white lab coat from the local uniform-supply store, and the stethoscope that had arrived in the mail that morning, and now he put it on his ears and listened to his own heart. The sound was clear and strong, and Gopi felt overjoyed at how well he had done. Then he danced, just for a minute. Afterward, sitting down behind his desk, he grinned his little-boy grin. Then there was quiet. No strange creatures stirred in the walls, no one rang on the telephone. And in the quiet and the stillness, the sound of Gopi's own beating heart returned to him, and for a brief moment, the poor man saw himself as if from a distance. He saw himself as we see him, sitting alone in an office on an empty country highway. A doctor? He wondered if he should have started in a smaller way, working from a room of his house, prescribing medicines for his friends, writing doctor's notes for their children. But even that prospect now seemed absurd. His face grew warm with the dawning realization that he had made a ridiculous, a gigantic mistake.

As a tension began to form in his left shoulder and the base of his skull, Gopi tried to remind himself that he had to do this in the biggest possible way, so that people would feel that he was a doctor. But the panic remained, and Gopi felt desperately a need for the company of people, so he walked outside and stood among the men on the sidewalk.

"Good morning, fellows," he said to them. His hands were thrust into the pockets of his lab coat, and his stethoscope draped over his neck.

"Good morning," they said back. Gopi recognized Vicente and some of the other men, and when they saw him now in a doctor's white coat (he would have looked quite smart), one man said something in Spanish, and another said, "You're the doctor?"

Vicente added, "We didn't know you're the doctor. We thought you were making up the office for somebody else."

"I'm the doctor," Gopi said.

"Good morning, Doctor." Vicente smiled, and Gopi's tension disappeared.

Then Vicente's friend rolled up the cuff of his jeans and showed Gopi a rash of ugly white-and-black bumps on his shin, and all the men gathered around to look. And this is how Gopi Kumar, aka Dr. Raju Gopalarajan, got his first patients.

Like many of us, Gopi had wanted to be a doctor his whole life. Those of us who knew him back home remember how he thought himself a martyr for having abjured the field early on, after seeing the families of friends thrown into crisis by the necessity of paying enormous bribes to the medical school admissions committee. When his friends asked how he had done on the qualifying exams, Gopi, who had done abysmally, felt an indignant pride in telling them his score was irrelevant because he would never subject his father to the burden and indignity of groveling before those goondas.

He quit college and worked for a time as an orderly in a hospital in Madras. It wasn't work fit for a Brahmin, some people said, but he loved hospitals. He found them exciting. He'd had to lie to his father about what his actual duties were: picking up bloody dressings from the floor, handling the warm, wet test tubes of other people's urine. The doctors never liked him much—he didn't cringe and salaam, like the other orderlies, and they hesitated to give him the most menial chores, yet resented any slight resistance he offered when they did.

He met Manju around this time. At lunchtime and after work, Gopi had taken to sitting in the commissary of the college he had once attended, where he still had some friends, and talking to the girls there. He made headway with his imitations of various professors and his intimacy with the ins and outs of the college bureaucracy. And he bragged about the jobs he would one day get, the car and motorcycle and house he would eventually own, and about the life he would find one day in America. He said he had visited America once: the floors there were covered in soft carpets, and cool air and warm air was pumped from the walls, and anyone could become American, it was in the laws, and he knew it, and he would do it. And when he talked like this, in his confident manner, Manju thought he seemed, in a way, magical. It was weeks into their romance before Manju realized that Gopi wasn't a student—he was an orderly in a hospital who came to the campus only to meet gullible girls. But by then, she told herself, it was too late. Manju was in love.

Her mother, of course, would be scandalized. Even some of her friends back then were scandalized. Manju had always been a shy and proper girl, they say, the last person who should have gone in for a love match.

But her friends' surprise was based on a misunderstanding. If they had looked more closely, they would have seen that Manju's shyness was the mask of an intensely interested observer of the opposite sex. She noticed the unnoticeable, skinny, silly-looking boys who sat in her classrooms, and she surprised herself by wanting them. She knew that the answer to her mind's and body's questions could be found in these greasy-haired creatures, because it was they who had made her realize the questions were there. She searched the faces of her married cousins for some sign of difference, of the calm confidence of transcendent knowledge, of satisfaction.

And so she married Gopi, and they moved in with his parents, and Gopi took a job as a salesman so he could save money; and four years later, just as he had promised, they moved to America. And that is also roughly how long it had taken, after the move, for him to lose interest in her, and for her to lose faith in him—four years.

Gopi had jumped from job to job to job, full of schemes. He approached us once for funds to start a Big Boy franchise. If we gave at all, it was out of friendship for Manju; but what became of the project, we never heard. Even Manju couldn't tell us—Gopi refused to share the details of his business ventures with her.

Incredible enthusiasm, followed by wild and ridiculous efforts, followed by boredom and abandonment: it was the pattern he followed in all his endeavors, Manju realized; and it was the pattern he had followed with regard to her.

This, she thought, was the great ocean of the middle of marriage. The home shore had disappeared from sight, and what had appeared as infinite promise became instead a terrifying endlessness, a lonely, crushing isolation of two selves in the world.

For Gopi, of course, lost in his own head, the promise was still there, always on the verge of fulfillment. There was opportunity all around in platefuls, and one only had to take his helping.

Gopi told the man with the rash on his shin that he would take care of him the next day. Then Gopi would have gone home and consulted his library books (which he renewed every two weeks, as he planned to do indefinitely), concluding finally that the rash was either a bacterial infection or a reaction to the sun. He forged a prescription for topical antibiotic, and recommended as well an over-the-counter anti-itch ointment and sunscreen. He charged the fellow thirty-five dollars for the advice, stressing that the price was a discount because this man was the clinic's first patient. Gopi figured the sum was less than half what a regular doctor would charge someone without insurance. Within five days, the rash disappeared.

Soon, Gopi was consulting with the workers on a whole catalogue of minor ailments, and they began also to refer their families and their friends to him. He recruited additional patients in bus stops or at the mall, preferring immigrants who looked newly arrived, Indians if we appeared trusting and un-Americanized. He would strike up a conversation to get a sense of the person and then hand out one of the business cards he'd printed up. In this way, Gopi generated business with surprising speed. People with very serious-sounding problems—old men with severe chest pains, for example—Gopi reluctantly turned away, but those with more minor ailments he gamely treated, or tried to, and after two and a half months he was able to cover his monthly expenses.

Those first months were giddy ones for Gopi. In the evenings, over dinner, he might tell Manju, "I sold seven televisions today."

"Very nice," she might answer. "Bring one home for us one day, that would be something."

"Soon, my dear," he would tell her. "Soon we will have big-screen televisions and nice vacations, too," and he would grin in his unaccountable way, so pleased with himself. "Don't you trust me? It'll happen, Manju. Why not? I say. Why not for us?"

Manju had become by this point more or less a sensible woman, but she would find something in Gopi's manner so infectious, so suddenly appealing—almost like the Gopi of old— that she would get up and take her dirty plate to the sink just so he wouldn't see the smile rising irrepressibly to her face.

At night, he would push up against her and bite her playfully on the neck.

"Ouch!" she would yell, and give him a push on the nose. "Don't be stupid."

"Why not? One good reason," Gopi would ask.

And Manju would answer, "What would be the point?"

"The point?" Gopi would laugh. "Now you see the point?"

And Manju would finally relent, thinking, Okay, why not?

Of course, when Gopi squeezed himself between Manju's pudding thighs, in his mind he saw pictures of Deepika Shenoy, our doctor acquaintance Dilip's wife; or of his old favorite, Dolly Parton.

"Whose key is in ignition?" he might even blurt, in his exuberance, "Gopi the physician!" And Manju would have snorted a laugh and asked him what he meant, if she could have, but on those first nights, at least, she was too distracted by the discovery that having his warmth inside her should feel so good and familiar, even though so much time had passed.

After he fell asleep, though, Manju would experience an aftertaste of unplaceable resentment. His behavior had the effect, in other words, of sharpening her long-dormant appetite for happiness, without satisfying it. She sensed Gopi's newfound sense of purpose but didn't understand it. She saw the outline of a different life together, but the content was missing. And in this state of directed longing, of contoured emptiness, Manju began to suspect that she was pregnant.

It was entirely plausible. Manju had confided in some of us years ago that the doctors had only ever said it would be difficult, not impossible. And now, she thought, perhaps a child had finally arrived to pull Gopi back and create the love they had never properly had. Manju could scarcely believe it, but something Gopi had said kept echoing in her mind: Why not? Why not for us?

When she made the doctor's appointment, Manju decided not to tell Gopi, or any of us, until she had gotten an answer for sure. The doctor was kind to Manju, and patient, and interested in listening, so Manju would have told her all about her body's changes, and the discomfort, and the intermittent sickness. And the doctor examined Manju and took her blood, and a week later called her back for more tests, and after this second visit, she was drawn and pale from the strain of spending long hours in cold rooms, half naked, stared at, pricked, pried open, and fingered by more people than she could clearly remember.

She drove home that day hoping that her husband at least would have done something about dinner. But when she opened the front door Gopi was hunched over a torn sofa cushion, its foam stuffing strewn over the floor.

"What in the world are you doing?" she asked.

"Nothing," Gopi yelled in alarm. "What do you think? Only fixing the cushion." Gopi had sliced it open with a knife and removed its innards, and now he was stuffing them back in and trying to stitch it all up as cleanly as possible. He was practicing. The following day, he was scheduled to perform his first surgery.

Vicente was the patient. Gopi had noticed that the young man had a lump on his forearm the size of a kumquat. Vicente said he'd had it for years, that a doctor had told him it was harmless—simply a fat deposit—and that it would cost nine hundred dollars just to remove it. Gopi said it was an ugly thing and ought to be gotten rid of, and that he would do it for a very reasonable price. Somehow, the boy agreed.

Vicente arrived at the office with a young lady whom Gopi recognized as the woman who always rode in Vicente's car. She was short and thin and wore loose blue jeans, a white T-shirt, and sneakers. Vicente introduced her as Sandra, and Gopi smiled and shook her hand; from the way he behaved, you could not have known how nervous he was. "Mucho gusto," said the woman, and Gopi corrected her. "I'm not Spanish, I'm Indian," he said. "But that's okay. Se habla español. Right, Vicente?"

Sandra made a noise that sounded to Gopi like *Hmph*.

"Do you want to watch?" Gopi asked her, indicating the examining room. Sandra looked to Vicente, who translated the question for her. She laughed and shook her head. "Oh, no," she said. She sat down in the waiting room.

As they walked into the examining room, Gopi asked Vicente, "She your wife?" Vicente grinned, embarrassed. "Not yet, Doctor. Can't afford to get married yet."

If any of us had seen him then, we might for a moment have doubted that this was the Gopi we knew, and not a surgeon long used to taking knives to human flesh. He smiled and spoke so calmly that Vicente himself was not at all nervous when Gopi told him to sit in a chair and roll up his sleeve and lay his arm on the examining table.

The novocaine had come in the mail from India months previously, but Gopi had not had occasion to use it until now. He opened the box and found his hypodermic, then filled the syringe with the drug, eyeballing the measurement. He injected Vicente in three places around the lump and stared gravely, waiting for the arm to numb.

After eight or ten minutes, Gopi poked the arm with his finger. "Can you feel that?" he asked.

"Only a little," Vicente replied.

Gopi didn't want to take any chances. He refilled the hypodermic and injected the young man again. After a few minutes, he directed Vicente to close his eyes.

"Am I touching you or not?" Gopi asked him.

"Don't think so," said Vicente.

"Now?"

"Unh-uh."

Finally, Gopi touched Vicente's arm. "How about now?"

"Nope."

Now Gopi couldn't help himself. He giggled. Then he thwacked Vicente with three of his fingers. "Did you feel that?" he asked.

"I heard it," said Vicente. "But I didn't really feel it."

"Okay then." Gopi squirmed his fingers into latex gloves and swabbed Vicente's arm with iodine. He had sterilized the scalpel by putting it into a bowl of water that had been microwaved on high for fifteen minutes, and now without hesitating and without giving himself time to grow afraid, he sank the blade into Vicente's skin.

The blade sank softly. Gopi sliced a thin line along the center of Vicente's lump. Blood welled slowly from the line, and Gopi wiped it with cotton gauze. Vicente didn't appear to feel anything. It was magical, Gopi thought; it was impossible. Gopi cut smaller, horizontal lines at each end of the vertical one, and then he took a breath and with his gloved fingers pried up a flap of skin. The lump was loosely anchored, and Gopi unmoored it with tentative scalpel cuts until it slipped out, slick and rubbery, into the palm of his hand. Gopi showed it to Vicente, who took one look and slumped down in his chair.

Gopi tried to catch Vicente up as he fainted, but in doing so he dropped the lump. It slid along the floor, and Gopi dropped Vicente to stop it with one foot. He picked up the lump and put it in the sink, making a mental note to flush it in the toilet later. Then he lifted poor Vicente off the chair as best he could and shoved his limp body onto the metal examining table, which seemed designed to hold, at most, a large dog. Vicente's legs dangled off awkwardly above the knees.

"Needle and thread, please, Nurse," Gopi chuckled to himself, and then he picked up the surgical needle that he had laid out earlier on a tray, already strung with clear catgut medical suture.

Vicente woke up halfway through the stitching, and Gopi talked to him reassuringly. "Feeling better?" he asked. "Don't look. Almost done." Gopi tied a little knot and appraised his handiwork. The sutures were cragged and haphazard, but Gopi marveled that a man whose mother and wife had never let him so much as stitch a button on his own shirt could have done such a relatively clean job. Gopi covered the wound with a bandage. He washed his hands and took Vicente's cash, and advised him to go home and take lots of Tylenol. Then he gave Vicente a firm handshake, making the poor man wince.

"See me back in a month?" Gopi said.

When the two men came into the lobby, Sandra stood up. Her face was blanched.

"¿Qué pasó?" she asked.

She and Vicente spoke to each other in quick overlapping sentences, and Gopi interrupted. "Why is she excited? What happened?"

Vicente turned to Gopi. "She heard the commotion in there," he said. "She thought something bad happened. That's all."

"Nothing wrong," Gopi said in English. He took Sandra's hand in his. "He's a good boy. Take care of him."

Sandra frowned. As she and Vicente turned around to leave, Sandra cried out again: the back of Vicente's shirt was covered with Gopi's bloody fingerprints.

After they left, Gopi sat down. We see him as the adrenaline slowly ebbed, and he began to realize what he had just done. He had used a knife to cut into another man's body, and the man had been helped, not harmed. He had performed a surgery, and what's more, while doing so he had not had a self-conscious thought. He had become a doctor, unselfconscious, and at this realization, Gopi floated with elation. He floated above himself and understood that he was enjoying a delicious and slightly terrifying dream. And in this state of queasy exhilaration, Gopi walked outside, eager for the calming society of the men in the parking lot. But they had left already, so he visited the dry cleaner next door, hoping to make conversation with the teenage-looking girl who worked there ("Where do you get so many hangers?"). She had gone to lunch, so Gopi walked in the gravel by the side of the long road until he reached the field of grazing cows. He talked out loud to the dumb, death-destined animals, and somehow this calmed Gopi down.

When he went home that night, before making love to his wife, he asked her, "How is it we came to be here, you and me, all alone in this country? Isn't it strange? That we thought certain thoughts that led to certain actions, and a lot of other things happened just by chance, and the net result is me lying here on top of you?"

"It is strange indeed," replied Manju, who, we would learn, had gotten some news from her doctor that day and, unbeknownst to Gopi, was experiencing her own private wonder.

. . .

At temple, on the festival of Krishna's birthday, Dr. Dilip She-noy surprised Gopi by beckoning him over to sit at his table in the lunch hall.

"Sit with me, Gopi," we heard Dilip tell him, with uncharac-teristic friendliness, and Gopi wondered if this was a sign of the uncanny success of his deception—the unfriendly doctor now instinctively recognized Gopi as one of his own.

Dilip poised his thin fingers against his Styrofoam lunch plate. "How are you, Gopi?" Dilip said. He had a long, serious face, and his gray hair plumed up softly. "Let's talk. What's going on?"

"Just the usual," Gopi answered.

"Really? Nothing new?"

Dilip's intent stare, his tone, began now to strike Gopi as odd. "But how are you, Dilip?" Gopi asked.

"Let us not talk about *me*," Dilip replied. He smiled, just a little. "Because, Gopi, it seems that you are the much more interesting fellow."

Inside the temple, Manju was looking at the boy Krishna in the altar, the black stone Krishna with wide gold eyes and a wise grin, blowing with his blood-red lips into the flute he held there. A lovely, playful Krishna; a mischievous, hilarious Krishna; and all at once, Manju thought, a terrible, mocking Krishna, grin-ning at all the capricious misery he had spun.

"Krishna, Guruvayoorappa," Manju prayed. She clasped her hands and clenched her eyelids and moaned the words quietly, trying in vain to muster the fever of trust and abandon to which she could sometimes move herself at this spot.

Manju looked around at all the other people in the temple, she looked at us chatting and praying, and thought how strange it was for us to behave as if all this were so normal. Her doc-tors would have given her months, maybe weeks, and now she looked at us as though we were a million miles away.

We didn't know what she was going through—she never once mentioned the word *cancer*—nor did she have a husband she could trust or tell, who could share the weight of her dying and make her less alone. She was by herself, floating far above us, and when she turned back to Lord Krishna it was with grief but also with this lonely, exhilarating anger. Is there really no hope? she asked him in silence. All my life you have given me only what you have wanted to give me and not what I have asked for. But that's another way of saying you have not been there and that you have never listened to me. Is there any sign to show that you are still with me, or that you ever have been? That after loving you so much my whole pointless life, you haven't abandoned me to die?

It was Deepika Shenoy, finally, who had the presence of mind to walk softly up to Manju and put her arm around her, and to whisper in her ear and dab the tears discreetly with a corner of Deepika's own green silk sari. She took Manju out to the lunch line in the dining hall and made sure she got a little bit of everything, and brought her to sit down with their husbands, and by then Manju was looking reasonably calm.

We ask ourselves at what point it became inevitable, and perhaps it was then. Gopi looked up from his food and was grateful for the new company. He greeted Deepika and complimented her on her sari. She had always been Gopi's triple-deluxe dream; it was embarrassingly obvious. Looking at this dream Deepika, Gopi wished Manju would eat better, smile more, wear some jewelry. Deepika laughed at something someone said and put her hand on her shaking bosom. It was a gesture that normally would have made Gopi giddy with pleasure, but now he managed only a wan smile.

Then Manju tried in her way to make small talk, but her husband interrupted her as usual.

"Not now, Manju," Gopi said, because Dilip had reached his hand into his shirt pocket and pulled out a business card, and was talking now, oblivious of the women.

"My nephew was driving to our place last weekend from College Station," Dilip was saying. "You see, he studies hard, just like I did. People like us slog for years. Don't you find us silly? He was driving home and he stopped at a gas station, where someone gave him this business card." Dilip paused now to stare sharply at his acquaintance; but Gopi's eyes stayed fixed on his plate. "Someone who looked very familiar gave him *this card*," Dilip repeated, extending the business card, clipped between two bony fingers, toward Gopi.

Gopi refused to touch it. And Manju looked at her husband and looked at the card. And at last, she herself took it from Dilip's hand.

"DOCTOR RAJU GOPALARAJAN, MD," Manju read slowly. "MEDICAL DOCTOR SPECIALIZING IN ALL THINGS SPECIALLY WOMEN'S HEALTH MATTERS."

Dilip finally turned, exultant, to Manju. "But you already know Dr. Gopalarajan, don't you?"

Manju shook her head no.

"You don't?" Dilip gave her a mordant smile. "But he's the great doctor specializing in Women's Health Matters. One of the most difficult specialities in the world, and he is an absolute master."

"Aha?"

Dilip raised his finger in mock severity. "If something cannot be cured," said Dilip, who had always been more insinuation than action, and who, after scaring Gopi, was content to leave things there at that. "If something cannot be cured," Dilip said again, turning back toward Gopi, "then ask Gopalarajan, and Gopalarajan will find the cure!" Was there any hope for poor Manju, for either of them, after that?

The next morning, when Gopi's office phone rang—it's hard to believe, but in a way it isn't—he didn't even recognize his own wife's voice, at first.

"Who's calling, please?" he asked, and she spelled her name as he had heard her spell it so many times to others.

"M like Mary, A-N like Nancy, J-U-K-U-M like Mary, A-R."

Gopi had not prepared for this moment, but for a few seconds his quick wits came to his aid. He drew in his breath and almost without thinking asked, "Something wrong with you, madam?" He spoke in a gruff tone he hoped his wife wouldn't recognize.

"Yes," Manju said. "That's why people call doctors, isn't it? Can I make an appointment, please?"

Gopi was surprised to find that Manju's voice, transmitted over the anonymizing phone, had an authority he had never appreciated in real life, and Gopi felt suddenly uncertain of his ability to bluff through the situation.

"Hello?" Manju asked.

The silence grew, and now Gopi panicked. He hung up, and when the phone rang again, he ignored it.

He had only a few minutes to wonder what in fact was wrong with his wife when he was interrupted again, this time by Vicente and Sandra walking in through the door. They held each other's hands stiffly.

The look in their faces struck Gopi with alarm. "Sorry to bother you, Doctor," Vicente said. "But seems like, maybe, there's a problem."

"I did everything well," Gopi said. "What problem? Everything is fine." Sandra's face turned red, and Vicente looked at her, then at Gopi. And then Vicente began to cry.

"He has pain," Sandra tried to explain, as she and Gopi waited for Vicente to compose himself.

Gopi saw that the young man had tied a white cloth around his forearm, and the cloth was soaked through with some dark fluid, and his hand and fingers below were plumply swollen.

When he unwrapped the bandage in the examining room a few minutes later, the smell hit Gopi so hard he staggered to the door and leaned out of it for a few moments. When he came back, he tried to breathe through his mouth. He already knew from his reading what had to be done, and that there was no time to waste. As Sandra stood anxiously at the far end of the room, Gopi anesthetized Vicente's arm and began to cut away the blackening flesh. He cut and he threw the sloppy matter into the trash can and closed the lid, but still the stench didn't go away, so Gopi cut more. Blood oozed from the cavity in Vicente's arm, filling the hole and spilling to the floor. Gopi spooned out the blood with a plastic cup and cut quickly before the hole filled again. Sandra held her hand to her mouth and cried, and Gopi told Vicente, "Tell her to stop moaning, won't you?" but Vicente's eyes were half closed and his head was nodding backward and he didn't say anything. Gopi cut more and became very frightened when finally he encountered a length of white bone.

After he and Sandra laid Vicente in the back of his car, Gopi watched Sandra drive away (on her way, we know now, to the Manvel General Emergency Room). Then he stood on the pavement, damp and terrified, and let his head slump down to see the footprint-spattered trail of red leading from inside the examining room all the way to the parking lot, to terminate there, at Gopi's feet. Inside, minutes later, he didn't notice the sound of the front door opening, or hear the footsteps leading to the examining room door, or see his wife walk in until she was two feet away from him.

Manju and Gopi stared at each other in silence. She studied her husband's bewildered eyes and looked at the lab coat he was wearing. She saw the gore-caked instruments, and she remembered Dilip Shenoy's odd expression at the temple the day before, and the voice on the phone when she had tried to make an appointment. She clutched harder the library book she held in her arms, and remembered Gopi's strange jokes in the bedroom, and the increasingly implausible stories about his advancements in television sales. And she remembered the lies Gopi had told everyone all his life.

And Gopi—exhausted, for once guileless—quietly pried the book from her trembling hands, bookmarked and dog-eared, and stared dumbly at the picture it showed: a woman's ovaries, bloated and blistering, laid out on a dissecting table, with a label that read INOPERABLE. The dull fear in his eyes was obvious to Manju.

"What's the matter?" Manju asked. She wiped her nose with the back of her hand. "You're such a famous doctor. Can't you help me? Hm?"

Gopi was unsure, for a moment, if his wife was credulous or mocking, but something in her tone seemed to demand an answer.

"I can try," he said simply.

There are those who will never accept what must have happened next. They don't understand what Manju saw in Gopi, for a few moments, here at the dying-ember end of our story. But there is a reassuring certainty to some unlucky lives, which is to say that fear has no place for persons already doomed; and a kind of calmness descended on Manju, seeing her husband covered in some other man's blood, seeing him drained and frightened. And isn't it possible that Manju herself found in Gopi's examining room the iodine and the novocaine, the knife and the needles? Manju herself lay down on the examining table, just as the Manvel General doctors, having gotten the details from Sandra, were phoning the police station.

Gopi was still nervous, no doubt. It took him some time to fathom the hopeless clarity of the situation. But Manju's calmness would have calmed him, and soon he understood there was no help for either of them outside of that room. The news stations had even somehow gotten hold of the story—didn't some of us hear the name on the radio and wonder who this doctor was, and if maybe we had met him at a function somewhere? And on his own, without asking, Gopi picked up the scalpel, knowing the red and blue lights would soon be shimmering through the cracks in the window blinds. We are with them as he picked up the scalpel and looked in Manju's eyes, knowing what the police would have no choice but to do when they came through the door and saw him doing what he was about to do.

But now those anxious police officers were still miles away along the highway. Vicente's friends had left for work already. The dry cleaner's clerk was late as usual. Only the skinny cows in their dirt-patch field could know what noises came from that desolate office building, and so there are some who will always have doubts—who will cling to their versions with the same shiftless confidence with which those cows stood waiting under the midday sun, dulled to their own fate or anyone else's—and who will never believe what happened when Manju looked down, and followed the sure movements of Dr. Gopalarajan's fingers, and smiled.

FOUR RAJESHES

DIRECT YOUR ATTENTION, RAJESH, to this yellowed photograph you purchased in a South Indian antiques market, a portrait of my own distinguished self: a turn-of-the-century Brahmin standing outside a mud-walled train station, wearing a crisp white vaishti edged in gold and a dark shut-coat buttoned smartly to the neck. My handsome face is capped with a majestic white turban; in my stern gaze and thin, unsmiling lips, you detect an autocratic temperament and anxious dignity reminding you of certain men in your own extended family. Around my neck, a garland of roses lies heavily, and the markings on my forehead show that, like you, I am an Iyer. Moreover, my name—R. Rajarajeshwaran Iyer—written across the portrait in a fine hand beneath my feet, seems a version of your own. (A grander version, to be sure.) Yet another coincidence: Painted on the building behind me, in block English letters, above some fuzzy chalk marks, is the word ROMBACHINNAPATTINAM—the name of your own ancestral village.

Who was I, you wonder? Some distant ancestor, some early echo of yourself? What were my days like? To answer you: I was manager of Rombachinnapattinam's first rail station, and, for all our similarities, my life was nothing like yours. For one, I lived in Rombachinnapattinam, a hamlet that had changed but little—prior to the introduction of the railroad—in its four hundred years of existence. The things you care about had nothing, and yet everything, to do with me. What do I mean? Allow me to tell you, in explanation, about a singular and profound incident in my life, to wit, my relationship with a peculiar young clerk in my office, to whom I will refer simply as R. (*Allow me* to tell you? My dear boy, having imagined my voice into existence, you give me little choice!)

I was still new to my post when I met R. I sat writing at my desk and spied him peeking awkwardly into my office door. He stood there in vaishti and topknot, his face round with boyfat, barefoot and totally shirtless. He was a Brahmin, clearly, but a poorer sort than I. At once, I took him for one of the countless busybodies and bores who loitered at the station of a lazy afternoon to watch the *Madras Mail* arrive, pause briefly, and depart, and I was a little peeved that my attendant and factotum, Dhananjayan Rajesupriyan, had not intercepted the lad, to direct him on to the platform where he should more properly have waited. Little did I know what impact this humble visitor would have on my life! But at the time, I fancied myself too busy to give him more than an irritated thought. I called out curtly, "Can I help you?"

He did not answer, but continued, annoyingly, to stand there.

"Young man, the *Madras Mail* arrives at three thirty-eight. You are early."

He shyly shook his head. At this point, thoroughly distracted from my work—I was preparing a letter, tactful but firm, to my nominal supervisor, who was also my fiancée's uncle, the Manager of Outbound Trains and Village Personnel in Madras, petitioning him hastily to fill the position of administrative secretary in my office, a post that had been too long vacant, resulting in my having to perform such unpleasant tasks as penning with my own hand these letters of complaint, rather than dictating them, as would be more becoming to someone of my position—thoroughly distracted, I rose and approached my visitor. (By the way, there is no such thing as a "Manager of Outbound Trains." You are taking strange liberties. Anyway, let it be.)

When I approached him, R. folded his hands in respectful greeting. I realized that he was not a mere boy, as I had first suspected. In fact, only a couple of years separated us.

"Namaskaram, sir," he said. "My name is Rombachinnapattinam R., father being Rombachinnapattinam N———, grandfather being Rombachinnapattinam V———. I am knocking on doors of kindly recommended Brahmin professionals because—"

"Yes, yes."

"—because I am badly in need of a job to feed myself and my good mother—"

"Your good mother . . ."

"My good mother, good sir, and my good wife, myself being recently engaged for marriage. Being recently engaged, good sir, I do not know what to do, and come humbly to you for guidance and the generosity of your good offices, as I have been highly recommended by the late Dr. T. Lumbodharan, headmaster of Rombachinnapattinam Higher Secondary School, who had oftentimes told me that the order and capacities of my mind are not those of the average or commonplace person."

"The order and capacities of . . . dear fellow, do speak slowly!"

"Good sir. My name is Rombachinnapattinam R. Father being Rombachinnapattinam N———. Grandfather being Rombachinnapattinam V———."

"Good God."

"Good sir!"

"Ha!"

Immediately, I forced a cough to mask my impetuous guffaw. A sweaty, twice nervous, villagey youth like R. come begging at my office would normally have earned from me a brief hearing and a curt dismissal. But there was something about this hapless fellow that made me a little hesitant to show him the door too quickly. I felt an unaccountable warmth toward him. His pitiable shyness, his touching excitement on meeting a man so far above him in accomplishment and station—a nervousness that amounted to a strange exuberance, his simple courage in thus approaching me, and the fact that he was a needy Brahmin and had been recommended by my own late headmaster—all this disposed me to deal gently with the odd fellow. He stood before me with hands clasped meekly on his ample stomach, looking up with large, beseeching eyes. A drop of sweat rolled in and out of the furrowed flesh of his brow, wormed its wet way down the crest of his capable nose, and hung for one pendulous moment.

Before it completed its descent, I had made an impetuous decision. "How is your handwriting, young man?" I asked him.

"Quite legible, sir," he replied.

And on the spot, I hired him as my secretary. After conveying to him the particulars of the job, I asked him to report the following morning, presentably, in shirt and sandals.

Why did I take such a decision? It was one of those moments when the electric current of instantaneous affection arranges in its circuit a haphazard constellation of objective facts, arranges them in one's mind into an apprehension or intuition, that is less than a reasoned judgment but more than a whim, but which has the feeling of a definite conclusion.

In short, I have no idea why I took the decision. But I had no qualms about my choice, and I called for Dhananjayan Rajesupriyan to bring us tea, as a sort of celebration. Dhananjayan had been outside sweeping the platform, and when he came in carrying a platter with two steaming tumblers, he glanced at portly young R. sitting across from me, and promptly spilled the scalding tea all over my desk, soaking my moot half-finished letter, and sending warm dribbles onto R.'s lap.

Such clumsiness was unlike Dhananjayan, so, rather than

thrash him, I only twisted his ear until he yelped. Then I apologized to R. with profusion, and the good man good-naturedly took his leave.

Dhananjayan Rajesupriyan was a lad of nineteen. A Vaishya from a poor and backward family of tinsmiths, he had been with me since the opening of our railroad station in 1908, some twelve months previous, an event which truly was the most exciting occasion in the memory of our southern village of Rombachinnapattinam. True, it was not much of a station—a mud hut with one large office, and a palm-roofed platform, but it bore the seal of the Great Indian Peninsula Railway. And I was its manager. Yes, its manager—at the tender age of twenty-four. See, we Rombachinnapattinam Iyers have a comfortable kind of greatness in our genes, a tendency toward the early achievement of plummy bureaucratic positions—a trait I urge you (wouldn't writing be easier if you found a sinecure?) not to squander. In my case, success was the consequence of certain strategic positionings on the part of my mother. Through her extensive network of distant family connections, she had secured for me a marriage to the niece of the aforementioned Manager of Outbound Trains. The engagement ceremony was some months hence, but I was already enjoying the fruits of the union.

My managerial post was made immeasurably more pleasant by the presence of my cleaning person and Man Friday, Dhananjayan Rajesupriyan. Dhanu was diligent, neat, and responsible; indeed, I delegated to him much of the drudging work of managing the station—selling tickets, cleaning and maintaining the tracks, raising and lowering the flags—and he ably handled it all, on top of his more menial chores. But his youth made him sometimes impulsive and irritable.

For example, later that day, he apologized to me most gravely for having spilled the tea. I assured him it was no matter, but then he frowningly added, "But I don't like that fellow."

"Don't like him!" I asked, surprised but not a little amused by his effrontery. "Bold boy! Why not?"

"Because I think he is *odd*."

"Why, Dhananjayan Rajesupriyan, he is no odder than you, my good man," I laughed. In truth, I was a little touched. Dhananjayan was very protective of me, and he felt obliged to be skeptical on my behalf.

"Dhanu," I asked, in a mood to express my appreciation, "after work today, take me to your father's tin shop."

"But my father is not there today," Dhananjayan protested.

"And do you need your father for everything, silly boy?" I asked. "Can't you do me a simple favor by yourself?"

As my peon and I walked away from work that afternoon, and found ourselves alone outside the empty tin shop, and I had glared into silence the nakedly staring neighbors, some of whom had the temerity to shout rudely at me as I passed; after we were inside and had closed the door, Dhananjayan did not bother to point out that my roof was of tile, not tin. And after I had taken from Dhanu the rough, sweet kisses and greedy caresses for which I relied on the boy, I removed two annas from my cloth purse and pressed them in his palm, telling him all the while that he was a badly behaved young man, who, unless he shaped up, would amount to absolutely nothing—our respite over and my tenderness requited, my manager's personality was again ascending.

(May I interrupt myself? The preceding paragraph is unspeakable, disgusting, implausible, and totally unlike me. You have a vulgar imagination! I know that to you I am just a man in a photograph—and indeed, I appreciate your efforts in bringing me to a kind of puppetlike life and transcribing my words as I speak them, even down to these too clever asides—but please consider that no doubt I was a real man, with an impeccable reputation in my time. What will people think? In any case, I am eager to get through this and have done with it, so leave it be.)

Like you, Dhananjayan—diligent, dutiful chap—smiled grimly, ignoring my admonishments. He endured my affectionate pinch on his nose, and clasped the money perfunctorily. What was going on in young Dhanu's head, I don't know, but I meant those annas only as a token of affection, not as a price for his silence!

And in any event, the next day, Dhanu and I spoke not a word of our pleasures the previous evening—pleasures which in the moment seemed each time simple and necessary, but which nevertheless gave me afterward a queasy feeling, a sense that I was doing something secretly monstrous. This morning held a particular distraction: when I arrived at work, R. was already there, cheerfully seated on the floor, scribbling in his tea-stained and stiff-paged notebook. The shirt he wore was threadbare, long faded of any decipherable color. He'd pushed his sleeves past his elbows, but when he rose to greet me, they slipped two inches past the tallest of his fingers. On his feet were thin and cracked chappals, and his vaishti was the same one, tea-spattered, that he had worn the previous day.

His appearance filled me with pity—he must have been poor indeed, and before even seating him, I instructed him on the location of my favorite tailor, and pressed a few annas from my own purse into his hand, telling him it was an allowance provided by the Railway for the outfitting of its employees. Then I showed him to his desk, advised him on the locations of our files, explained the timetables and the receipts. I have a very particular method of organization, which I described in no small detail, and he absorbed it all with great equanimity. I directed him on the arrangement and processing of the bags of mail that we were charged with transferring, letters from the people of Rombachinnapattinam to other towns throughout the Madras Presidency, and vice versa. He observed everything closely, and I could already see that he would be an attentive and fastidious clerk to me.

I then provided him with inkwell and pen, and without delay commenced my first dictation to my superior in Madras:

"To the Manager of Outbound Trains and Director of Village Personnel, Mr. P. Seshamurthi,

"Dear Sir,

"In numerous previous letters I had written to you explaining my urgent need for a personal secretary. As I had told you, I have already set aside money from the budget for this necessary addition to my staff. You, sir, insisted that, after reviewing available applications, no suitable candidate could be found. Because no suitable candidate could be found, you advised me to give up on the idea of having my own clerical assistant. You explained that all other village managers were making do without a personal secretary. Of course, you made the mistake of thinking Rombachinnapattinam a 'village,' whereas it should more properly be called as a 'town,' but leave it. You also urged me to return the funds to the general budget from which I had removed them.

"I am now happy to report to you that our trouble has been resolved. Just yesterday, the young man penning this very letter walked into my office and presented to me his curriculum vitae. His credentials are impeccable. He has held numerous high-level secretarial clerkships." Here, I paused to exchange a wink with R., but R., thoughtfully engaged with his work, did not even look up. While writing this letter, R. had shed the previous day's frantic energy, and was applying himself with transporting calm. "Moreover," I continued, "his diction is superb, his manner refined, his appearance meticulous." I continued in this vein for some time, heaping praise upon my new hire.

"In conclusion," I said, "I very much look forward to seeing you on the occasion of my engagement to your niece some weeks hence. Until then, I remain your humble servant," & c. Upon concluding, I asked R. to show me the finished letter.

R. rose and placed the piece of paper in my outstretched palm, and I observed that the first page was beautiful: he had written precisely what I had said, and with an elegant and flowing hand.

But at the top of the second page, the handwriting became jagged and uneven. Then the line broke in mid-sentence, and the rest of the page was filled with—how shall I describe it?—bizarre and outlandish marks that fell upon my eyes with a certain kind of violence. The bulk of the page was entirely covered like this. For a moment I panicked, worried that my vision and focus might suddenly have left me; I rubbed my eyes and blinked, and strained hard at the page, but it did not change. It was entirely unintelligible.

I thrust the paper toward R. "What is the meaning of this?" I asked him.

He stared blankly at the page for some seconds, as if not seeing what I meant to show. Then, slowly, his eyes resolved on those appalling marks, he nodded his head in acknowledgment, and calmly he told me, "Yes, I see. My mind must have wandered."

His explanation was so simple, unadorned, and unbothered that I began to doubt myself. Was my initial shock unwarranted? Perhaps this was a simple mistake, something like an inkblot. After all, up till this moment he had been, in all things, anxiously meticulous, somewhat in my own mold. Yes: It was his first day, after all, and didn't I owe him some time to adjust? I decided to let the matter pass. He sat down again, and again I dictated the latter part of the letter, and indeed, this time his transcription was flawless.

I put the strange incident out of my mind, and for the next several days R. was in fact an exemplary employee, early to arrive, late to leave, dressed now in a properly tailored shirt. I found myself drawing Dhananjayan's attention to R.'s punctiliousness, his energy, his cool and alacritous demeanor in the face of all tasks and challenges. "Study him," I told Dhanu. "You should strive to behave more like R."

"Am I not also a good help to you?" young Dhananjayan plaintively asked.

"A good help? You? Ha!" I replied, with unwarranted irritation, unwilling, as I inexplicably found myself some days, to spare a compliment for this speck of a boy. "Dhananjayan Rajesupriyan, you are a bad help. You walk slowly, and your nose is always running. You remind me of a donkey." (Pardon me, but need you paint me so rude? It is true, I was strict with this boy you've imagined, and I regret it; but he would have his revenge in time.)

Only in retrospect do I realize that during all this uneventful interval, R. was required to perform little or no *writing,* and absolutely no dictation. It is also possible that I failed to notice further indications of eccentricity, for during that time my life was too full of distractions. Several months previously, a train had derailed at Maniyachchi, crushing some three dozens of people; and since that calamity, there were rumors of unannounced and random inspections at all the village stations. It some days caused me unbearable worry to be in charge of this station and this steam-powered juggernaut in which so many entrusted their lives. I was, after all, only twenty-four, and by nature susceptible to fretfulness and mental unease. Some days, I required Dhananjayan to reassure me four or five times in the space of an hour that he had thoroughly completed the "all-clear checklist for safe passage of trains through the station." Consider that hundreds of people now passed through Rombachinnapattinam weekly. Strangers—at one time an occasional phenomenon—disembarked and entered our village every afternoon. (Our *town,* rather.) We were almost overnight connected with the whole of India. As much as I embraced progress, one sensed something unnatural about the arrangement. I had the ever-present and growing fear of disaster on my watch. And even as I worried over my small domain, people called on me through the day and into the evening, asking favors for themselves and their family members: discounted tickets, delayed departures, personal tours of the train. I was, indeed, a big man in our town (better!), and it was an image I struggled to maintain. I did not care to disappoint my community.

I was to see the majority of that community at my engagement ceremony, mere weeks away, and in truth, this prospect caused me further strain, articulating itself as an unpleasant, simmering gurgle in my stomach and innards. What if I didn't like the girl? What if she expected me to visit Madras and buy her saris, as I had seen some husbands doing, now that the train made such a journey conceivable? What if the girl demanded conversation and attention? I had resolved to impose strict limits on her behavior, but really, I hoped to have very little to do with her whatever, and that, like new household help, she would be the sole province and responsibility of my mother.

It was with all of these worries and pressures building up inside me and compounding themselves, and with my mind clouded in a kind of fog and gloom, that I thought to write again to my supervisor and formally request some days off, to give me time to attend to myself, to clear my mind and rest properly before and after my engagement ceremony.

Sufficient time had passed that R.'s previous lapse scarcely passed through my thoughts when I called to him to take down my words, and as per normal usage, I asked to review the document only after I had finished the dictation.

He put the paper in my hand and when I turned down to look at it, I felt something collapse inside me, as if a heavy stone had tumbled from a chamber in my heart, to land with a thud in my stomach. R. had not completed even one neat and elegant line when the page again became suddenly filled with the same . . . outrageous and unintelligible . . . the same inhuman scrawl and monstrous gibberish. Like a toddling child on his first day in classroom, I stared at the page and could make no sense of what I found there. How can I give you a picture? These were not the random markings of an animal or an imbecile, no; there seemed something purposeful about what he had put down. It gave me pause. I fleetingly wondered: Were these dense markings a somehow accurate transcription of things I had unwittingly uttered? Did the garble on the page represent a garble that had come from my own mouth? Of course not, I quickly concluded. But what if the words were perfectly legible and English, and it was I who had turned idiot, and lost my ability to read them? On further study, I determined that this awful letter was written neither in English nor in any language. It was entirely inhuman, illogical, and unfamiliar, and it gave me a twisted feeling inside to look at it.

"R.!" I called, I bellowed. "R.!" I could scarcely speak. I only held the paper before me, hoping it might speak for itself.

He observed the letter meekly and in silence.

Finally, I was forced to ask, "What does it . . . what does it mean?"

"What does *what* mean, sir?"

Now I felt the first tickles of rage. This chap was taking me for a fool. I saw it clearly now: I was the butt of some elaborate joke. But I could not understand the joke, nor even articulate its scope and purpose, precisely, and this agitated me all the more. Certainly, whoever was behind this joke—whether R. himself, or some enemy I had unwittingly made here at the Railway, who was using R. as his agent, some secret inspector—whoever it was could not have found a more straight-faced jokester, for R. was not in the least perturbed by my alarm. The bold chap looked at me with a quizzical, altogether innocent expression.

"Don't test my patience, R. Tell me, what is the meaning of this? What are you up to? What is going on? I will not be made a fool in my own office." Now he took the offered paper from my hand and began to read it, calmly and with interest. After waiting some moments in silence, I asked, "Do you still not see what I am referring to?"

R. did not answer—he seemed lost in the perusal of his creation, as if those bizarre markings held some deep, engrossing significance, and although he had written them, he was being edified by them anew.

"Come on, R.," I said. "You can pretend that you are reading something there, but I won't be duped." But he still did not look up from the page. I laughed, and in my unsteady laughter I heard my own uncertainty and growing terror.

In the ensuing silence, I knew I should throw him out on his ear, but he seemed so transported with his letter that I admit I somehow hesitated to disturb his profound reverie! This moment of foolish hesitation had the benefit of rewarding me with the idea that I should really corroborate this insanity, to reassure myself that R.'s equanimity was indeed an act—that it was he who was behaving outrageously, and not my own perceptions that had been shattered.

I went to the window and called to Dhananjayan. When he came inside, I politely asked R. to show Dhanu the letter, and R.—finished, apparently, with his reading—obliged.

"Dhananjayan," I asked, in the calmest, most agreeable tone I could muster, as if nothing at all were amiss, "would you please tell us what you think of this letter that R. has transcribed on my behalf?"

Dhanu looked at R. and at me, with a bemused expression. Then he raised the letter to his eyes. I could not see his face behind the paper, but from the small clearings of his throat and mutterings of interest, I imagined him squinting and perusing, eager, as I had been, to find some meaning in what was clearly meaningless. He took a great deal of time in the perusal, and I must say, I was on tenterhooks, frightened lest he might have found some explanation for the madness on that page, some meaning that was plainly there, but that I, from some fundamental defect of intelligence, was unable to see.

Finally, he returned the letter to my hand, and gazing now with assurance at R. and then at me, rocking his head with satisfaction, he offered the following analysis:

"It's a fine letter. Very fine, sir."

"Very fine?" I could only repeat, in a voice that sounded, to myself, small and distant.

A horror was creeping into my soul, for here was sure evidence that I was mad, or that my eyes had lost reliable function. How many other things, I wondered, held meaning for everyone in the world but for me? Was it because I had been pampered by my parents, sheltered all my life in this hamlet, that the incapacity was not brought to my attention sooner?

Only slowly did the explanation come to me, and lift, like the iron lid of a government well, the anxiety that rested heavily on my heart. Why, Dhananjayan was perfectly illiterate! Letters in written English were no more recognizable to him than letters written in language of birds. In my agitation, I had allowed myself to forget it: the boy had no idea whether he was looking at straight gibberish or the sonnets of Shakespeare!

So again, I had reason to twist him up by the ear. "Talking out of your nose, Dhanu, eh? How many times have I told you not to speak when you don't know what you are speaking about? I should be rid of the both of you now, should I not?"

I released Dhanu's ear and turned to R., reaffirmed now in my conviction that there was no option but to fire him, chuck him, blast him, discard him on the spot, cashier him, expel him, and expunge him. A secretary who could not take dictation, and moreover, pretended to take dictation while instead perpetrating outrageous crimes and wastages of ink and paper, could not and would not stand in my office.

"Dhananjayan's appraisal notwithstanding," I told R., "can you tell me why I should not dismiss you here and now?"

R. did not answer, nor did he seem in the least discomfited by my tirade, and in the again growing silence, I realized I did not have quite the "fire in my belly" to proceed. For courage, I drew closer to Dhananjayan, who stared at this unfolding scene, rubbing his tender ear, in perfect amazement. I patted Dhanu's shoulder—no hard feelings—and said, "I've scolded Dhanu in good fun, but I'm sure even he would make a better secretary than you, R. What do you say, Dhananjayan Rajesupriyan? What would you do were you in my position?"

Seeing now which way the wind was blowing, Dhanu did not hesitate to offer his opinion. "I would twist *his* ear and make him howl. I would. Then I would thrash him cent per cent, and leave him crying at his door. Shall I do it for you?" Dhanu picked up his broom and held it aloft in a threatening manner.

I restrained the boy with another tug to his ear. "Not your place, Dhanu," I reminded him. Then I turned to R. "R., you hear what we have said. Now what do you have to say for yourself?"

But R. said nothing. Instead, this Bartleby (this who?) only stared into my eyes, neither angry nor afraid, neither defensive nor beseeching. He seemed to be still afloat in the calm of having written and then read his nonsensical pages. With peaceful indifference he looked at me, lacking the slightest residue of malice, or any trace of awareness of the misdeeds he had committed. In the face of R.'s overwhelming tranquility, my will began to waver. Perhaps, I thought, he had not acted deliberately after all, and his mishandling of my letter stemmed from some blind, inward compulsion. This inner defect prevented him from performing his duties, to be sure. But here was the picture of absolute innocence. It is inherently difficult to act harshly against innocent characters, and I still hesitated to say the words I was determined to say.

I found my mind searching for some reason to avoid having to turn him out into the hot afternoon. Again, I remembered his poverty, his pathetic appearance when I first met him, the poor mother he cared for. Would the credit I had earned by giving gainful employment to a needy Brahmin be lost if I let him go? Would it be seen as bad luck, or bad manners, to turn him out so soon before my engagement?

And there was also something else R. had told me, something else which suggested, perhaps, a painful affinity between us. "Myself being recently engaged for marriage," he had told me, that first day we met, "being recently engaged, good sir, I don't know what to do. I don't know what to do."

I could not, of course, assume that R. shared my own hideous passions. But here was someone, clearly, like me, set apart from the common lot. Here was someone who found the regular world a little bit . . . confounding. And while I had found a way to function in it (the common world)—found a way, in fact, to thrive—R., like an inverted version of myself, remained on the outside looking in.

It soon seemed to me that any one of these reasons counseled against dismissing R.—at least until I could help him to find some other means of supporting himself and his small family.

"R.," I told him, speaking gently now, "this letter you transcribed is not at all the same as the letter I related to you. Now, whether you can admit it or not, you know this is true. Can I have your assurance that you will endeavor henceforward to do as you are supposed to, and keep your mind focused to the task at hand?"

I saw his eyes responding to my words; I saw that he understood.

"I will, sir," he told me.

"Now, there's my man," I said, beaming, proud that my measured tone, quick mind, and commanding presence had negotiated the shoals of this strange difficulty, and been rewarded with a concession. I had salvaged R.'s job despite himself. R. and Dhanu—such people relied on decisive and reasonable managers such as myself. How would our villagers eat, how would trains run, how would the world move without managers!

Now, even having gotten R.'s reassurance, I thought it best to keep him away from paper and ink. These commodities were dear and not to be squandered. I could manage to write my own letters for a while until a more agreeable arrangement could be found.

"Dhananjayan," I said, "from today and for the time being, R. will help you to execute the operations of the station. He'll do my filing. But, R., I beg of you, don't go near the pen."

R., of course, received all this news with the same impassive face with which he had absorbed my previous admonishments.

(My dear fellow, allow me to say, you have written this part of the story quite passably! I find myself strangely moved by the scenario, and by the grace of my own actions. Carry on.)

As it were, more than a year later, looking back on the episode with the dimness of memory and distortions of hindsight, Dhanu would insist, "I was not bluffing when I complimented his letter, sir. I never liked R., but his markings were beautiful. I don't think I would find such strangely pleasing things even painted in the palace of Mysore Maharajah."

R. gave me no serious botherations in the days between that incident and my engagement ceremony. But I had little attention to spare for him in those times, with the headaches, entanglements, family demands, and organizational difficulties of the ceremony and subsequent wedding to concern me. The worries of being a groom, so it seemed at the time, far outweighed the pleasures. I looked forward to the transition to manhood that my betrothal signified, yet it caused me enormous stress. I had met my betrothed once or twice, so I was told, at family functions, but I scarcely could recall her face. Some days, I burned with curiosity about this woman with whom I would have to spend all my days. But in a way, it hardly mattered to me what she was like; I knew that regardless of the woman, I should recoil at having to accommodate a new and unknown presence in my life.

These thoughts I carried with me as I rode to my fiancée's

home, the December afternoon of my engagement ceremony. Watching the people and houses pass behind our cart in the dappled sunlight, the weather almost alarmingly beautiful, these concerns seemed to grow inside me, until they achieved something like anger. This anger was completely unrelated to the figure of the little girl I was to marry, but as soon as I saw her—the heavy sari draped over her shoulder, the glint of her nose jewels—this anger attached itself to her figure.

At the hall, a coterie of family members came to the cart, holding flower garlands and sandal paste and a vessel of rose water, and before I had even stepped out of the cart they began to sprinkle and anoint me. Inside the compound, young women peeked at me from behind their friends' shoulders; children came to touch me and hold my hand until their mothers pulled them away. Indeed, silliness and horseplay were strictly prohibited in my general vicinity.

"Like a rajah," people whispered, admiring my appearance.

A chair was offered, as others sat on the floor. Sweets on a tray appeared. Chips and savories. Coffee or lime juice? Coffee *and* lime juice. Because I didn't finish my coffee, my bride's father scolded his wife, the wife yelled at the cook, the cook berated the servants. I began to have an inkling of what was meant by the expression "to be treated like a bridegroom," and when time came to leave for the temple and begin the ceremony itself, I had left behind entirely the gloom and anxiety, the anger, with which I had begun the day.

We walked toward the temple on a route that took us within a few meters of the railroad station. I had left the station that day in Dhanu's capable hands, with R. as his help. And while I had total confidence in Dhanu, I did have a small worry he might use the occasion to pick some quarrel with hapless R. I walked down the road with my parents flanking me, and the bride's family all around. Behind me stood the very uncle-in-law who was my nominal supervisor in Madras, and alongside him were my future brothers and cousins, everyone in a grand procession with me, resplendent, at the center.

At what point did it become clear to me that something was amiss? In retrospect, there was a strange agitation in the street, an excited general chatter, but at the time, of course, I assumed this excitement was a result of my own presence on that street.

When the railroad station came into view on our left, I noticed that there was an unusual crowd on the platform for so late in the day—why were they milling about? Only then, strange to say, did I notice the elephant, so to speak, on the horizon: the massive *Madras Mail* sat idling on the tracks, one full hour past the time it should have departed!

"What is this?" my new uncle asked me, in surprise.

I began to make abject and nonsensical explanations, all the time puzzling through in my mind what might be going on. I spotted Dhanu through the crowd, and called to him, and when he came running toward me, he was in actual tears of agitation.

"I flew the green flag, sir. I promise you. I cleared the tracks."

"Tell me plainly, what happened?" I grabbed him and shook him by the arm, to calm him. "Why is the train standing here? What have you done? What are all these people looking at?"

We were tacking toward the platform now, redirecting the entire engagement procession, pushing our way around the loitering mob, who turned but briefly to acknowledge us. And then I heard Dhananjayan confirm what my eyes were only then showing me.

"It's R., sir!" Dhanu said. "It's R., it's R. who's done this!"

R., you see, was doing what he had always done: he was writing. He had broken off a piece of white brick from the outhouse wall, it must have been, and was using it as a chalk to scrawl all over the dun walls of the station. His abhorrent scratches covered the doors, the windowpanes, the very floor of the platform. Running out of space on the building, he was writing now on the fat trunk of a neem tree and even the unpaved ground, and would soon begin on the train itself. We had denied him pen and paper, and he had made the whole earth his canvas.

The same obscure, convoluted designs that had been shown only to me were now scrawled in the open, writ large for everyone to see. It was as if all that was private and awful had been drawn into sunlight, grandly revealing its horror.

Passengers had disembarked to smoke and chat and watch the spectacle, and laugh at our own variety of village idiot. The dawdlers ignored poor Dhananjayan's entreaties that they return to the train. The train conductor himself leaned leisurely out of the window of the engine. He shook his head at the marks, observing to those assembled, "He must be a learned fellow, to be able to write so many interesting things. Myself, I have never learned Sanskrit." In response, one listener spat, "Sanskrit—how ridiculous! That fellow is clearly from Calcutta, and he is writing in Bengali. A very ugly language, as you can see. My uncle has visited Calcutta, so I should know." And to this, another laughed. "You're both mad. The Britishers have ordered improvements to all our village stations. Hadn't you heard? This man is just a simple housepainter, painting in the British style." And from within my own engagement party came the reply: "Housepainter? 'Vandal' is more like it. And we should beat him about the head if he were not a Brahmin."

Oblivious to their attentions, R. hopped about from place to place. He had tied his vaishti high and tight to afford ease of movement, and it slipped looser and lower as now he squatted and now he stood, and wrote and wrote. Thus, for all to see, was the eminently qualified fellow I had hired as my own personal secretary! Some passengers could not contain their mirth: the maddening, haphazard scratches seemed to tickle them deep inside, so that even their eyes showed surprise that they could not control their giddy giggles. "It is so pretty," one small child squealed foolishly to his mother—and perhaps this is where Dhanu got his idea, much later, that those horrific marks were pleasing to look at. Meanwhile, the train conductor revised his original appraisal: "It is not Sanskrit, it's English. Just look how carefully that foreign gentleman over there is reading." The foreign passenger in question was indeed monitoring the scene gravely. He turned, finally, to his also British companion and explained, with sage dispassion, "It is best not to interrupt him," indicating R. "You see, the superstitious symbols he is making are deeply meaningful to the Hindus of this region."

My new uncle-in-law, for his part, had grown quietly furious. He stared at R.'s display as if those lines spelled something of direct offense to his dignity and soul; he dripped and pulsed with sweaty indignation. He called out darkly in my ear, but I could not hear what he said, for on the other side, Dhanu had dissolved again into helpless, childlike tears—the boy seemed to have been pushed past his limit.

I could not turn to face either of these people, but instead, adorned all in flower garlands, I stormed up to R. I screamed oaths and imprecations at the back of his head, demanding an explanation. But the man calmly continued writing as if he hadn't heard me.

Finally, I grabbed him by the shoulder and swung him round by force. He stared at me, calmly blinking. Did he recognize me at all? I grabbed the chalk from his hand and flung it into the tracks.

"Get out of my sight!" I said. I am ashamed to say that I struck him across the face, in front of all of my guests. But this blow had the effect of finally bringing him back to reality.

"Get away from here, you imbecile, you fool! Never come to this station again."

He seemed to understand what I had told him. He gathered up his vaishti and walked away.

I turned aside in disgust, only to find standing before me and blocking my path a slick-haired photographer supporting his grotesque contraption. My in-laws had hired him all the way from Madras, and he had only now disembarked from the train and found our company. "Let us have it over with," my bride's uncle instructed me. So, steaming and humiliated, I moved to the part of the station least sullied by R.'s offenses, wiped off his marks with my hand, and stood with any and all dignity I could muster—at any rate, I knew I looked smart, with a magnificent new shut-coat given me as part of my dowry. After several minutes of tedious immobility, while the frenzied crowd settled down to stare, the fellow finally uncloaked his head, the crowd hoorahed—hadn't they enjoyed quite the show this afternoon!—the engineer finally blew his whistle, and we continued our tense procession to the temple. (Would that I had imagined you then as I do now—I might have bashed that camera! There is something altogether too ticklish about your reanimating me and setting me in ink . . . even as I suppose there is something revealing in it. Nevertheless, carry on.)

After this incident, my bride's uncle was understandably concerned about my management of the station and my prospects in the Railway, and consequently, my suitability for his niece. My judgment and character were called into question. For a few anxious weeks, there was some uncertainty as to whether I would continue as Rombachinnapattinam's stationmaster, and indeed, whether the wedding would still go forward. To have a wedding canceled for a scandal so public would have been disastrous to my family's reputation, and to my personal prospects. In my secret heart, I had hoped for some reprieve from the wedding, but now it had come I saw the horror of it. Social death was not a price I could pay.

I saw my whole life passing from the plain and legible world to that of ugly incoherence. Things were reversed: the wrong side was facing out. During these days, as my mind obsessively rehearsed the steps toward my predicament, trying to pinpoint its first warnings, and how it could have been avoided, I kept alighting on one scene: I sat smugly at my desk, relating an eloquent and well-considered letter, as R. scribbled dutifully; then R. quietly handed me back a piece of paper that bore no resemblance to what I had composed, that was not at all what I had expected to see.

That letter began to seem filled with uncanny portent; those bizarre scrawls seemed the sign and analogue of my own inner turmoil, my emptiness, my lack of power. The indecipherable signs on that page spoke of some mystery inside me and all around, in plain sight yet stubbornly inaccessible. I felt very alone, and the image of my loneliness was also lost among R.'s unreadable characters.

And now, ironically, I might share R.'s fate. I wondered what had become of him since I had publicly scolded him, since our simultaneous humiliation. What had happened to his poor mother, to the wedding he had spoken of? Had his family been plunged into poverty? Had I sent him to go begging in the streets?

Some afternoons I found myself wandering in the particular Brahmin quarter where I knew R. to stay. I made inquiries with his neighbors, found out which humble house was his, but I could not bring myself to look in on him. I was too guilty. I had hit him in public. But deservedly so! For I was also terribly angry with him—to recall that scene on my engagement day filled me with a humiliated rage I could not bear.

Don't get the wrong impression: I was judicious in my anger, and not lacking in compassion. Just ask Dhananjayan if you think I was incapable of tenderness. Just ask Dhanu if you think I was incapable of love!

Well, come to think of it, don't ask Dhanu, because what did even he know about me? As it turns out, I also understood very little about him. He was just a boy, after all, and how much could he tolerate? But Dhanu was to have his revenge on R. and on me, and when it came, one evening not long after my engagement-day fiasco, it was spoken softly, in tones of love, even while he held me in his embrace.

"I have some happy news," Dhanu told me, with his sweet voice.

"Yes, Dhanu? Good. Tell me."

"He has disappeared. You can relax now. He won't bother you anymore."

"Who has disappeared, Dhanu?" I asked.

"Mr. R., of course," and at the sound of his name, I felt a seizing in my guts. "Mr. R. I thought you must have heard."

"Heard what, exactly?" I asked, trying not to betray the feeling of foreboding inside me.

"Why, heard about Mr. R. About the manner in which he left."

"What *was* the manner in which he left, Dhanu?" I asked again. In this way, cruel Dhanu made me struggle for every scrap of information. Finally, I managed to gather that R. had come to the station the previous day and bought an open ticket, one way. "You were away on one of your long afternoon walks," Dhanu took care to note. "Otherwise you would have been there to see him." Without a single piece of luggage, alone, and without uttering a word, R. climbed aboard the 3:38 *Madras Mail* and vanished.

"Vanished?" I asked.

"Yes, vanished."

I laughed uncomfortably. "You make it sound as if it were something mystical that had occurred. Surely he has simply gone to visit some relatives somewhere. Where did he tell you he was heading?"

"He didn't say. I tell you, sir, when he stepped on the train, he vanished almost like a cloud of steam. He talked with no one, and his face had the look of someone who has no intention to return."

Now I could not hide my agitation; I threw off the boy's arm. "So R. is gone? For how long? Why didn't you stop him? Why didn't you make him tell you what he was up to? Dhananjayan Rajesupriyan, did you just stare dumbly and watch him go?"

"Always you tell me not to ask pointless questions," Dhanu said. "I felt it was not my place." Then he paused. "Could it really be, sir, that you are upset Mr. R. has left? Didn't he cause you only distress and worry when he was here?"

"Well, yes, Dhanu," I had to acknowledge. "Mr. R. has caused me more distress than anyone I have ever known. He almost ruined my life."

"Then, sir," Dhananjayan asked, blinking his eyes, "shouldn't you be quite happy that he has gone away?"

I could not find an answer. The devious boy knew he had me in a corner.

(Briefly, may I take this opportunity to call into question *your* judgment and character? As dramatic as all this is, I must reiterate that it puts me in a gratuitously unflattering light. What, finally, is the point? To have one's life reflected back so unrecognizably, so bizarrely is a form of torture. Interesting, to be sure, but hellishly so. At any rate, hurry and finish.)

To shed some light on the strange events narrated by Dhanu, that evening I finally visited R.'s house (it was a room, actually; a dark room rented in a shabby home) and looked in on his poor mother. But what I learned there only deepened the mystery of R.'s disappearance, for R.'s mother had even less knowledge than I did of the boy's whereabouts. The nearsighted and anxious old woman told me that she had awoken previous morning to find R.'s bed neatly rolled, his shirt and notebook missing, and absolutely no sign of the boy. He had left without leaving any note, without any indication as to where he was going. He had, indeed, so far as she knew, simply disappeared.

The old woman was distraught and amazed to hear that R. had been observed boarding the *Madras Mail*.

"Mami," I tried to reassure her, "surely he is only gone to some neighboring town to visit relatives, or to seek work."

"What relatives?" she cried. "What work? He doesn't know anyone; he doesn't know to do anything. You understand this as well as I do, sir."

The lady was inconsolable, alternately worried about her son's fate, and furious with him. "His wedding day arrives in three weeks, sir," she told me. "I was lucky to find a bride willing to marry a boy like him. It would have been understandable if *she* was the one to disappear."

"Surely he will return in time for his wedding," I ventured. "He is not . . . *totally* incapable."

"Just look at this, sir!" The old lady opened a cabinet. "These are his things. This is my son." The shelves were stuffed full with loose papers, torn and wrinkled scraps and salvaged bits of newsprint—hundreds upon hundreds of pages. I began to take them out one by one and examine them. They were each completely covered in the same indecipherable scrawl—page after page. "This is my son. This is the boy we are talking about!" the old woman wailed, as my very skin began to crawl.

That week I telegraphed all my contacts in the Railway, all up and down the line, even in Madras, to see if anyone could report on R.'s whereabouts. But no one at all, anywhere, could recall even having seen him. Dhanu's imaginative description began to seem more and more apt: R. had stepped onto the train and somehow evaporated.

Three weeks passed. The date planned for the boy's nuptials came quietly and went with no word from him. Despite my concern for the boy's fate, I resolved to carry on with life, to let none of it bother me. Whatever had happened to him, I insistently reminded myself, was no fault of mine.

A month passed. Then three months. I heard meanwhile that the bride's family, furious, had demanded the return of their small dowry from R.'s poor mother.

It was pitiful to think of R.—lacking all social graces, who had never before left our village—lost and alone somewhere in vast South India. I imagined him driven to extremis—starving on the roadside or throwing himself in despair into the ocean. In my heart, I cursed the train for having spirited the helpless boy away. Why existed such a thing? Where was ever the need to travel so quickly? I even wondered if Dhanu had planned the scheme, and somehow deceived R. into leaving; but my conversations, later, with people who had been on the platform that day confirmed that R. had clambered aboard the train of his own volition, without uttering a single word.

Fighting down my anxiety, I continued to reassure myself that his disapperance had nothing anymore to do with me. But then, walking home one evening and happening on a series of lines and scratches in the roadside dirt, I felt an excited panic. Were these R.'s designs? Had he here returned to us? I stooped and studied the marks and scuffs, trying to draw a familiar feeling from them. I pointed them out to two passing ladies. "What do you think it means?" I asked. In their disturbed glances, I realized my own foolishness, for these were only the frantic pawprints left by some copulating street dogs!

I felt a plummeting disappointment. The boy was profoundly gone; and I saw then that despite my outward disavowals, my own preoccupation with him had reached a worrisome level. I had become infected with an idea: that R.'s writing had held some message for myself. Analogue and cause of my predicament, his writing was also the key to escaping it. Now, because of my own actions, R., and the meaning of his message, were lost forever.

Deeply distressed, I began spending long mornings in the Krishna temple. I watched the priest doing puja, then I sat and chanted Gita verses with some other scholars there. I found solace in the monotony of prayer, in the thought that my muttered words might find connection with the spiritual realm. But in the quiet of meditation, my mind wandered. Could R.'s markings, I considered, themselves have been some kind of prayer? And just as my prayers brought me closer to God, could I now find R.'s whereabouts by praying to him? I tried: I meditated on his face, I repeated his name—until the sacrilege of what I was attempting too much disturbed me.

And one day in the earliest dawn, unable to sleep, I walked to my office and confronted the canvas bags of mail that had arrived from Madras previous day, some to be distributed here, others to be sorted for transfer to other stations down the way. Suddenly it occurred to me that therein might be some message from the boy. I upended the bags and spread the mail across the floor of my office—so many correspondences, so many people with things to communicate to each other! None of it mattered. I sought only one letter; it would be written in an unintelligible gibberish, but it would contain a profound and reassuring message, for it would mean that R. was alive, that he was trying to reach me! With patient madness, I sat on the floor and searched missive after missive, until Dhanu arrived for his morning duties. He laid his hand on my shoulder, guided me gently from the floor to my desk, where I sat and quietly wept while he cleaned the place. (Sat and wept? Looking at my photograph, my chap, do I really strike you as one who would give in to softness of mind, to weeping?)

Why had I turned R. away so harshly? I saw very painfully that my concern for the boy had come too slowly, piecemeal, and too late, and that this lapse could no longer be remedied. Indeed, after that time, R. was never again seen in our village. Why had I not looked out for this boy who had always been—but was now so irrevocably—lost to the world?

The final occasion I went to visit his mother, taking with me some small money and a packet of food, as I walked along the road, I heard the sound of her wailing through the window of her quarters. Amid the old woman's cries of lonely grief, those who shared her house and lived nearby continued blithely about their daily tasks. Whether she was really crying, whether R. was really gone, one could not have told for all the concern shown by the people on that street. But perhaps they could not be bothered to acknowledge what they could not first of all understand: R.'s absence was as complete, as profound, and as indecipherable as those intractable letters he had composed in my name.

My own wedding, you will be relieved but not surprised to hear, was after all not called off. My position with the Railway also remained quite safe. The bride's family of course realized that they would have suffered as much scandal as mine had they been part of so public a fiasco as a canceled wedding, and we were therefore united in grand fashion before some two hundred of guests.

Married life was both more and less than I had expected. At first I found my wife quite a nuisance. Coming home to contend with this new person was like lying down to sleep and finding the bed covered in mosquitoes—one had longed for comfort and familiarity, but found only irritation. Shall I give you an example? So many times I came home from office, and had not even had time to wash my feet, when she would call out peevishly from wherever she sat working, "Aren't you even going to say *hullo* to me?"

It is true, over time I did become somewhat fond of the girl, like a friend, or a sister, or the sister of a friend—someone whom I teased and abused, but who became very useful to my mother, and on whom, finally, I also began to depend.

Our relationship only fully began to sour perhaps two years or more into our marriage. I was leaving the house one evening, hoping to find some relaxation with a new friend of mine, a young man named Rishikesh, who had come to our home twice or thrice to whitewash our kitchen walls, and who also proved adept at clambering up the palm tree in the garden, and cutting down the coconuts. This talented young man Rishu proved to be a kind and affectionate friend to me, and a more agreeable presence than Dhananjayan, whose daily appearance in the station I could scarcely anymore abide. In fact, I was quite seriously considering replacing Dhananjayan with this alacritous Rishikesh, although Dhanu had tearfully implored me to keep him on, saying impudently that all of his neighbors looked at him askance now that he had worked for me, and he would have great difficulty ever finding a comparable position.

In any event, as I walked out the door to visit this new friend Rishu, my wife called to me and asked where I was going.

"What is your interest in asking?" I responded. "Why shouldn't I go where I wish to go?"

"No matter," she said. "I already know where it is you're headed." Then, as I turned again to leave, she added (and with a note of such spiteful derision in her voice!), "But other women's husbands—other *men*—don't do such things."

All the anger that had ever been in me, all the humiliated rage, rose up again at that moment, and I gave my wife such a thrashing as you can scarcely imagine. Then I walked quietly out of my home, leaving her to my mother's ministrations.

(I must say that my relationship with my wife is not something I would have preferred for you to have mentioned. I fear you have finally gone too far. You think you have license based on the distant chance she was some great-great-grandmother to you, or someone whose life otherwise sheds light on your own. But you don't understand the least of it. And neither did she understand me. We lived a life of utter intimacy, yet how little she knew of my secret heart, and I of hers. I grew to be a fiend in her eyes, I'm sure; and she always remained an inscrutable problem for me. She suffered a lot. Yes, you have gone too far, but I suppose the remedy would be to go further still; if you write another story, perhaps you ought to write one about her.)

Very glum and sour of mood following this altercation, I walked out that evening to meet with Rishikesh. As I walked, I felt that my outwardly easy life was in fact entirely insupport-able. And upon entering that poverty-stricken and unpleasant part of our village where Rishikesh lived, I heard people call out in the darkness and I suspected they were mocking me. A pebble hit me in the leg; I yelled angrily toward the shadows. Had I become nothing but a laughingstock, propped up only to be played the fool? Was the world in cahoots against me?

Rishu tried but could not extract from me the cause of my unhappiness that evening, and in my bitter mood I had half a mind to give him a thrashing as well! I asked out loud why I had even bothered to come there, for I suddenly seemed to have lost all affection for the boy.

And it was in a similar state of glum and angry dejection, the next afternoon, at the station, opening one of the newspapers from Bombay, that I read a brief article that caught my eye:

INDIAN SOLVES LONG-STANDING MATHEMATICAL PUZZLE

Rogerson, a scholar of Indian extraction at the University of Harvard in Boston, America, has published an article in the latest *Journal of the American Society of Mathematicians,* that is said to solve the Leumens Paradox, a conundrum that has confounded scholars since the time of the Ancient Greeks. The head of mathematics department at Harvard, Prof. Wlm. Oxswett, BS, PhD, FASM, FRSM, has said: "This is a paper that will be hailed as one of the three or four most important papers in the history of mathematics. Rogerson is a man of unparalleled genius."

I know nothing of maths. It was my worst subject in school, and of course I had never heard of this "Leumens Paradox" nor of this fellow "Rogerson." It did not even seem an Indian name. But I was intrigued by the story, and I studied the picture that accompanied it: a skinny young man in a dark-colored American suit, a wide nose, a spotted cravat, a thick black cream of hair. His eyes were large and sunken and strangely, sadly calm, and they seemed also familiar to me.

Yes, I had seen eyes like this before. I knew that gaze: focused beyond the thing at which it was looking, angled at some unearthly perspective, but earthbound and sad, bearing up quietly to the world's eternal misunderstanding. I had once looked deeply into such eyes, and they had disconcerted me. But at first, the precise resemblance escaped me.

It was only sometime later, before leaving for home, when I glanced back on that picture, that it occurred to me: Could those be R.'s eyes?

But R. was no mathematician, was he? Moreover, the face in which R.'s eyes were sitting in that newspaper was nothing like R.'s face. R. had been full-cheeked, not wan and sharp-cheekboned, like the man in the picture. R. had sported a shaved head and short ponytail. He had no well-groomed, flowing mane of hair, like this "Rogerson." His nose was bony and round at the end, as I recalled, and not so wide and flat. R. was daily attired in nothing but the shirt I made him buy; and when not at work, he wore no shirt at all. He would not have known what to do with a cravat! And the markings R. was wont to make looked like no mathematics that I or anyone else had ever studied. And, of course, R.'s name was not "Rogerson."

That day, I read eagerly through the other papers for some mention of this story, some corroborating detail, but found nothing. Finally, I tore the photograph from the page and hurried out of the station.

Later, I chastised myself for my foolishness. The prospect of R.—who could scarcely dress by himself, or walk the half kilometer from his home to the railway station without getting lost—somehow finding his way by steamer to America, gaining a post at a famous university, solving an ancient mathematical Paradox (I had asked my old maths teacher on the Leumens

Paradox, and while most of his answer escaped my understanding, I gathered roughly that it had to do with the impossibility of forming a square or perfect "parallelogram," as it is called, by connecting four given or imaginary points, which occupy similar or identical positions on each of several grids, but which are separated from each other by actual or imaginary dimensions or factors of impossibility, separated from each other even by space and time—an impossibility unless one formed a shape that appeared to exist but did not in fact exist)—the prospect of R.'s having solved such a puzzle, and earning international acclaim thereby—why, it was all so wonderful that I felt I must be crazy to believe it. (Not crazy, I must interject. Perhaps mistaken, but not crazy. Are *you* crazy, let us ask, to imagine that you can imagine me? To think, upon finding some ancient photograph which excited your nostalgia, that you could fill in the gaps using your twisted imagination? Are you crazy, to think that you can draw this strange story, create this absurd conversation between us? That despite my indubitable deadness, I am so close you can imagine to feel the breath of my voice in your ear? Perhaps you and I are related; and so are all people related. More likely I am imaginary; but mustn't all people be imagined? Crazy? Just as I am lost to you, R. was lost to me, irrefutably—how people so close to us can become so unreachable, how people unreachable can feel so close: there's your paradox—and yet I longed to have him near to me; in my longing, I *brought* him near to me. Not crazy—as you hear these words, as you reach past the years to touch my face—not crazy, no.)

But at any rate, no: those eyes staring at me from that newspaper, familiar though they seemed, were not—could not be—those of R. It was with regret that I came to this conclusion, for what a solace it would have been to know that R. had achieved such a success. How elating to imagine that those blurred and garbled markings—not just those markings, but my whole life, the world—had unknotted into crisp and legible clarity, full of happy meaning! What an amazement to consider that the boy had been purposeful all along, and his scribblings had only lacked that audience capable of understanding them. A pity: our R. was no genius but a madman, at whose center were not the secret keys to mathematics but a garble of nothingness.

No, this was not R., I told myself. But then why did I find myself inquiring into the cost of a passage to America? Why did I secretly sell a necklace from my wife's wedding trousseau? Why did I need cash on hand, if not to purchase a ticket? I had never, before that time, seen the great deck of a cruising ship, nor the wild, deep, transforming ocean, nor the gray towers of cold and sunless Boston. Why, then, did I picture these things as feverishly as if they were my destiny?

(. . . Why indeed? Was it he in the photograph, or was it not? Did I travel to America and meet him there, or did I stay in India, to father some child, who authored another, who created a third, who perchance gave birth to you? What is it, Rajesh? You hack, you tyrant: Don't leave off the story here, blame you! Conclude it!)

I AM AN EXECUTIONER

I AM AN EXECUTIONER. TELL ME, is it disgusting? Something too shameful? When I am engaging in a practice of useful caring benefits, on your behalf and with your monies? Short times ago when freshly married, I brought home my new wife, Margaret. Prior to our wedding day, Margaret and I had met only in the computer, where we were enjoying delightful interchanges. But when she realized of my profession, she became so angry: "You dupe! You ape! You trickster! You foul and dirty person! I never would have agreed to marriage had I known!" Nose-jellies meantime were squirting from her nose.

In our small and famous country, I am Chief Executioner. In fact, Only Executioner. Is it a small post? A foul and dirty post? An ape's post? I could not meet Margaret's bloodflushed eyes and tearglistening face, so I aimed my eyes to the cockroach in the roomcorner. "Quite plainly I told you," I told her. "I am civil service member, rank four, grade seven, serving in Ministry of Justices, Punishments, Appeals, and Probations some fifteen years, making such-and-such monies per annum, including pensions and associated benefits. It is tricky maneuvers to catch a wife at my age, also being one time divorced, but please don't call me a liar. *Life of truth is its own reward,* my papa always he told me. Even your mummy-daddy were smiling to hear of my job. To be frank, your mummy-daddy were most eager to marry you off, using wordings for you like 'winter chicken' and 'Christmas cake in the month of January,' to which I personally took exception. For you to this point go on complaining, dear Margaret, when you are perhaps occupying no such position, and after everything already is good and settled and nothing to be done, is moot, silly, and not at all fair. Wipe." I stretched to her my kerchief for her nose-jellies.

"Pah!" she spat, spanking down the kerchief.

May I speak frankly? In those moments, the chiefest goal of my mind had been to make the marriage totally official, come what may. I was paining very much to do it. So long it was since I had a wife! (Or anything of that nature.) I tried to change away the subject of my job. I brought my eyes to face-to-face her. To my lips, I yanked up a smile. "Margaret, you are such a plump and pretty bride," I told, holding toward her the imaginary mirror of my palm. "Always brides are sad on the wedding night. It is so charming in its way, and not at all unusual. You are only missing mummy-daddy. And maybe you are little wary regarding the supermysterious duties and requirements of the wifehood. I assure you, dear Margaret, it is only so much pleasure there. Softest and darkest of the pleasures. Do you like chocolates? Do you like sweet curds? Wifely duties are like that only. Come on. Let us retire now to bedroom, and I will show to you. To start us up, will you demonstrate some of your athletics, calisthenics?"

"What are you talking about?" she asked to me.

"In your computer profile, you wrote up you are enjoying such exercises daily?"

"Pah!" Margaret spat again. She ran into the bedroom (my bedroom) and bolted up the door. The doorslamming sent Catty to scurry under the sofa, leaving me solo in the room. Still there was a smile in my face, for what purposes anymore I did not know it, so I wiped it off. I thought: She is not very much a shy and blushing bride, my Margaret, nor is she on the saucy side. She is bolder than I imagined, and not at all demure. But only so much time could I give to such a pang and a heartache, because next day it was my serious program to care for a new prisoner.

A new prisoner in the death row always brings excitement. Although it means lot of work and challenging duties, whatever said and done, those chaps are often the chiefest friends of me. So after the big crash-crash of Margaret's distressful objections, I was eager for a return to the comfortable death row, even though the new prisoner was so unusual, a young girl and very quiet.

I woke up early next day, night's darknesses remaining everywhere. I had contented myself with sofa-sleeping, and wearing only yesterday's clothings, such was the difficulty imposed on me by my Margaret. Catty only waked to care me, ruffling my leg in little tippy steps. Margaret I could hear making some rustlings in the bedroom. I cut the bits of chicken and feeded it to Catty and was off. By 5:00 a.m., already I was in the prison. I clicked the lights in the death row, and swept nicely. That girl was the only prisoner there. When I reached with my broom of her cellroom, I stopped and looked on her.

Normally in the life, people always marvel how I am maintaining cheerful demeanors and positive outlooks despite what they are perceiving as disgusting and upsetting responsibilities called upon me by my duties. For example, just now a little girl sat in the floor of her cellroom instead of the cot there. She was scratching the nose-crusties and itching the short hairs, gazing round with bewildery looks. Normally she oughted to be in the schoolhouse studying quietly, or picking flowers under the sunshine rays and playing hopscotch games with her mummy-daddy-friends. She had none of the eye twitchings or evil grimacings like sometimes persons of guilty conscience will demonstrate. It was very odd the situation, and true it made me to fill my head with thoughts.

When first this girl had arrived in here, she dragged along the heavy chains. The guards on either side was lifting her up by the arms, and beneath the jute-cloth frock, her little feets was not even touching the ground. I myself looked to Warden with wonder. My eyes was asking: This is like a big and serious criminal? For the death row? But Warden never explained to me. He only slapped me the back of my cranium. "Look strong. Are you become a woman? A dog ate all your testicles? If you show fear, she will be walking on top of you."

So I had only to execution that simple girl some days hence, no questions could be asked. But did this lead me to conscience-pangs and depressions? Nothing could be further off from true. I reminded to myself: If the deathrow prison is a good place for me to work my days, then it must be a good place for little girls to stay, isn't it so? Even when fate will happen shortly, life is the life, whether in prison cells or sunshiny hillsides, and I provide the good careful honest execution and it's a good thing for all the concerned. I tell no lies, I am the good friend to them, and sometimes they are even thanking me.

Not many people are capable of pursuing such unpleasant work day after day with alacrity. (I am reading now from my semiannual psychologic review paper issued by Ministry office.) *Although his tone and manner are frequently disturbing, he does not demonstrate visible or dangerous indications of stress.* How happy am I each time to read this: that some higher-ups had recognized that for me, executioner is a service and a calling, if not one of the higher of the callings, then certainly one of the humbler of the callings, but a calling all the same. On the top of which, it is the only calling for which I am qualified and also providing sufficient remunerations. It is in this way only, and with such attitudes, that I consider it and pursue it.

So, as I pushed the broom besideways that girl's cellroom, I showed the shiny smile with good alacrity, displaying nil and zero indications of alarming distressfulness. I rested the broom against the wall and put my hands on the cellroom bars.

"Remind me of your name, little one?" I asked, smilingly. She looked up to me like I am a Frankenstein standing there, then crouched off away from me.

"Don't be scaredy. Is this your first time in our capital city? Did you come from some country place? What an excitement!"

Still she sat all silencey. I wondered, what to tell? Should I mention of one special fact, which for some people it is upsetting (my wife) and for others they never believe it until they see it happening to them? I gave a try:

"Little girl, you are wondering who am I? I am not only prison sweeper. I am going to execution you. But don't worry your head: I am not a rough fellow. I treats my prisoners nicely, if only you could ask of them. Chummy was my last one before you. He was sad and weepy on the last days, but I sat inside there and held his hand like the papa. Sometimes Chummy could be a hard fellow with me, but on the last days he came so emotiony. I asked him, why you don't allow me to call the priest and so on? Many prisoners find a comfortable thing in that. I asked him, is there anything I can do for you, any messages I can convey to friends and so on? I wanted only to care him. He said, only thing to do is, you don't execute me. Even while he asked it he was clinging of my hand. Of course, you can look at it as, who else is he going to cling the hand of? I am the only fellow there. Anyway, I said, my good friend Chummy, I am asking you seriously, so don't funny me. You know what he replied? He said, blast you, you goddamned bastard, go to hell, or something like that and so on. Can you imagine it? After all I have done him. But did he let go of my hand? No. I had to struggle to unsqueeze my hand from him."

I finished my talking and waited that girl to reply me something, but only quietness came from her face. So I continued my talking: "Don't worry, lot of people behave unhappy first time they arrive in here, even the big-time criminals. New place always means difficulty. I myself remember when Papa was gone and Mummy was all by her scaredy and she took us to the new town; I went first time to the schoolhouse and how vomitty I felt when master he scolded me and no friends was there because nobody would friendly me. I played only with my brother-sister, I acted to them the care-for. Why it falls to me, to be the know-person, to be the care-for? So be it, I won't complain. Anyhow, maybe you don't understand English, you are the poor uneducated country girl. You need some time to accustomize. Sit there, relax yourself comfortable. Nobody will bother you very much." Then I smiled her and waved her goodbye.

When I got to home that day, I was little nervous of my new wife, but Margaret already had unlocked the bedroom door. It lightened me big-time. I entered inside to wash up my face and change my clothing. Margaret satted herself quietly on one side of the bed, staring there as if something very interesting in the wall, preventing her gaze away from me her husband. In the mirror, I could not stop my eyes from adoring her rounded bottoms making the big double dimple in the mattress. I wanted only and immediately to take myself up with her, but I had learned from many years back in the first marriage that this is the bad approach when it comes to strategy.

After first wife had left me, I tried to maintain practice by visiting to the friendly house. I liked that house because the girls there was friendly and never minded what was my profession. Even they asked it, still all they did was to friendly me, or flicker the eyelash and say ooh-wah-you-scare-me-you-big-strong-muscleboy, and if they cried or acted real-life scaredy or had bad tempers then Madam would punish them.

But one time there had been a bad happening in the friendly house. Madam had a new lady, one short plumpy girl with whom I liked to do squinchy-squinchy. She had the big mouth, so Madam all the time was chiding her. "Large stupid fatso," that girl called to me, making other tongue-droppings, finding herself very funny, even though she was the more fatter one than me. I took it in a stride, so long as she did friendly to me. But one time some new man came there, he didn't like it none her nasty stupid name-calls, that reason alone he beated her up good. Afterward the man was sleeping, that bruised-up bleeding girl took Madam's kitchen knife and stabbed him everywhere. Why she did like that? Why she didn't leave that place or ask Madam, kindly tell this man don't beat me? Any case, she stabbed him to the death, bloodied up whole of the room, the coppers they taked her away, time came to pass, judge and juried, she showed up in my death row! How happy I was to see a friendly person in the death row, who had been known to me in the good-times-gone-by. But it was not like that to be. In the death row, she was always sour of mood, her tongue was pouty, she would not friendly to me or look my face in the eye, or even call me as "fatso" or other funny wordnames. Her whole liveliness had gone her, making my feelings also to go down. By the time I hanged her, I felt even some relief. At the execution time, Madam and some friendly-house ladies visited the audience chambers, but they did not wave me hello. Could it be they didn't recognize me none behind my execution mask? That was my first bad warning signal.

Time came to pass, next time I went to the friendly house no one would friendly to me no more! They wouldn't take my monies, Madam never smiled my face and instead told me to flee out of there before she asked her big bruisy to bruise me.

"What I did, Madam?" I asked. "What you thought I was? Where you had imagined my monies were coming from? This is my good living, Madam. I can't be executioner one day, then the dogcatcher some other day simply as it is your lady in the death row. There is only one of me. We are a small country, and no one else is capable of my duties but my own self."

Madam would not hear it none. "You get out of here, you terrible-and-so-on, never show your face to me again." Even she kicked me in the leg her pointy shoe and spit me. She called for her big bruisy and I ran out of there, even leaving behind my good hat that time. Friendly house came to be a past memory.

That is why I big-time wanted the wife. I thought that having the new wife will solve all that problems, but now I had it and no it didn't. When my first wife disappeared me, I cried myself, even everyone always wondered what happened to that wife, even her family people they blamed me and spit me.

I wondered, this time is they going to blame me and spit me, although I am the different person now? Margaret was sitting there in the side of the bed, and even I felt like rushing her, I reminded to myself this was not no friendly-house lady. Better me to do things careful. Better me to wear my thinking cap and find the best way of hugging her. Answer was: I had to begin it slowly. I had to begin with talking.

In the death row, talking comes so easy to my tongue—even fierce and terrible killers provide sympathetic ears. *Captive audience is best audience,* Warden always jokes me. But somehow standing before this new wife of mine, my tongue became like the tube sock. My stomach twisted knotty, as if only one or two pegs of Johnny Walker could soften it up. There she was, sitting in the bed, awaiting. I thought so hard, yet was unable to come up with a single item conversational. I concluded: Okay, I will ask *her* to converse *me.*

"Listen here, dear Margaret," I told. "Don't you sit there sulking and skulking. I myself am in a drabbish mood. Talk your husband."

She remained muted, eye-facing to the wall. I began to feel little sadly for her, sitting so far from her native place with no familiars nearby. No wonder she is pouty. Again I gave a try. "What you did today, Margaret? Please tell." Only then I seed it: the suitcase pulled up from beneath the belly of the bed, sitting out with some of the shiny women's jutties piled up already inside of it like coconut shavings.

"What is this?" I exclaimed.

Margaret still provided silence.

"You are leaving now already, is it?"

She gave no reply, only staring away.

"Where you going? Your mummy-daddy's living very far from here. Will they be so happy to see you after only last week spending numerous thousand bank notes for a hotel wedding?"

Continually she kept mum.

"How you going to go home, Margaret? Who will pay for the boat ticket? I don't have so much money."

Now I heard a funny noise, like water squeaking at high pressures from the insides of a cat. I worried for a moment—had she did something awful to Catty? Where was Catty? But then I realized that sounds was coming only from my wife, from Margaret.

"Oh, there-there-there," I told to her. "I meant nothing by it."

I went quickly to where Margaret was sitting in the bed and putted my hand on her shoulder. But she curled her shoulder in a big circle to disperse me. I offered to her the kerchief but she ignored. Then she closed all her eyes hard like squeezing a lemon and insufflated noisily the nose-jellies.

She sat with her face crisscrossed with all the ribbons of sticky fluids, making only a little bit of whimpering. Finally, I coerced my mouth to start talking. And I talked to her of the only thing that was in my head: "Hey, Margaret, the new prisoner arrived in the death row. We comfortabled her so much as possible. Shortly she will be off. Young girl, very young little miss."

Had I been more thought-provoking, I might have been carefuller than to tell my wife of my job, as it was only my job which had so much disturbed and upsetted her from the beginning. Now I stood up and tied a towel over my bottom part so I could change my pants and jutties. Even she was my wife now, I was little shy concerning Margaret.

"She looks so soft and flimsy, Margaret. Almost like it was her first days in the village school."

Then I heard Margaret turn her body slight bit. Through the mirror's inside, I seed she was staring me with some expressions in her face. Her big eyes was giving off a blinky shine, and the eye tears and nose ribbons was not flowing, but drying rather. Could it be my talking offered something to curious her? Her face gaved off a puffy glow, which very much appealed me. She was lost in her thought bubble; I could not wonder what it was she was thinking.

Finally, she speaked. "Why is a little girl in the death row?"

To my ears, Margaret's voice was like a small box within pink wrapping papers.

"Even I asked that question, Margaret!" I told to her as I squirmed off my thingies. "Warden shoved her such a rough way down. That Warden sometimes is so bad. So strange it all is, Margaret." And then I was combing my hairs in the mirror.

Wordlessness again came from Margaret. She shuffled her bottom once more. And seeing Margaret's wall-facing body, her bottom making bed-crumples there, made me feeling even more, that I have a wife now and it is time to enjoy her. After some more time, she spoke me a very interested voice.

"But what she did to end up in there?"

This was a shocker to me: two questions from Margaret regarding my job! I wondered, why had she this interest? Was she only seeking to fire up her angry? Or was she really the friendly curious wife of me? I was too much confused and excited. I wanted to catch her into my hands and tell her all the stories, but I grew nervous.

"What she did to end up in there," I told to her, thinking myself carefully what to tell, "what she did to end up in there, Margaret, is she committed some crime."

"Don't simply say she committed some crime, fellow. Tell: *What* crime has she committed?"

Now I seed she was looking at me full interest. I splashed little bit of the after shaves against my cheeks to finish the grooming. I felt my leg start to give a tremble, so to calm myself, I satted in the bed near to Margaret.

I observed that when I satted, she did not shift off away from me.

"You want to know what she did, is it?"

"Tell!"

Being close to Margaret made my armpits to give water. Even I had just splashed the after shaves, I could smell my own flesh odors rising up. I knew that I could not hold on very much time longer, and so I took a bold move: I put my hand on gentle Margaret's thigh. I found it big and firm and dolphin-shapely. I steeled myself for some shove-off from Margaret, but what a wonder to me: She did not push away my hand. I said to her: "Dear Margaret, human being's heart has capable of great and terrible passions. Who can explanate? It's my lot in life, to witness it in a daily basis. In the end, what differences to me? I do my job-duty only. What did she do, didn't she do, young, old, guilty, innocency is not my issue. Duty is there for doing, simple as that, not everyone can do it save for me. If I have any special talent in it, modestly I accept it."

I observed that what I was saying had some effects in her. Jealous Catty jumped into the bed behind us, but only we ignored. I moved my face very close to Margaret's face. Her breath smelled to me of warmed potatoes, and I detected a jiggle-tremble in her lips. My eyes went downtown to see what's inside her blouses.

"But what did she *do*?" she asked.

"In just plain facts, Margaret, such informations oftentimes they don't tell to me."

"Hunh!" Margaret said. She pushed off my hand and moved to the farthest Antarctica corner of the bed.

. . . .

Some people always assume that because of natures and necessities of my job, my heart must be hard and jagged and full of holes, like old and tored-up city roads. Nothing could be further off from true. When I was a schoolboy once in days of yore, I read a poem, the gists of which I still remember. I used to be very moved by poetry, those days. It is true! My papa always yelled me for having too many girlish eye tears. (My papa was tall and liked to speak of too many things, so that the government taked him away and never returned him. This was in the olden regime, before the liberation of our good and famous country. My papa's hero name is the only reason I received my appointed job, Warden always he jokes me.) Anyhow, I liked one poem. Near the lonely path, one grass leaf is dying. That is, the poem I am remembering. Leaf is thirsty for water that leaf is dying. One dewdrop feels sadly for that leaf. Dewdrop rolls down and feeds itself to that leaf. Dewdrop did such a good deed. But on the time sun raises next day, grass leaf is any case dead, also Mr. Dewdrop has sunk away into forever. Nobody will ever hear of him: So brief is the life, so brief.

I observed that, even Margaret was rejecting me, I had to go on my job. It was my patriot's duty. Every day I saw that little girl, I watched her and cared her. I asked to her, "Would you like the refreshing water?" I asked to her, "Why you didn't eat your food that was brought for you? Was it too cold for your tongue?" I told her of the things what was happening in our country on the TV newses what she was not allowed to watch. One time I brought a candy that I had and kept for her. She ate it! I liked to see her face then. Even she didn't show the emotionals, I knew she was finding it sweet.

But never having had someone so strangely young and solitudey, showing neither sad nor happy indications, I asked myself: Maybe would she like something different? What is it to be a little girl sitting in a strange place, nothing to do? Maybe she would like some amusements?

I liked that idea. "Hey, can I give to you some book, magazine?" I asked to the girl. "Can I give to you some amusements?"

That girl gave no answer. Still I went on. I remembered that my last prisoner Chummy left behind several magazines after his hanging. There was something interesting in them, so I had not thrown them off, but secured them in my own locker for the safekeeping. I went and retrieved them to give to the girl.

Chummy and me was such good friends. He was a dirty fellow with regards to several missing females, so it was said in the TV newses, but to me, he could be the soft character—although sometimes he was tongue-bitey, before the final days came and he started to become regretful. Sometimes together we worked the newspaper crosswords of the daily papers—Chummy knew so many words than me. One time, we even played the words game of "Hangman." Another time, I mused to Chummy, "It will be very quiet after death, don't you think so?" (Chummy had complained of my talking-talking.) "No, it won't be quiet," Chummy told. "Because your jabbering will stay in my head eternally." (He knowed of such fine words: *eternally*.)

And I wondered: Is it true? My talk-talk will go on echoing for eternally? Before I dropped the floor on Chummy, I undertaked an experiment. When he was standing in the gallows all ready for go, I whispered something to his ear. I gaved him a secret only I knowed, something I never ever told to no one. And before he could say some responses, I hanged him.

And then, I wondered, still is my secret sitting outside in the world? Or where is it gone? Is my bad secret ringing eternally in Chummy's ears someplace? Or is it disappeared to nothing?

"Here you go, small madam," I said to the girl as I handed her the magazines of Chummy. At that moment, I remembered too late, those were the wrong magazines for that girl! Those magazines were only for the growed people's eyes, and I became blushed when I saw the girl look over the bad pictures.

But then I thought myself: If she's going to die, then what is the harm there? Let her see something, anyway, before she goes. I observed that girl's face in anticipation for the expressions there. What an excitement, first time in a child's life to learn of the intimate things. How happy I would be, if a youngster, to receive such magazine gifts. What a happiness I am bringing to her!

But that dulled little girl gave no such happy expressions. She sat there only glumly turning one page, then another. Then chewing at the page corner like something salty is there. Then closing magazines and snuffling again like she is crying without the tears.

Anyhow, maybe it will take some time, I thought so. I will try again during tomorrow. I went and taked back the magazines to myself; she had no interest now, so why waste it? And again, I locked away the door.

After a certain number the nights of sofa-sleeping (one or two is perhaps acceptable, but five-six?), a man in his own house begins to feel draining off away from him some nonrefundable reserves of what it is called *dignity*. No matter what every man is doing for his professional job, still and all, must he not have dignity?

Am I doing bad things? Is my tone and manner disturbing the people? Is my personality disgusting, like my first wife had told to me? I was in the times of youth in that time, and even I did some of the bad things in life, doesn't everyone? But I thought them over and sweated myself. Is all the women only going to disappear me?

I took my magazines home with me. Truly that was all there

was for me in the today of my life. I had to keep the magazines beneath the sofa cushions of my own house, so that my wife will not disgust herself. (In those magazines, I discovered several last letters to Chummy's attention I had stored in my storage locker. Oh no, I never delivered them! It looked like lovermails from some ladies who loved him and believed of his innocency. They proposed of marriage to him. It tickled me, so I kept them aside to read it later.)

Meantime, my wife, Margaret, what was she doing all the day long? Every day I came home, she was wearing same dirty clothings like yesterday, not having moved very far off from bed, so lost in her own downbeat head-thoughts. She did not bend or cower me, like my first wife had did. What had she eaten? What had she done all the day long? She never even spent five coins to go and do the Internet Web surfings. What there was in life, to make one person so frowny?

But even still, every day seeing Margaret laying her thick bosoms down on the dirty bed cloths, even she was greasy and messy, it was hard not to help myself. Her hair was sprawling in the bed sheets going every swishy way, like oily silk curtains for the lovemaking. Oh, my God! The sour waftings from her warm pits and her potato breathings, everything, everything of dirty Margaret was so much appealing me. But she wouldn't even look to my face. It made me to feel so lonely.

One consolation remained to me, that one thing would put some lively bubbles into the flat water of Margaret, even it discomfortabled me and confused me as to why. That is to discuss strange and hard things regarding that very thing which in the first place upsetted her, which is to say, my job.

One time watching the TV newses where the police cops was chiding against the rowdy sign-holders, Margaret shifted her head from the hangdog slouch and asked, "Was it you who hanged all the protesters who were executed some years back?"

I turned to Margaret then, little bit pleased but also little bit worried. That time yet I wasn't sure would she enjoy the answer yes or the answer no? Oh well, I head-or-tailed it, it came up honesty.

"Yes, Margaret. Fifteen of those fellows I had to hang space of one day. Tiring work, let me tell to you!"

"Fifteen!" she exclaimed, her face all jumpy. "How? How did you do so many?"

"Three by three I hanged them. It took me time till full evening." (Meanwhile, advantaging myself of her distraction, I shuffled myself one small inch closer to smell her more nicely.)

Next day I was frying the meat in the oil for the meat salad, I blurted her, "You know that one time a bad raper was sitting in the death row, he gained up four hundred kilo. He was eating too much meat salad and drinking the oil for a drink! His family was paying extra to the cook, I think so."

Margaret's eyes popped up from beneath the hairs. "Oh, God. How can a rope hold such a heavy man?"

"Rope holding up is not the problem, Margaret. Rope is strong, but neck is not. At such a weight, his head is sure to rip off!"

Letting slip such a very vivid details, even I started to blush myself for what effects it might have on her. But only she elevated the eyebrows and bolted herself upright, waiting anticipationally. I knew she wanted to hear more, but I did not want to, somehow I felt squirmish to tell. I thought: Let her ask it.

And finally, she asked it: "Did it happen? Did you off his head like that?"

I sat next to her that time, and even she letted me to pat her back soothingly, as I thought in my mind of how to storytell it. "Oh, I worried very much, Margaret, trying to think of proper way to kill him. Can we not kill him the other way? I even asked to Warden. What if some name person is there in the viewing gallery and sees the off-tearing of his head? It will look very bad, won't it? Bloody and so on. But law sentence is the law sentence, Warden reminded to me. It was written as 'hanging,' so it cannot be alternated. Anyway, I did not off his head finally. He died of heart attacks before I could drop him."

"Hm," she snuffed, as if my happy ending was too quick and bummed her. And then off she flumped back into the bed, no more talking, no more touching, nothing doing.

I wondered: Why is it she perks so strange to hear the most weirdest aspects of that very thing which also disgusted her, in other words, my job? In my life, my job is my duty, I don't have shames and I don't practice no regrets. But her questioning was making me to feel something queasy was there. And for a fair woman to express such an interest seemed somewhat disturbed and unwomanly. But very well, at least it was something in the positive ledger. Some certain tangible progresses thereby was being made in my wifely relations with my wife, so let it be. Such was my foolish thinking.

But in such a situation, what else was a man to do? How long could I crawl off to some corner and pull up Chummy's good magazines? This was my everyday life.

Time moves so quickly sometimes. I realized one day, no more hours was left for magazine browsings, for idling death row chitchats with that little girl. In fact, Warden told to me, "How long you going to stand there in idling chitchats? We going to execute in some two days." And he clapped me the back of my cranium. "You did your preparations, man?"

The girl was sleeping that day under her scratchety woolen blanket, because always they are keeping the air condition too much. I thought: It is a solemn duty I must wake her up with, but if I keep up my natural cheerful nature, it needs not be so unpleasant. Beneath my arm I held the weighing scale, and around my finger rolled up a length of string to take the measure with. And so, with solemn and cheerful face, I unlocked the door. "Hey, hey, wake up, small madam!"

That girl did not stir. I seed she was deep in some nasty dream, her face all wiggled up like angry dogs. I considered: Okay, better not to disturb her. Let her sleep, poor thing. But two days only and she will be dying, and I must preparate. Anyway, I can take her measure without awaking her.

Very quiet, I taked off her blanket. She was lying there total nakedness, that tiny girl. This how she sleeped in her home village, most likely. I taked that string and tied it round her big toe, and stretched it out to the top of her head.

Now I had the measure, okay. I put it into my notebook. Next, to weigh her. After that 400-kilo raper breaked the small scale Warden was keeping, my sister in Australia sended to me one pressure-sensitive battery-power electric scale. It was my pride and joy in the death row, while the batteries still was working. Even Warden liked to stand in it and see the number light up some fancy way.

I had put this new scale in the cellroom floor. But how to take her weight without awaking her? Okay, I lifted up that poor girl and curled her on top of the scale. What a light girl! What a light girl! She lay there flopped up on top of the scale like flounder in fishmonger's shop, and still she did not wake or stir.

Okay, now I had the weight, I denoted it. With my mind, I calculated lengths of rope and so on. Still I had trouble to leave that girl. Anyway, some more questions I had to ask her, but she was sound sleeping.

I had to ask the prisoner, who is the next of kin? Who is going to come and take her after it is finished? Or what she preferred us to do with her, bury, burn, or et cetera? As I could make some allowances for the various religions.

All this I must ask to that girl, but how I'm going to ask it without awaking her? This was inside of my thought bubble when I looked down and seed her eyes was wide open now, blinking me calmly.

"Hello, small madam!" I smiled to her.

Again, she looked like she didn't know what to do with my smile.

Now I felt little anxious. How to explanate? "You see, little she," I began, "normally in life, tackling necessities and trivialities of tying up the last scene can be postponed indefinitely. One is aware the coming-towardness of the ending, but since no time certain is fixed, there seems always some more time coming, even though we might not know the ending would hit our nose this minute. Not so here in the death row. Because date and time are fixed certain, indefinite eventuals become immediately necessaries. And so it is with you."

I don't know a single word if she understood.

"Okay, plainly: You have a mummy? You have auntie? Who is going to come pick up your deadened body?" I knew even I asked it, there was no happy answer here. Had that girl had any friendly person of useful caring benefit to her, he/she already would have arrived. And so I was not so much surprised when that girl's face started tumbling minute I asked the question.

"Oh, there-there, little girl." I was not used to her face showing so many emotionals. "I'm very sorry. But I can't preventicate it and neither can you, isn't it so? So why not try to be cheery?" But even still, the eye tears had started falling.

At my job, I am a professional. People grow sad on the death time, such is their nature. I am so steady and I care them. I leaned down and picked up that girl because she saddened me.

I sat her slippery bottom in my knee and stroked her comfortably, and she turned and looked in my face. She looked up at me like she knew something more than I did, and I felt that moment the first time that this little she was not so little as she looked.

What a queer feeling! I asked to myself how this girl had been surviving herself in the Regional Prison before coming to the death row? How she lived with so many of the older prisoners, and the rough-talking, badly uneducated regional prison guards? What had she to offer them?

In her eyelook, it appeared she already knew my thinkings. Like she is used to these ideas, and even she didn't like to do it, she would do it no questioning. And so much she seemed to expect it, the flat fish resignation in the eyes, that I began to feel discomfortable with myself, and my armpits started to give water.

Maybe it would be an okay to do with her? my mind asked to me. After all, when life is short, things go out of order. It is a way of caring her, in one way to think about it. And I could not help but consider that she will die two days hence and any shames would be dying alongside her.

To top it all, I had a wife in the home, yet I could not have her. She refused to give to me. I was a man without normal relations. But here is something soft that I could have and moreover she would give to me. Why not I do it?

This time it was only Warden's imaginary voicecalls, and some faroff doorslamming that made me finally to see how badly I was thinking. I called that tiny girl some dirty names and pushed her to the ground and got little bit heated with her. "Who you think I was, that you can place me in such positions?" I asked to her. "Do I look like a man as to imagine such things? What if Warden seed me with a naked girl sitting me?"

I clanged the door on her and locked it. Then I left the prison in flusters and traveled home. I felt sorry to be so heated and rough to that girl. Inside of me gurgled a sea of agitation. I went straight to my bedroom and began shedding my clothings. Then I seed my wife Margaret. She was standing upright facing the mirror, staring her reflection like she is making herself so disgusting. Her brown hair was going down near the bottom.

"Hey, it is me, your husband," I announced to her, even I knew she could see me plain as sunshine rays. "Talk me!" I said. My fluster was hot. "I am your husband. How long can you go on without talking me?"

I was thinking myself, I have to take off the feelings of that little child sitting inside my arms. I was thinking also that the only reasons I was put in such positions is that, here my wife is standing and withholding it. Even my head spoke to me that she is my wife, after all, and no one else's. Why shouldn't I take it if I want it?

"This is how you treat of your husband?" I asked to her. "All day long, I work too hard. All I want is to love and care you, and you won't even face-to-face and talk me? You won't even say, hello husband, welcome to the home?"

Meantime I was walking closer and closer behind her. She stood facing the dressing mirror but not looking me. I became so close now I could feel her petticoats. I looked her face in the mirror and she was grinching her eyes hard as to keep it from seeing me.

I said: "I always am a good man. But what it makes a husband to feel like, if your behavior to me is not happysmiles, but crying? How it makes a husband to feel like, if you cannot even face-to-face me? Everything I does is to your benefits only. My life its own reward, is that it, Margaret? I can't ask you for nothing, is that it? You know, in one day and some few hours I will be executioning that little girl? Do you think it makes me to feel good and happy to execution such a poor girl? But does I ever go on complaining? Does I ever lie on the bedcovers all mopey in my dirty clothings?"

When I mentioned of that girl, I saw that her breathing changed. I saw it, she was interested.

"What a light and little girl she is," I said to her, remembering the feelings of the little one. "I hope we have enough the lengths of rope. We need a long lengths to snap such a light girl."

And in the mirror, I seed Margaret's eyes open little bit, like slits. And she was biting her lips and breathing with energy.

"A long rope?" she asked to me.

When Margaret asked me the question, I felt like I could not help it, I began putting my hands to her petticoats. I felt new determinations that day. I had no shyness about what I wanted, honesty was my best policy, so I began rubbing myself against her clothings. "Oh, she will almost be hitting the floor, that is right."

In Margaret's slitty eyes I seed her interest; I seed, if I talked correctly now, I might have everything I wanted, minimum of fighting. It was hard for me to feel it in my stomach. It was too much exciting. I pushed her plush pillow. My own voice I could not control it. It came a whisper and sometimes it came shouting. "What you say, Margaret? I have to order her the last meals. I forgot to ask her what she likes. What is it I should feed to her?"

And now I looked in the mirror and saw my face was as disturbing as Margaret's. The toiletries and powderings and shaving oils all was jumbling down from the dresser.

"Please, Margaret. What you say? I am your husband. What can you give to me? Power's in your hands. I am a grown man and still I can beg, and still I can cry."

Margaret very long time was silent. She was with one hand pushing back the mirror to keep herself upright there, and one hand trying to shove me back and keep down the petticoats. In the mirror her face was looking me directly.

"Can you take me there to see her?"

In the mirror, I seed her spitty mouth. I seed Catty's tail flicking from the dark space beneath the bed where she was hiding and cat-staring us.

"Of course, Margaret, of course. I can do anything, anything, anything!" And mirror was shaking so that maybe it would drop in both our heads and end all the miseries.

"Take me tomorrow. Take me, I want to see her."

She pushed her elbow backward, paining me sharply and creating some gap between me and her. She slipped downward through that gap and next thing suddenly she was on the farthest ends of the room. (It was too clever. There popped a realize bulb in my head: Maybe she had been watching movies?)

She wiped her face, looking like she is the man now. "Take me then tomorrow."

"Okay, Margaret," I was panting, out of my breaths. I wanted to run to her, but I tripped myself to the floor, paining my shins. "Damn it everything, Margaret. Okay. Tomorrow. But after that, then no more waiting. You must give to me everything."

Please don't think me a rude man! I only tries to be like my papa. He was the big strong truth-telling man, whereas I did many bad things. I am not tall like I put it in the computer ad for enticing Margaret, also the picture was some twenty years back. Many other things I did it wrong all the time in my life. Always the womenfolks bring it out from me.

Anyhow, now I had promised to Margaret. Anyhow, maybe all of it would work to the best. And next day, it seemed Margaret had forgot all my bum behaviors; whole of morning she was easygoing to me. She cleaned her hair and put on the nice frock like the normal wife who is leaving the household. "Do you like to take the fried chicken's egg?" I asked to her, and she nodded me, so I fried up the egg. I asked, "Why not you take some milk to drink?" and she did it. I feeled I was caring her almost like she was sitting in the death row; it tickled me warmly! We boarded the bus and sat side by side in the bench, thigh of me touching thigh of her. Bus was full of everyday peoples and Margaret and me looked like the normal boring married couple off for the workday, how it pleased me. We offed from the bus, and Margaret waited herself outside the prison, a dirty place in the edge-skirt of the city. I told, "I will go inside making sure everything is possible now for the visit."

Then she smiled me. A real smile! I thought, yes, this whole thing is rolling like coconuts. After all the mistakes, my rude advancements and so on, finally, some progresses was being made in my wifely relations with my wife. "I am sorry my mood yesterday," I said, and gave her the tender strokings in her cheekbones, and she offered no protests. Despite strangeness of it all, I thought things was going again in my direction.

I stepped inside of the prison, stopping straightaway in Warden's office.

"Warden, sir," I said. Warden was distracted with reading the gambling numbers in the newspaper. "Hey, Warden."

"What is it, man?" Warden yelled.

I tried to simulate the smiling casualness. "It looks our little madam has a last-day visitor."

News of someone's arrival made Warden to put down the newspaper. "Damn it. Where is the visitor? Why you didn't tell me? Where was he scheduled? You didn't clean the hallways. Damn it, fellow." He began straightening his shirts and combing his hairs.

"Hey, not to worry," I told. I myself had been nervous, but now Warden was the nervouser one. "No worries, sir. She is outside still. It is a next-of-kin, auntie, or somesuch. A country lady only, no one to worry. I made her wait on the outside. She came from faroff and didn't call, just now only she arrived. I will go and bring her."

Warden continued flustering inside as I went out and brought my wife inward. She followed me slowly, staring very strongly left and right, and I saw that when Warden seed her, his whole face went still.

Warden stepped me aside. "Madam," he said, acting like some different person and not at all Warden. "Madam, don't be frightened, a gentle woman as yourself must feel very strange in this rough prison. But come this way. You will see we have taken very good care of our charge. You will be perfectly safe with me."

He jutted his elbow for Margaret to hook herself there (it did not happen). Simply they began walking to the cellroom. I followed them behind, but Warden turned backward: "You wait here in the front office, man."

What could I to do? I watched them both disappearing round the corner toward the girl's cellroom. I jangled back and forth.

I could not bring myself to sit my bottom. I wondered myself: What if that girl reveals something about my previous behaviors? Well, that is not a worry, I reminded me, as that girl never talked to no one nothing.

I tried to listen what was going on in the cellblocks, but I could not hear it. I fretted, what if Margaret tells to Warden she is my wife? Then maybe my job is quite finished.

I peeked my face around the corner to see their doings, but I could not eye-catch it. Margaret had bended down somewise, with Warden standing off. What was happening? What words thereby were they saying? Oh, God.

Finally they turned their heads, and I removed my head backward. I satted myself in the office and feigned the perfect indifferentness as their footsteps approached me.

Warden arrived first. His face showed no anger, and only normal Warden facial expressions, and so I knowed it, everything was okay. I had a big relax. But then Margaret came, and moment I seed her, I feared I had made the big-time mistake. Her eyes was brimmed red like tears had been dropping there, and she would not look my face in the eye. Was all progresses I had this point made to my wifely relations with my wife hereby abolished? I could not say it.

"Just one moment, madam, I must give you some paperworks," Warden told. He went behind me, and Margaret only stood there with a look in her face like she is in the weird dream, and I could not tell who it was inside her head.

Then Warden called to me, so I went backward.

Warden whispered, "Ask her some gratuities, man."

"Hey, Warden, I cannot do that. You are the one who taked her there, maybe it's better you to ask."

Then Warden clapped me my cranium. Boy, it hurt! "I don't ask you like a question, man."

So I had to go back, very sheeplike, to my own wife Margaret. Without looking her face, I told to her, "Excuse me, madam."

Now only Margaret looked her face to me. Her far-looking eyes finally focused there. I edged my glance to see her: her expressions was wide like a girl's face, but tired like a woman's. She looked very new. Is you still the same Margaret, I felt to ask of her, but I could not ask it. I could feel Warden's eyes also staring me. Very quietly, I said, "Madam, can you please give us some gratuities? For we the caretakers of the prisoner? For the food we gaved her? For the waxy painless rope?"

In her expression, it taked her a moment to understand. Finally, she reached her purse and dropped some sad coins toward my hand. I looked down at it as I did not want to see her anymore. What was her thoughts of me? I feared to know it.

Later in that same day, Warden took me to the side. "You done all your preparations for the hanging?" he asked.

"Yes, Warden."

"Go back and undo it. We not going to have no hanging for that girl."

I looked to Warden with my face like a question, but I feared I knowed his meaning.

"Ministry says we have to kill her the other way," Warden told.

That day was very difficult one. I called the Ministry peons and spent many hours driving the truck through the bad countryside roads to search out appropriate stones. I removed the gallows and rearranged all of the execution room.

And that night Margaret wouldn't touch to me, spite of my best efforts. Even though I keeped to her my honest word and never did to her like I did to my first wife, even I asked her and poked her: "What you had promised me? Don't you remember it?"

"Yell, then," she yelled me. "Beat me. Go on! Kill me, even. And when they find you for murder, you can execute yourself."

"What foolish talk," I answered her. "No one can execute his own self solo. How can anyone do it proper?"

But even she kicked me and scratched me like Catty, I would not go this time for sofa-sleeping. Even she taked her blanket and slept on the floor, I would stay in the bed that was mine.

And next day, I waked before morning. I stepped careful over floorsleeping Margaret and pressed my white smart collarshirt and blue shortpants. I wore the belt and the white socks. It was my execution day uniform. I polished the black shoe and wore them and went for the prison. I felt anxious to my stomach about Margaret, but so much thoughts filled my bubble: Was all the big stones in place? Was the chambers clean in case of dignitary visits? Was prisoner properly attired and so on?

Prisoner was not properly attired. I had to hold her tightly while Warden pulled over her the dark frock. The little girl had finally understanded the natures of her situation, and now she snarled like tigers. No traces of the soft girl was left; she showed the teeth this time. As I bounded up the hands, she spat and called me filthy dirty bugger, and such names. I looked to Warden's face, but to my great relax Warden considered it as a normal prisoner namecalling, and not a truefact accusation.

"What, little madam?" I asked to her, in my nicest voice available. "What you was thinking? That you can go on sitting your cellroom for eternally? What you think you was doing here? Who you think I am to you? I was your kindly friend, and I never did lie to you."

One or two cracks was necessary from the billy club, and then she calmed herself. What a shame. I don't never like for it to be like this. But finally that girl came the quiet way. Now only the fear was in her eyes, the blood was gone her cheeks. Even she made some accident inside the frock, according to the smell in my nostril.

Before we came to the execution chamber, I had to do one thing. I took my black hood and pulled it down my face. There is only three holes in the hood, for eye, for eye, for mouth. It looks so solemn and scaredy, I think so. I put it on my face in case one or two name officials or families should be there in the viewing gallery.

This case, of course no name persons or families would be there, only the same jobless people as comes to all the executions. The sentences was changed only in the last moments, so no big crowds would come and crowd me. We walked toward the chamber. In that girl's ears, I whispered some things that was in my mind. I said, "You are quiet now, that is good, little girl." I said, "Don't be scared, but this is a different way we are doing it. Sometimes we do it plain and sometimes different. Ministry says you and your family has did very bad things. Your papa is a bad man. Is it so?" She didn't answer me nothing. I looked to her face to see if she was still angered or scaredy. I could not catch it. Her eyes was weird and gave no plain indications. She would not look my face or respond my finger pokes. I began to wonder myself: Is life gotten too confusing for the little girls in our good country in these days?

We arrived in the executioning platform and stationed there. Warden came up then in his shirt-tie, and in some special big-man voice read out the law sentences. I didn't always ear-mind it, with all the big words, *forsooth* and *therewithal* and so on, and *it is so ordered*. I was thinking of that girl. But so what if Warden was talking there some foolish nonsense in his big pretend voice, it meant one thing only, it meant the blinky green light and one thing to be done and one person only to do it. The beats came faster from my heart and my mouth came dry. A previous time in this moment the advocate had came running in the execution chamber holding new sentences and grabbed Warden, saying judge had granted their big appeals; then and there we halted the executioning. But this time even I waited it to happen, it did not happen. I was not especial disappointed, except it meant a hard work for me and a hard final end to my friend, so it goes every time, so what does it matter?

For the record, Warden asked the prisoner had she any last

words? At first the girl speaked nothing, and Warden walked off and left me to the work. But after a moment, the girl had some last words to speak of. She cried out her filthy curses. And then she stopped her cursing and was quiet.

Oh well, I said to my mind. I did her my best and only thanks she has to give is filthy wordnames, so what can I to do? I pre-parated. This time, there was no readynoose to place over the girl's neck. I saw that the stones was in place, and the fulcrum lever. Then I looked up and saw one extra person was in the viewing gallery, one woman she sat there, guess who it was, my wife, Margaret. Why she came there? She was wearing same clothings like yesterday, her hair crazy. It made me heated to see her, but what could I to say? I could not tell to her anything without Warden would know she was a known-to-me and not a next-of-kin.

Margaret stared at me full in my face, my mask, my smart uniform. Her eyes deeped so strange, like she was sticking her look all the way inside me. It made me feel bad tickled. Who was I to her this moment? I wondered. Was I the fulltime stranger? Was I her husband or something so different? And then Margaret looked away from me to the prisoner's face. Meantime, I slipped gently over that girl's face the hood that was finally covering her eyes.

When she was in the jute-cloth darkness, then only I bent down and whispered into her ear. I had to bend low down for that small girl. Very quietly I whispered to her something, my mouth so close to her shelly ear that even through the cloth I feeled the warmth there. Very quietly I telled to her, taking as long as it is the telling of it taked.

What I telled her was too secret; I don't want nobody ever to know. I put in her ears the words—like dewdrops, like dewdrops. I was the last one for her in the whole world, that moment.

As I talked, still that Margaret she sat there. Nothing she

could hear of what I said, but any case she looked like nothing more in the world was left for talking. I finished telling that thing to that prisoner's ear, and before the girl could give answers, I pulled the lever of the floor, and she cried out and fell down to the bottom chamber.

I looked down, and she was moving and making some crying noises down there. I moved my hands to the fulcrum stick and strength-lifted one heavy stone over the end of the floor, and it hit her with a sound. Still she noised, as I levered the other stone on top of her. And then the other and the other.

The life of truth is its own reward, my papa always he told to me, before they disappeared him. Thereby, I am an honest executioner. I take good care and I don't tell lies, minimum of possible. And each time I pushed down that rock, and it landed with the bad sound, I thought myself: Truth! And I thought, in that way, I do a good job. Until she stopped noising and was quiet, and buried she was under the rain of stonedrops, and there was no question she was smashed and dead.

I did my work no fussing, I am very good in my job, and in the end of it, I looked up, believing Margaret already would be gone, maybe her eyes could not watch it, after all even Warden had left in the earliest so as not to look on it. But no, still she sat staring me so awful until finally she got up and walked away. Okay, why should it bother me?

All around me was dusty and silent, and to myself I wondered: Was my words still here? Where my words went? My dewy words. A moment in the ear, a moment in the brain, and then the brain became smashed. What is the effects of it, after all? It made me wonder the universe, even we was here many years, eating, sleeping, now one wife, now another. The bad things we have did and all the things our eyes have seed and all we have gone through. It heavied me, like that large pile of stones was piling on my insides. Even my big secret in her ear felt like a small-time.

And when the execution was over and done, and with the peon boys' help I lifted out the poor broked-up girl and snapped her photo for the morning newses and boxed her, I went home solo, via the bus ride. Nobody thanked me my good job, as per the usual, never did it bother me, why should it? It is only a job not something unusual. Way I see it is, once I did it, then all of us have did it, all because of me, and that is thanks enough to get.

And when I got to home all dirty, Margaret was sitting there again, silent at the table, so downbeat like she had been wearying me and patienting me for one thousand years. "How long you plan to sit there like the only innocent one?" I asked to her. "You have seed me what my job has me capable, so what more does I have to do, to say to you?" Any case, I was hungry, I did not ache my head and worry. I cooked the potato bowl to eat it. "You want some potato bowl?" I heard myself voicing; she nodded, so I gave her from the potato bowl. We sat there eating. We didn't talk nothing, and I wondered myself, what can I tell to her, who is always going to be there in the following days remembering it? I took bath, and even she would scream and fuss, I determined myself to sleep my own bed, because at long last I seed that in these times, each man must take for his own self some dignity, no one else is going to give to him. Any case, she made me some edge-space. And next morning and all the mornings in the thereafter, I am coming back to my good job. For all is said and done, what else is there for we to do? All is said and done, Margaret is my wife, and I am an executioner.

DEMONS

WHEN THE PHONE RANG THE NIGHT before Thanksgiving, Savitri Veeraghavan was doing her best to forget that her husband, Ravi, lay dead on the living room floor. A pot of tomatoes and lentils and water was boiling, a simple dinner, and Savitri had put a stainless steel wok next to it on the stove, turned the heat to medium, and poured in a yellow pool of vegetable oil.

On the phone's first ring, Savitri threw into the oil a handful of jeera, and the oil responded with its usual eager sizzle. On the second ring, she sprinkled in two teaspoons of mustard seeds, and the oil coughed and spat and spluttered so that even Savitri, prepared for just such an outburst, took a surprised step backward to avoid the burning spatter. Then the spice found its home in the oil and the heat, settling into a slow sizzle, and the smell of a meal well begun wafted out of the wok, over the kitchen, and into the living room, where Savitri's husband's cold nose failed to notice it.

She picked up the phone.

"Hello?" she asked.

"What?" the voice said bluntly.

Savitri recognized Poornima's voice instantly. "Hi-yee," Savitri said in the weary singsong she reserved for her close friends. "What? Tell me."

"What time you coming tomorrow?" asked Poornima.

What's tomorrow? Savitri thought quickly. Poornima's luncheon, that's right. "I can come anytime. You tell me," Savitri said.

"Come early," said Poornima. "You can give me some help. Ravi and Radha can come later if they like."

Savitri shook her head. "Radha won't be here. She has so much work to do at college, all her activities."

Poornima hmmed in surprise.

"Will your Arun be there?" Savitri asked.

"Oh, yes."

"Really," said Savitri. "Just for the weekend? All the way from Harvard?"

"It's Thanksgiving," Poornima explained.

After Savitri hung up the phone, she thought, Thanksgiving! The way Poornima says it. As if it were our own holiday. Actually, it's the one day our people *don't* have any plans, and that's why she's having a party. Savitri threw into the wok six handfuls of chopped okra and stirred them around with a large metal spatula. Okra was Radha's favorite, and Savitri tried to imagine Radha was coming home for the weekend, something reminding her to think only good things, only good things. Savitri pulled the back of her hand over her forehead, prickly with sweat, then rinsed her hands under the kitchen faucet.

As the cool water ran through her fingers, Savitri felt fear creep into her lungs like smoke. She was forgetting something. Something beyond the kitchen door, something worse to think of even than Radha's not coming home, and Savitri's arms trembled as she lifted the wok in both towel-wrapped hands and poured the simmering okra into the pot, now boiling, of tomatoes and lentils. She covered the pot, turned off the heat, washed her hands carefully once more and dried them, and walked into the living room.

It was still there. It lay on the floor, bent at the waist so it was cocked into a V. He looked so uncomfortable (but that wasn't the right word) twisted there on his side. He had fallen just short of the brown plaid sofa where his bottom and hers had worn two threadbare, distanced indentations. He wore a plain gray blazer and green polyester-blend trousers grown shiny from wear. Ravi's left arm was pinned under his torso, his right arm was flung backward as though he were winding up to bowl in a cricket match, his fingers curled fiercely around an absent ball.

Savitri took two steps closer. She became aware of a faintly acidic smell. Ravi's black eyes were open, focused at some indeterminate point. She noticed, trailing from the corner of the frozen grimace of his mouth, a trickle of mealy yellow liquid that was drying into a crust on his cheek. She smelled it, too, and she covered her mouth with her hand to fight down her revulsion. This was Ravi's final meal, she thought. The pizza he must have had at lunch, two slices with olives, onions, and red chili flakes, eaten alone and in a hurry.

Savitri looked up and away. Certainly it was terrible for him to have died so young, she thought, before his daughter had even finished college or started a family. But was it Savitri's fault? She couldn't take all of the blame. After all, he was such a simple-minded man, frustratingly so, and stubborn. But hadn't this also been his virtue? Hadn't his family always been the first and only thing in his heart? Savitri pictured him sitting at his desk at seven in the evening, reconciling numbers, earning money he would never spend on himself. And now for it all to end like this, on the floor. Savitri looked down again and saw that she was anointing her husband's body with a drizzle of tears.

Savitri's husband, Ravi, died after picking her up from work. She had been among only a few of her colleagues who volunteered to stay late with Phillip, her boss, before the long weekend. Savitri had no special plans for the holiday, and besides, she enjoyed her job. "Phillip is perfectly happy to drop me at home afterward," she had told her husband.

"I don't like you taking rides with strangers," Ravi had replied.

When she reminded him that Phillip wasn't a stranger, Ravi revised himself. "There's no need to ask other people for rides," he said. He had said this before, but Savitri knew that it was not "other people" Ravi objected to. It was people like Phillip, with his big-toothed smile, his American confidence. The way he took people easily into his trust, speaking to them with jocular familiarity, presuming some common language that Ravi was not privy to. In Phillip's presence, her husband felt very small. She saw it in the way Ravi folded his hands over his stomach and smiled mawkishly, nodding along to everything Phillip said.

But Savitri didn't push the issue. She treated the subject delicately. She agreed to let Ravi wait outside her office in his white Tercel as she sat inside at her workstation in her blue face mask and rubber gloves, applying a delicate tweezer to the circuit boards she tested and assembled, blue to white, white to yellow, yellow to red. It was not as easy as it sounded, no, not nearly, and Savitri had a steady hand. What's more, she could hold her own among the Phillips of the world.

"Go home," Phillip had told her, standing over her in his white lab coat. "Your husband is outside. Tomorrow's Thanksgiving. Go home."

"My husband will wait," said Savitri, looking up, smiling behind her mask. She couldn't ask for a nicer boss, and so handsome. Almost every day he complimented Savitri on her work. She wanted to take him home and cook for him. If only he were Indian, she would have introduced him to her Radha.

When she finally came out, Ravi had been difficult. "Been waiting an hour," he said. "My neck is hurting, my stomach is hurting."

"Who asked you to wait, then?" Savitri said, her annoyance overlapping and indistinguishable from her concern. "And with the heater off just to save gas. No wonder you're getting sick." She reached over to touch his forehead. "You should have gone home and taken rest. I told you I would get a ride."

Turning the car toward the freeway entrance ramp, Ravi said, "Don't worry about me. Look at that traffic. Would have been fine if you came out when you said you would."

They stopped at Kroger to pick up milk for the next morning's coffee.

"I'll come later by myself and get it," Savitri told her husband.

"No need," he said. "We're here now. It takes two minutes."

Ravi idled the car by the curb as Savitri went inside, took a minute to survey the produce, and picked up the milk. The store was crowded with holiday shoppers, and when Savitri finally got to the checkout counter, the boy bagging groceries produced a whole turkey from underneath the counter and slid it into her bag, next to the milk.

"What's this?" Savitri asked, aghast. She and her husband were Brahmins, lifelong, neurotic vegetarians.

"It's free," said the boy. "A gift for Kroger cardholders."

Savitri couldn't stomach the idea of the cold, slick turkey touching her milk and was about to ask the boy to take it back. But then she thought better of it. She could give it away, maybe as a Christmas gift for some American in the office. "Please put it in a separate bag," she asked the boy, and she carried the two bags gingerly out of the store.

"What did you buy?" Ravi asked her.

"Just milk," she said.

"Took you that long?"

"Yes, took me that long," Savitri replied. "I can't jump ahead in the line, can I? If you are not feeling right, then why did you bother to pick me up? If you are in a rush, you should have let Phillip drop me."

This only made Ravi angry again. "Why should you go about taking rides from people when I am here? As long as I am here, what is the need?"

And then a thought skittered across Savitri's mind like a stone across water: What if you weren't here? Would it be so bad? No more arguments on the ride home. No more of your fussy demands, unrealistic expectations, strange insecurities. I could live without you to monitor everything, I could live as I alone wanted.

These musings, Savitri now insisted to herself, were born of her momentary annoyance, but they were also, on some level, serious questions. Ravi was forty-nine. He didn't eat right, didn't exercise, was susceptible to long hours of simmering ill temper. What if he kicked the bucket?

Then a voice must have spoken, lost in the wind or buried in the putterings of the car's engine, Savitri would believe later:

Asthu, asthu. Make it so.

Fifteen minutes later, as they pulled into their subdivision, he had said her name in a strange way, as if just her name were an urgent question he expected her to answer, or a disbelieving accusation: "Savitri?" She didn't turn to him but continued to stare stubbornly out of the passenger window, waiting for him to continue. He hadn't, so she simply ignored him.

They turned into their driveway. The electric garage door opened with grinding, excruciating slowness. Then, halfway inside the garage, halfway out, the car jerked to a stop. Savitri turned and saw her husband's face stuck in an exaggerated grimace. She called his name but he didn't answer, emitting instead a strained, spittly whistle. Savitri told her husband to stop it, to finish parking the car and to stop his stupid games. When still he didn't respond, she herself put the gear into park. Ravi's face was pale. With great effort, he lifted his hands off the steering wheel and stepped unsteadily out of the driver's side door, leaning on Savitri so heavily that he left a bruise on her shoulder. Savitri helped him into the living room, but then his wheezing and gasping stopped with an audible finality, and she could hold him no longer, and onto the floor he slumped. His body jerked in short spasms, his face turned purple, and then he was still.

Long ago, when Savitri was a child, she had, within hearing distance of her parents, told her little brother that she wished God would smash his face to a pulp. That very day, crossing the street on his way home from school, her brother had been knocked flat by a bicycle rickshaw, losing consciousness for several seconds and earning a minor laceration on his forehead. Savitri's mother had been furious. She dragged a tearful Savitri by the ear and made her bow down a hundred and one times before the family altar. "Stupid," her mother had screamed at her then. "Don't you see? The asura ganas uttered *Asthu* to your wish."

The asura ganas, Savitri was told, are small demons in the air all around us. Bastard cousins of the gods, they mutter at odd intervals *Asthu, asthu,* a powerful word in their ancient language. Whatever a person is thinking or saying at a given moment becomes reality if at the same moment the demons happen to utter that magical word.

Savitri had been impressed with the lesson, although she would never admit to believing it. She corrected herself whenever an evil thought rose to her consciousness. She'd had many occasions to remind her own daughter of the possible consequences whenever Radha spoke ill, gossiped or conjectured, used an infelicitous euphemism, or in anger wished some bad fate on her parents.

Savitri hadn't thought about such things for years, but as she stood over her husband's contorted form, she understood that her evil nature had finally caught up with her. She saw it clearly for a brief, terrible moment: her husband was dead and she had killed him. All was panic and pressure, and then she found herself in the kitchen, cooking.

Now, hours later, with the outline of events deepening its imprint on her mind, a feeling of overwhelming fear and guilt returned. Savitri thought through her tears, If only Radha were here. Together we could figure out what to do. Radha doesn't have any sense, but she has one thing, she's brave.

Savitri wiped her eyes on the back of her hands and inhaled loudly to clear her nose. She picked up the living room phone and dialed her daughter's dorm room.

"Hello," a girl's voice said.

"Radha, it's Mummy," Savitri said. "Radha, you have to come—"

"Mrs. Vee . . . ," the girl's voice said. "Mrs. Veeraghavan. This is Lisa."

"Oh." Savitri hesitated. I must compose myself, she thought. I mustn't let Radha's roommate know what it is that has happened here, what it is I have done.

"Lisa?" Savitri said in a voice barely controlled. "How are you?"

"I'm fine," said Lisa, tersely.

"Going home for the holiday?" Savitri was trying now so determinedly to act cheerful that she smiled at the receiver.

"Yeah," Lisa said.

"I'd like to meet you sometime, Lisa," Savitri offered. "I don't know why Radha never brings her friends home. I could cook you some of our Indian specialities."

Lisa was silent.

"Lisa, can I please talk to Radha?"

"Radha's at the library," Lisa replied.

"Studying? But tomorrow is holiday."

"Well, that's where she is," Lisa said.

Savitri paused. "I want to know where she is," she said, her voice now serious. "If she is there, give it to her the phone. If she is gone to somebody's house for the weekend, give me the number there, please."

"With all due respect," Lisa started, inauspiciously, "you call her, like, five times a day. It's not normal. You have no right to control her."

"Lisa," said Savitri, maintaining her composure, "I am her mother, isn't it? And this situation is different. Tell me where she has gone."

"I'm sorry, I don't know."

"Is she gone to some boyfriend's house?" asked Savitri, her voice becoming gradually unsteady. "Has she left already? Tell me what is the number there. Just give it to me the number, Lisa."

"I don't know."

"Darnit!" Savitri yelled. "Lisa, this is an emergency. A big-time thing, you know? Concerning her daddy. Will you tell her please to call me? Just ask her to call me." Savitri fought to keep from crying.

Lisa again was silent.

"Lisa, you will please do that, won't you? Do that please. Promise me."

"What happened?" Lisa asked.

Savitri calmed herself. "Nothing, nothing happened. Don't worry. Just tell her I called." Savitri remembered that she should behave normally, and she added, with desperate sweetness, "Hey, sorry I yelled, Lisa. Don't forget to come over some weekend, okay? I'll cook you my sambar."

When Savitri hung up the phone, she instinctively braced herself for what her husband might have been about to tell her: "Why you always worry over Radha? She's a good girl." Radha was Ravi's pet, and he refused to have even the slightest suspicion of her. He believed, honestly, that when she graduated from college she would marry someone he would approve, a

Brahmin boy from a good family. Ravi couldn't see that Radha was already very far away from this way of thinking. But Savitri heard the impatience in the girl's voice whenever she had to speak even a few words to her parents.

Radha hadn't always been like that, distant and rude. As a child, Radha amazed her mother. She was outspoken, sometimes out of control, but fearless. She had been a smart girl, too, and good to her parents. When Savitri applied for her first job, Radha had helped her to write the cover letter. Savitri felt that she and Radha shared a special bond, because they understood things that Ravi never would.

In her mother, Radha had someone to laugh at the jokes she made at her poor father's expense, about his embarrassing habit of going outside in his lungi to check the mail; about how he didn't like to eat out anywhere but Pizza Hut and Indian restaurants; how he never thought of visiting anyplace in the States where there were not distant relatives or friends of friends from back home they could stay with. And Savitri hungrily sought her daughter's opinions on many things, because the girl had knowledge that her mother lacked: what American clothes to wear to work, which books were good and which politicians worthless, how Savitri should respond to her coworkers' confusing jokes and expressions.

They never should have allowed Radha to go away to college, but the girl had been so insistent about it, and so persuasive. Maybe Savitri had grown too reliant on her, had confided in her too desperately, had pried too frequently, but these days Radha behaved as if her parents' very presence suffocated her. After she went to college, she became a different person. Strange boys began answering her phone, she took any excuse to avoid coming home. Savitri had married Ravi in a family arrangement at the age of nineteen, and now at the same age her daughter was having experiences Savitri couldn't even imagine. Studying anything she liked, going to parties, dating handsome boys. What must it be like? Ravi too easily believed the girl was simply busy with her studies. But Savitri saw how quickly Radha was growing away from them. She was growing away, and she was leaving Savitri behind.

The doorbell suddenly sounded its bright electric bling-blong, and Savitri's mind filled immediately with panicked apparitions. She had been found out, she knew it. She hurried to the living room window and peeked carefully past the curtain. It was her neighbor, only her neighbor, Doug Naples.

She went to the front door and unlocked it, opening it just a crack, and stared at Doug, her heart pounding.

"Did you know your car is outside?" Doug asked. "It's been sitting there for an hour, the engine running. I just thought I'd come tell you, case you forgot about it. It's sticking out the garage."

"Oh, yes," said Savitri. "Forgot all about it. Thank you, Doug." She was pleased to hear that her voice still sounded steady. She felt the panic and unease of moments ago dissipating again into a strange and calculating self-confidence. Doug clearly had no idea what had happened. Here he was at the door, talking with her as on any other day. She opened the door wider. She asked Doug, "How are you these days?"

"Oh, I'm all right," said Doug. "I just thought I'd come by because, well, you never know. Types of people been moving in around here, somebody might just see that car sitting there, the keys inside, and decide—oh my Jesus." He paused. "What's up with Mr. V.?"

"What do you mean, Doug?" Savitri asked, stubbornly holding her smile.

Doug pointed to the floor behind Savitri. She turned around and saw her husband's legs protruding from behind the love seat, skewed at awkward angles.

It's finished, thought Savitri. I'll just tell him. Spell it out very calmly and sensibly. Maybe Doug will help me, tell me what to do. He'll talk to the proper people on my behalf. He'll confirm that I am not responsible for any of this.

Or maybe Doug Naples was not the best help in this kind of fix. Six weeks ago, Savitri remembered, he had offered to help Ravi repair the latch on their fence door. At Ravi's insistence, even Savitri had grudgingly gotten involved, shuttling to and from the house with odd tools and cold glasses of soda. She could see full well they were only going to make a mess of things. And sure enough, the men had ended up inexplicably ripping out the entire length of wooden fence posts, leaving the lawn naked, the above-ground swimming pool exposed like a dangerous temple, an open invitation to a lawsuit. Any neighbor could probably sue them for intentionally endangering their hapless children, and for emotional distress, and on top of that for bad taste and poor landscaping and strange smells wafting out of their kitchen. Every day Savitri feared walking to the pool and finding the pale, bloated body of some little American child floating faceup among the leaves and dead insects. Savitri and Ravi would have a lot of explaining to do then.

Oh, but be careful what you think, Savitri. Be careful.

So instead of telling Doug Naples the truth about Ravi, Savitri took a deep breath. She said, "Ravi is doing yoga. Yoga, Doug. That is, you know, one of the things we do in India. A very good thing."

Doug raised his eyebrows and exhaled an impressed "Huh." He nodded and lowered his voice to a whisper. "Yoga, isn't that something. My doctor says I should do it, too. Good for my sore back. You know, I smelled that Indian food you were cooking, and there's old Vee doing yoga. Isn't that something."

"Come over sometime, Doug," said Savitri. "We'll show you how to do yoga, too."

"Sure," Doug said. "That would be something. It sure smells interesting. And when he's disposed, tell Vee anytime he wants to take another crack at that fence, let me know. My nephew is here for the holiday, we would have an extra hand."

"Thanks, Doug," said Savitri. "I'll tell him."

She shut the door and watched Doug walk back to his house, where he sat at home all day, unemployed, and waited for his fat wife to come home. He was just the type of American her husband would attach himself to. Like her husband, Doug had the air of someone who had been dropped here from another planet, fascinated but flummoxed by the most basic practical processes, like how to fix a fence or find a new job.

Savitri walked out to the garage and parked the car. She took the milk and the turkey from the trunk and brought them inside. She put the milk in the fridge, and she wrapped the turkey's cellophaned and bagged flesh in an additional plastic bag, cleared a space at the margin of the freezer, and slid it in, careful that it touched nothing else.

She saw now that she had the capacity to carry on as normal, that her guilt was not plainly visible on her face. She had only to pretend that nothing had happened, put it all out of her mind. No one knew that Ravi was dead, no one suspected that she might have killed him. If she allowed herself to ponder her situation, then the thoughts would overwhelm. Better to try not to think too much about it at all.

She walked to the living room, stopped, and drew a breath, but couldn't avoid looking down again at her husband. Oh, she couldn't bear to see him lying there, his mouth agape, his eyes wide open in the same naïve, uncritical, awestruck gaze he'd had in life. He was staring at the living room, as if to take in all the furniture, the old and ugly things. As if to say, I bought this all for you when we were young and dumb and content with each other, and this room was enough for us.

She had killed this innocent man, her husband, who loved her. She had thought of it, and it had come to pass.

Savitri walked hurriedly past him and into the bedroom, shutting the door behind her. She stripped all her clothes off onto the floor, had the fleeting thought of taking a hot, hot shower, but instead crawled directly under the covers of her bed. She was so tired now, tired of thinking, of cooking.

Savitri remembered the only other dead relative she had seen, her grandfather, when she was ten or eleven. He had died of a heart attack at an old age in the old house in the village, and they had stretched him out on the bedroom floor to clean him. Then they wrapped him in white cotton and covered his forehead with sandalwood paste and white ash and red kumkum. They moved him to the sitting room floor and laid him there. His sons didn't shave, the stoves remained unlit. The neighbors brought over simple foods. A vadhyar came to the house to pray over the body and prepare the soul for its journey. All her grandfather's friends and neighbors came to pay respects, coworkers and former students, before they took him away to be burned.

Savitri had not witnessed her own parents' deaths. Those had been "phone deaths" that happened while Savitri was in the United States. And now Ravi slept with his head on the carpet, still in his dirty clothes from work. Even death has become less, she thought. Was it her fault?

Where was Radha? She picked up the bedside phone and dialed her daughter again. The answering machine played some song, black music, as Savitri called rap music, and then Lisa's and Radha's voices, alternately. "Hi, this is Lisa . . . and this is Radha," and then simultaneously, "do your thing at the beep and we'll get back at you. Peace."

"Hello, this is a message for Radha," Savitri said. "It's her mother calling. Hi, sweetie. It's me. Listen, I'm not mad at you. Okay? I am not anymore mad. Call me. I just want to talk to you. I love you. There is one thing I need to talk to you, an important thing. Don't be worried, okay? Something happened, wanted to ask your advice about it. Not—" She got just this far when the beep of the machine cut her off. Savitri hung up the phone and closed her eyes.

Ravi should have been in the bed next to her now, or in the bathroom, brushing his teeth. She thought of his face, smiling. About two months ago, she remembered, they had been invited to a dinner party. Savitri had made Ravi change his entire outfit before they could leave. She made him wear one of his few nice shirts, told him to comb his hair with oil. And when she was through with him, she had been struck by how handsome he looked. Even Ravi seemed to enjoy the attention she gave him, despite the nagging that came with it. And at the party, Savitri found herself doing small things for him—refilling his coffee cup unbidden, complimenting him in front of the other husbands.

Why had she asked for his death? She still smelled his odor lingering in the sheets. When she went to the toilet, she should have found the seat wet from his washing, evidence of his presence. She missed his five-dollar haircuts and fifteen-year-old suits. She missed walking on Sundays side by side through the department stores, sullenly vetoing each other's choices, the quiet but certain understanding they shared. She missed his messy way of eating, food oozing from his fist, his relish understated but evident. How other times he might take one bite and say, with simple sincerity, "Nice food, dee." Why had she ever wanted more than this?

At one time in her life, Savitri cried if Ravi came home late from the office. Staring out the window, waiting to see the headlights of his car, she had longed so much to be with her family and friends back in India, where there was always someone in the house to talk to, where you could walk to people's houses. Savitri realized then that if they were going to stay in America, things would have to change. She would have to learn to drive. She needed to start meeting people, Americans. She couldn't sit alone in the house forever. She wanted even to take a job like some of the women she had met at temple. But then, for years, she had given up so many things to stay at home for Radha.

Now, finally, Savitri had begun a career. She still hoped to have more education, more money. She wanted to see things and to travel. Ravi didn't seem to share these ambitions. Savitri knew that her husband still harbored dreams of moving back to Madras. But she thought there was so much more to be had in America, so much they hadn't even understood yet. Was she wrong to think this?

Savitri felt she had to ask someone for advice; the situation was impossible otherwise. But who else could possibly understand such a predicament? Take Poornima. Poornima lived a life like Savitri's but, Savitri felt, with so much more grace and ease, so much less struggle. Poornima had a way of willing things to fall into place. It sickened Savitri to think of having to confess to such a person, such a perfect person. But maybe it was her best option. Maybe there was some easy way out of this, maybe Poornima would tell her this unwieldy problem wasn't a problem at all. Yes, Savitri thought. She would go to Poornima's luncheon. Then, if she could master her guilt and embarrassment, she would confess to her friend.

Savitri didn't fall asleep until early in the morning. When she woke up, the radio newsman was reading the weather report as if it were any other day. It was already past noon. She got out of bed, a dull pain in the back of her head, and showered for twenty-five full minutes. Then she wore a blue petticoat and blouse, and a silk sari embroidered with gold. A little bit much for a luncheon, perhaps, she knew.

Leaving the bedroom, she caught an unwanted glimpse of Ravi's body, and, although she expected it to be there, Savitri gave a short cry of surprise. It seemed to have softened a bit and sunken into the carpet, to have lost its tension. She hurried past it to the garage, took the Tercel, and drove to Poornima's subdivision, a new one where a security guard in a redbrick kiosk took down her license plate number as she passed.

Poornima's house leaned high in creamy brick at the end of a cul-de-sac, edged by a neat lawn, accented by young azaleas and crape myrtle in red mulch freshly laid by the lawn men. Poornima's lanky son, Arun, greeted Savitri at the door, his black hair gelled down to a shiny, cropped shell. He held a glass in his hand.

"You're looking awfully beautiful, Auntie," Arun said, smoothing down his hair, making Savitri smile despite herself.

"So polite you are, Arun," Savitri said. "When did you suddenly get old enough to drink wine?"

Arun retreated into the crowd and Savitri wound her way through the party, finding Poornima in the kitchen, assembling a tray of hors d'oeuvres with manic accuracy, bhajis and chutney and samosas and murukkus. "Done. Take this, Tina," Poornima said, handing her tray off to the maid, and turned to Savitri.

"Sorry I'm late," said Savitri.

"Hello, dear. Don't be sorry," said Poornima. "Where are Ravi and Radha?"

"Not coming," Savitri said. "Didn't I tell you?"

"Of course. Very bad. They'll hear from me."

"I didn't tell you."

"You told me. Here, take this." Poornima handed Savitri a glass of white wine from a collection of several on a tray.

Savitri took half the wine in a gulp. "I didn't tell you," she said. "Ravi is dead." There, thought Savitri. Just tell her. Easiest like this.

"What?" asked Poornima. Her son wandered into the kitchen just then, with a girl Savitri had never seen before.

"Did you say hello to Auntie?" Poornima asked her son.

"Yes, I did," replied Arun, and indicating the young woman, "This is Nira."

Savitri shook the girl's hand and turned back to Poornima, but she was already gone, attending to other guests.

"How is Radha doing?" Arun asked Savitri.

"She is fine," Savitri said. "I don't know, really. She says she wants to take off from college one year and be an airline hostess. See the world and all."

Poornima turned from her conversation on the other side of the room and called, "Nira goes to Harvard with Arun, both of them premed. Look, I'm embarrassing them. Sorry."

Savitri turned to the girl, Nira, and took her measure. Taller than Radha, somewhat slimmer. Lighter complexion. Obviously smart, probably has rich parents. I see how it is, thought Savitri.

"You going to marry this girl?" Savitri asked Arun, and then immediately apologized. "Sorry, that was not a right question."

"That's all right, Auntie," Arun said, diplomatically.

"Because I always wanted, you know . . . I always thought that you and my Radha together would be good. You grew up together and all. And you're doing so well. I don't care that you are not Brahmins. You have to make compromises. Uncle didn't understand that, you see? He could be a stupid man sometimes, Arun. So stupid." Savitri felt a catch in her throat. She paused to regain her composure.

"But now you've got this girl, good for you. And Radha, well . . . There's only so much I can do, right?"

Arun stared for a moment, blinking. Then he smiled. "I think my mother might need some help," he said. He took his friend by the hand and left.

Savitri replaced her empty glass of wine and grabbed another from the tray. Then she veered into the party, almost running into Poornima's husband, Vasanth, himself holding a wobbly glass of scotch in one hand.

"Hello, lovely lady," he said, pushing his oiled locks out of his face with one hand. He had hair thick as an eighteen-year-old's and too long, licking down over his eyebrows, curling over his ears. "Where's the captain?" he asked. "Where's the young lady? Younger lady I should say."

"Both of them indisposed," answered Savitri.

"Indisposed? What is this? Working even today, the slave. It's Thanksgiving, I say, and he's left his wife all by herself." Vasanth smiled. "Someone should *tell* him."

What must it be like, Savitri wondered, to be his wife, to have his money? Did Poornima ever wish for Vasanth's death? Is this the sort of life Savitri had wanted?

Savitri heard the tinkle of ice in glasses, the gibbering voices of tiny demons all around her. Immediately she regretted her thoughts.

"Would be so much better if my wife were looking as young as you," Vasanth said, grinning wide. "She's not nice, Savitri. Every time I open my mouth she is giving me bad looks." Vasanth was so close that Savitri could see the thin red shaving cuts on his cheek and note the odors of sweet aftershave, hair oil, and hard liquor. Savitri felt sickened by his flesh, the smell of his potions, the slick wetness of him. She longed sharply for the plain, dusty familiarity of her husband.

"No!" Savitri said fiercely, shaking her head. "I don't want this. You hear me?" she called out to the room.

"Eh?" Vasanth asked.

"You hear me?" Savitri yelled.

She turned and left Vasanth behind, perplexed but with an uncertain smile on his face, eager to find the joke in the situation. Savitri moved through the crowd until she found Poornima in the kitchen. "I'm leaving," Savitri said to Poornima. "My husband's dead."

"What nonsense," said Poornima. "You can't leave before having lunch. I have to help Tina." Poornima walked toward the young maid, who hovered over the oven. Together, Tina and Poornima pulled from the oven a glistening, honey-brown turkey, assembled all round with red potatoes and green beans. Savitri guffawed in surprise.

"What is this you've done?" Savitri said. "You're a vegetarian."

"But the kids aren't," said Poornima. "Vasanth isn't. And the Nairs aren't, the Bannerjees aren't. It's Thanksgiving, Savitri. And Tina taught me to make the turkey. Actually, you could say she did most of the making. Tina!" she called.

Tina returned with a carving knife, and Poornima stepped to the side, letting the young woman take the turkey toward the dining room.

Vasanth entered the kitchen, drunkenly proclaiming, "It's Thanksgiving, but we have no Pilgrims. Only Indians, no Americans. Must have both for Thanksgiving, isn't it so? Americans in big black hats."

"You're drinking too much," Poornima said humorlessly. "And besides, we have Tina."

"But she's black!" screamed Vasanth. "Black doesn't count." Tina eyed him sharply, saying nothing. "Black is different," Vasanth continued. "Did you ever see a black Pilgrim? Tina is on the Indian side with us."

Arun stepped forward to put a protective arm around his father's shoulders, and Vasanth seemed to go limp, instantly calmed by his son's embrace. He looked up at Arun, who stood half a head taller. "Why don't you be the Americans?" Vasanth asked earnestly.

"Me?" asked Arun.

"You kids," said Vasanth. "Kids are Americans, parents are Indians."

"But that's wrong, Dad," Arun explained. "You were the immigrants, after all, so you should be the Pilgrims. We're natives, so we should be Indians."

"Backward!" Vasanth laughed. "My son turns everything backward! Clever boy." With one hand, Vasanth squeezed Arun's cheeks together until the boy's lips puckered. Arun took it amiably.

"Sweethearts, everyone, come to the dining room. We're cutting the turkey. Sorry, *carving* the turkey, carving it," announced

Poornima to the living room, and the crowd moved toward her. Savitri followed them, and in the mirror-paneled dining room, she stared at the reflection of all her people, beaming and glittering, husbands and wives, parents and children. Enemies gathered in truce around a decorated table. Poornima, with Tina's hand guiding hers, raised the carving knife aloft.

Savitri turned to the woman next to her, a casual acquaintance, someone she had seen occasionally at temple.

"My husband is dead," said Savitri.

"What?" gasped the woman.

"My husband is dead. I think I have killed him, unintentional. Actually, unintentional, intentional—I'm not sure."

"What are you saying?" the woman asked, a look of confusion grading into one of horror. She backed away from Savitri, farther into the crowd.

Savitri tried to explain. "I killed him, and he's on the floor. I killed him, you see!" The people gathered in the dining room stopped laughing and stopped talking. Poornima looked up, her knife and her smile frozen. The guests clutched their empty plates and turned toward Savitri. "I killed him," Savitri yelled to all of them, "and that's all there is to it." Savitri knew they understood. They understood, but she could see from their eyes they would never acknowledge it.

"Savitri, darling." Poornima set down her knife, approached through the stunned crowd, and put her hand on Savitri's shoulder, gripping it with gentle firmness. "What's happened? Why are you upset?"

Savitri didn't answer. She shrugged off Poornima's hand, turned around, and went out the front door. She got in her car and drove until she was back at her house.

Her husband was on the floor—she bent down and pressed the lids closed over his cloudy eyes; she brushed his hair into place with her fingers—and Savitri was very sorry. The phone was ringing.

"What happened?" Savitri heard Radha's voice through the receiver. "Lisa said something about Dad."

But he was dead, Radha's father, and there was nothing to be done about it.

"You having a good time over there, sweetie?" Savitri asked. "Don't think about anything bad right now. I want you to come home, then I'll explain. Food's already cooked. A turkey is in the freezer. Bring your friends, it's okay. You won't be upset with me, right?"

"What happened to Dad?"

"I'm sorry. You loved him, I know it. Remember he took you to school, and you wouldn't let go his hand? You were small then."

"Mom—"

"Hey, listen. We'll sort it out, everything. You and me, we'll figure out what to do," Savitri said, and listened hopefully for the arbitrary voices of demons.

NARRATIVE OF
AGENT 97-4702

1. INVESTIGATION OF SUBJECT 243-66328

I began surveilling Subject 243-66328 roughly seven months ago, concluding just last Tuesday, late evening. Surveillance was according to the standard procedure. It consisted of observation from the motorized phaeton, changing locations and costumes periodically, starting in the mornings, early mornings, 0500. On weekdays, the man, 243-66328, could be observed leaving his house, walking to the corner, waiting for the train, boarding the train. It was usually the same train car—I still remember the registration number of the car he boarded: [redacted].

The subject was going to work, presumably, but I wouldn't know for sure. I was assigned to remain at the location. After he rode away, he was tailed by another Agent, perhaps in the guise of a passenger on the train. But I am speculating.

My guess would be that the subject went to his office. I did not know which office. I did not know the location of the office or what he did there. I could only infer based on the train route; but of course he could have transferred to any number of different routes. About 1900, he would come back home, and that's when I would see him again.

Again, I don't know the number of the Agent who tailed

him, or who surveilled him the rest of the day, if it was the same Agent or a different one; I waited in the phaeton until evening. I even had my meals in the phaeton. I followed the full-intensity surveillance protocol, that is, there was no relief. I was on constantly—but never past the point of fatigue. "The Agent watches until he is no longer watching"—first Precept. So I brought a limited amount of food, approved foods. I brought the necessary equipment, prepared myself, so I wouldn't have to leave the vehicle for any reason, wouldn't have to go to the restroom, et cetera. It's not easy, of course, but I've gotten better at it. I was equipped with a photographic recording device, a portable Teletype for emergencies, as well as with [redacted].

The woman, that is, 243-66328's wife: Sometimes she came out of the house with the child, as the subject was leaving in the morning. Neither she nor the child was under surveillance, at least not by me, not per my directive. I would therefore prefer not to share my observations on the wife and child at this time. Again, neither of them was under surveillance, officially.

My impressions of 243-66328 are detailed in my reports. He is a middle-aged man: about forty-two, forty-three. Light skin, dark brown hair, healthy teeth. Just about five foot ten, roughly one hundred eighty-five to one hundred ninety-five pounds, depending on the week. Balding in a horseshoe pattern. A tendency to wear dark colors: black suits, navy suits, probably wool blend. Owned one brown tweed sport coat. His bow ties were colorful: pink, red. My guess is that he did not pick them himself. His wife on some days tried to fix his tie for him at the door, or to smooth his hair, whereas he never attended to such details, at least not during that interim journey from door to corner. And always he wore the same pair of black oxford-style shoes, as far as I was able to tell. I suppose his wife had given up where the shoes were concerned. Again, that's just idle speculation. At any rate, his outfits each day are carefully detailed in my reports. Sometimes they kissed, but it was not a usual thing.

He carried a briefcase, small black briefcase. It was an old briefcase. The leather was visibly worn and scratched. And he wore glasses. Thick glasses. Brown plastic frames. Carleton was the make. Thick lenses. And he had a slight accent. It is, honestly, hard for me to say what his accent was, because he would not talk much, walking from his house to the corner. Sometimes, he would turn and yell something to his wife. Such as: *Please don't forget to pick up my shirts.* He said that periodically, as he was running out the door. Referring to the cleaners, I would guess. Or, *I love you.* If his wife or his child had called out first, then he would say, *I love you, too.* This is all meticulously logged. So I can only say there was some discernible inflection, but I would be hard pressed to say what. I think it was foreign, but whether [redacted], or [redacted], or something else, I'm not sure. I have not completed the module on accent recognition. I applied for it once but my acceptance was deferred pending a referral.

When he reached the corner, he would often turn and wave once more to his wife—who always stood watching, with the child, at the door—before the train arrived and he boarded it and was out of sight.

I do not know what the investigation of 243-66328 was about. "The Agent does not try to understand what he is seeing"— second Precept. That is a job for the Analyst. So I tried not to speculate. Except to the extent that it seemed clear he must have been up to something bad. I thought this because the Agency parceled the investigation so carefully. The clearances were top. The lines were divided. Every little thing was "to be known only if necessary." I hardly knew anything. I mean, I was told to go to the location and observe the subject. And that was all I was told. So all this made me think it was fairly significant.

I have of course had plenty of other cases that were at a similar level of clearance. I have even served as a liaison for and helped to organize investigations where I did not know, strictly speaking, who the subjects of the investigation were. That is, in some cases, I was not a field Agent, but instead was stationed at [redacted] helping to direct the field Agents. Sometimes I was not even provided numbers of either the field Agents or the subjects of the investigation, much less names. In a couple of cases, I did not know what the subjects looked like or any biographical information but purely location coordinates. In yet other cases, it was set up somewhat differently. Each investigation was different. Theoretically, I suppose it could have been anyone. I suppose I could have been unwittingly directing an investigation of someone I know.

At about 1830 or 1900, 243-66328 would return home. Between the time he left and the time he returned, I would have logged my observations on the quarter hour. He was gone for a stretch of roughly ten hours. As there was no subject activity during that time, my observations were often limited to the number of neighbors who happened to pass by on the sidewalk; the registration plate and description of any vehicles—trains, phaetons, or sedans—in the vicinity; changes in the light and weather; the activities of various squirrels, starlings, and blue jays that lived in the oak tree in the subject's front yard. On a few afternoons, a group of children played stickball in the street in front of his house, which made things relatively lively.

I did this every day, for over six months, ending just about a week ago. I took notes every fifteen minutes, at a minimum. At the end of the day, I compiled my daily report, using my portable Teletype. I submitted my daily report to [redacted], and then I went home, arriving at my residence at about 2230. I live with my husband [J], as the Agency is aware.

2. RELATIONSHIP WITH [J]

[J] would be awake typically, waiting up for me, when I arrived home. We would talk, of course—I was usually exhausted, but

I would make the effort. I wasn't used to coming home so late, but it happens on some cases and we tried to make the best of it. We might open a bottle of wine and share stories about our day. Rather, he would tell me stories from his day and he would ask me about mine. And I would tell him stories, too, but, of course, I was careful that he could not—based on my stories—come to a real sense of what I had done. I have a cover, devised with the guidance of the Agency. My cover is that I work as [redacted]. Which of course I actually sort of do, when I am not on assignment. [J] also certainly understood—he understands, that is—I have a job that I can't talk about. He knows the general nature of the job, but not the specifics. He knows it can be taxing. My classification is Red; it is not White. Therefore I am permitted to give certain limited details to my spouse. If he were to press me on any detail—which he knows better than to do—but if he did, I would know exactly what to say. I've been well trained. I am mindful of my training.

[J] believes my cover. Or rather, he believes and he does not believe. Meaning, he knows I have assignments that I cannot discuss; and that sometimes, therefore, what I'm telling him about my day and my activities is just a story. That's for his protection, for my protection, for the integrity of the investigation, for the integrity of the Agency, and ultimately for the security of the City. He knows exactly as much as the Agency has permitted me to tell him.

To elaborate further on this salient point: When I tell [J] about my day, or about what happened in my life as a so-called [redacted], he believes and he does not believe. Like when you are reading a book or watching a movie, perhaps. He suspends disbelief: that's the phrase. He's tacitly participating in the fiction. But, unlike a movie, he doesn't know where the story ends and the real things begin. He trusts me to make those edges seamless. I would say that requires a lot of trust on his part. I admire that about him. It certainly makes things easier for me.

I wouldn't say I was lying to him, no, because he has agreed to it; he understands what's going on. Even if sometimes he might forget that he understands. Maybe you could say he doesn't know how much to believe, so he simply believes all of it.

Sometimes, when I'd traveled for an assignment, or I was on a particularly stressful investigation, I had a kind of game. [J] would say, "So what did you do today?" And I would say something as bland as possible, like, quite often, "Spent all day on the phone with the Mechanisms Department trying to fix the oscillator in my radio," something bland like that. "Didn't get any work done. And you?" This was a game, or a running joke, I suppose, primarily to amuse myself.

In all our conversations—I want to state this clearly—I never revealed protected information.

[J] is a consultant to the [redacted] industry, as the Agency is aware. He is currently posted at [redacted]. He has passed each of the Agency's periodic character investigations, which have typically been conducted without his knowledge. We love each other. There are no serious problems in our relationship. We have never been separated; we have never been unfaithful. We have been together for almost four years and are planning to have a child in the coming year.

Our last fight—to keep you perfectly up to date—our last fight was about eight months ago. I suppose it is a little embarrassing. I realize I don't have much of a private life that is secret from the Agency, but in any case: [J] was upset with me because I had failed to notice his new tattoo. He already had a couple, but this was a new one.

He is a little rough around the edges for a [redacted], I suppose. He used to serve in the Municipal Navy, if that explains anything.

And yes, I am trained to be observant, but I think it is precisely because I am so alert all day at my job, that when I get home, I sometimes simply turn it off. I have a strong desire to relax. The tattoo was on [J]'s forearm. And it was my name. My first name, in elegant script. He'd had it for about two days before I noticed it. Like I said: embarrassing.

He was very upset. He would barely talk to me for a week after that. "I notice absolutely everything about you," he told me, with some indignation.

3. PREVIOUS INVESTIGATIONS

When I was younger, before I was involved with [J], I would periodically engage in close work. It is something that is sometimes asked of Agents who are unattached romantically: to use emotion as a tool, to use sexuality as a tool. We are trained for it.

My shortest such investigation was, well, a few hours. The longest was about five years, but that was an exceptional case. It was the investigation of [Subject N]. For five years, I was seeing the subject—that is, carrying on a relationship with the subject—purely for the purpose of surveillance and accessing information. It was intense. It was a challenge to maintain distance, to continue observing for that duration. It took me a little while, of course, to get in the rhythm of it. I struggled at first, as the Agency knows. But it was also rewarding; I improved very much in my discipline and focus during that time, and I believe it showed in the quality of my later reports. And [N] was such an interesting subject, as I came to find out. It was on one level a relief when the [N] investigation ended, but on another level, as I have discussed before, it was traumatic.

In my view, such work is deception in the service of truth. I have always believed that anything I have done while with the Agency, anything that might have given me pause in a different context, was in the service of finding the truth. I do believe in the importance of finding the truth. Information adds up. It paints a picture. Any detail—every detail—can reveal so much. I believe in the importance of collecting information. And it is humane. I am attending to them—I mean, attending to my subjects in the sense of paying attention to them—more carefully than any normal lover. [N] will never again in his life have someone pay such close attention to him. I can almost guarantee that.

I care about the subjects of my surveillance. Yes, that is a fair statement. I don't think they would necessarily see it that way, of course. But I wouldn't do it if I thought it was harming people. It is helping people. In the long run, it is even helping the subjects of our investigations. It is ensuring that we see them more clearly, as it were.

4. ENTRÉE INTO THE AGENCY

I joined the Agency at the invitation of a friend of mine, [Agent S]. Again, of course, this is in my files. And surely in her files, for that matter.

I knew [Agent S] from university. I did not know back then that she was an Agent—if indeed she was, back then. We had been good friends. As a matter of fact, she later introduced me to my husband, but that is a different story. [Agent S] and I had both lived in the [redacted] and were spending a great deal of time together, socially. She knew a lot about the frustrations I was having in my previous career as a [redacted]. I used to confide in her to some extent. She is a little older than me. Very accomplished, very polished. I looked up to her. She was good with advice, a great listener, easy to talk to.

[Agent S] is the very Agent who later herself became the subject of an investigation, unfortunately—an internal investigation, you could say, although we don't of course have a separate division for that. To me, [Agent S] never actually said she was part of the Agency. She never out-and-out said it, until after I accepted the invitation to join. She was extremely discreet.

To this day, of course, she is—as far as I can be aware—the

only Agent whose name and identity I know, whom I have touched and seen, with whom I have talked face-to-face. All communications with other Agents or with the Agency itself, communications such as this, have been masked. That is, they have been conducted via Teletype or document drop or by means of blinded chambers at [redacted].

[Agent S] simply said to me, "Have you considered joining the Agency?" I was surprised. I thought she was joking.

I was suprised because, while it was plausible, in retrospect, that [S] might have been an Agent, I just did not think that I fit the profile. I was a bit disorganized. I was a very open person, by nature an open book. [S] had known me in university, which, as the Agency knows, were perhaps not my finest years. My grades were average. I did my share of drinking. I was not known for my discretion. So for someone to ask me with a straight face if I wanted to join the Agency—it seemed like she was trying to play a joke.

But when she convinced me that she was in earnest, I was taken aback. And then, as it sank in, I was thrilled. I was thrilled because, like any child, I had fantasized about being asked to join the Agency. I'd never imagined it could be more realistic than any other childhood fantasy, like becoming an astronaut or marrying a prince. My mother—like many parents, I'm sure—used to tell me the stories about it.

5. HISTORY OF AGENCY (AGENT'S PERSONAL UNDERSTANDING OF)

The way my mother would tell it is as sort of a fairy tale, a bedtime story. About the founding. She would say that, long ago, when our City became independent, the first Monarch worried about holdouts from the old order; he wanted to root them out. He also needed more information about the population than he was able to receive in the corridors of the Municipal Palace.

He needed nuanced intelligence. So he asked his trusted adviser, whose name we will never know, to be his confidential eyes and ears among the population—to be his agent, as it were.

This man, this first Agent, had two children, a boy and a girl. Over the years, separately and confidentially, he revealed his job to each of these children, and asked their assistance. Neither child ever knew that the other had also been asked to be an Agent.

As from time to time the threats to our City increased, each of these children invited some of their own trusted friends— separately, individually, secretly—to aid them in their task. And like this, over the generations, the Agency persisted, simply by each Agent tapping the shoulders of others, as it were. It was one of these first Agents, probably, who wrote the Precepts, which have proved to be extremely useful and durable as regulatory guidelines.

I'd often thought about it, in my fantasies as a child, what it would have been like to be one of the first. In my imagination (now, this is embarrassing) I was friends with both of the children of the first Agent—friends with one and romantically involved with the other, actually—and they both separately asked me to join. It was very dramatic because I couldn't tell either of them that the other had also tapped me. I had quite an imagination as a child.

You could say that this old story first got me interested in the Agency. Of course, it's just a fairy tale, but it is useful, especially given that the actual history of the Agency is kept in confidence. I have never myself heard the actual story. The fairy tale doesn't fit perfectly. Today we no longer have a Monarch, thank goodness; we have the Executive Committee of the Agency. Agents now work not for some powerful municipal ruler, but for the people, directly—as mediated through the Agency. We are agents, you could say, of our follow citizens. But at any rate, the story is what first piqued my interest in serving as an Agent.

As the Agency knows, I have not yet myself been permitted to invite anyone to serve as an Agent.

6. INCIDENT INCURRING DISCIPLINARY ACTION

The day after completing my assigned investigation of 243-66328, just last week, I was given another assignment. A short assignment: I was to conduct a blinded interrogation of [redacted], who was being held at [redacted]. So I went to [redacted]. I conducted the interrogation. It took me about a day and a half.

After I finished, I was met by [Agent S]. I did not find this unusual. Because the recruiting Agent is the only Agent with whom I can have direct contact, [Agent S] is often used to relay information to me. This has remained true even after [Agent S] herself underwent investigation. That investigation did reveal her to be personally compromised—specifically, she was thought to have suffered a mental episode, as I was given to understand. As a consequence, my understanding was, she was confined to [redacted]. But she was still operating as an Agent within the confines of [redacted].

She met me and simply asked me, "Would you like to see the files on 243-66328?"

My reaction was startled. I said something like, "See them? Are you sure?" I didn't even know, frankly, that she would be privy to where the files were kept.

And she said something to the effect of: "Yes, would you like to see them?" At which point, I reminded her, my clearances on this were apparently limited. I'd had no idea even that the records were stored here, and as I stated, I was surprised that she would just simply want to show them to me, when there had been so much secrecy around this.

And she said something like, "I know exactly what your clearances are." And I responded, "Is there some reason you want me to see them?" And she said, simply, sort of: "Come with me." Or: "Come with me, we're going to see them."

And at that point, I began to have a suspicion: She seems really intent on this. Perhaps she's having another episode, or something's going on here.

It did occur to me to decline. She is well above me in rank, but she is not technically my superior, so I was not legally bound to obey her. At the same time, there seemed no reason not to. I didn't see at the time that she would obviously be breaking any regulations. I thought maybe the best way to handle the incident was to comply with her—not to have an open conflict, not to excite her. And then, if anything seemed inappropriate, I could deal with it at that time. I can see now that I should have simply ended the interaction immediately.

To be honest, I was curious. I would have to say, frankly, I let my curiosity override my better judgment. I acknowledge that this was a grave mistake on my part.

She took me up to the [redacted]. This is a part of the facility where I had never been. She knew the combination to get us inside, and we entered an elevator and came out on another floor and passed through several secured doors—she knew all the combinations—and walked down a number of hallways and entered another elevator and emerged into another hallway. I think eventually we were in a sub-basement or sub-sub-sub-basement somewhere. I feel that we had walked maybe thirty minutes. And then we came to a large door, and again she was able to disengage the lock. It was a heavy door—it took both of us to swing it open, once it was released. We walked inside to find a vast room. It was enormous, high ceilings, concrete floors. The room had no windows, but it was well lit, the ceiling was covered with electric lights. It was just a very vast room—more than a square mile, I would guess. And there were rows and rows—and rows—of file cabinets, up to the ceiling. The whole room was filled with them. Files upon files upon files.

It was quite overwhelming. I felt that the files for the entire Agency must be stored here. I really hadn't ever known that this storage space existed. It was curious.

And [Agent S] knew exactly where to go. We walked down the rows of tall cabinets, we walked for another twenty or thirty minutes—I would have been hopelessly lost if not for [S]—and finally she turned left and walked to one particular cabinet. There was a ladder there—a rolling ladder—that was much higher than should have been safe to climb. But she climbed it all the way close to the ceiling. It took her a long time, and I couldn't even hear her voice when she got up there—frighteningly high. She seemed to open one of the wooden drawers and remove something from it. She slowly climbed down. Finally, I could see she had several file folders under her arm. When she reached the floor, she handed one to me. I started examining the contents, and I was amazed. I recognized my own reports, my own observations, although they were heavily redacted. I didn't have more than a moment with the file. Then she took that file abruptly from my hand and gave me another one. This was a report of one of the other Agents who was apparently following 243-66328. The logs were even more detailed than my own. It had also been redacted, but the file seemed to describe the sound and timbre of his voice, the incremental changes, over the days, in the length of his hair and fingernails. The duration and frequency of his bathroom visits. Every possible observable detail, it would seem.

She removed that file abruptly and handed me another folder. It seemed that each report was more exhaustive in its specificity. I believe I glimpsed logs describing the ways in which he tilted his head, what he looked like in the morning, the color of his socks and underwear, the smell of his breath, the flutterings of his eyelids, a taxonomy of his gestures on a certain afternoon. Things even more detailed and personal than that, I believe, but I can't be certain. This was all very quick, and many things were redacted, and moreover I was not reading thoroughly. At the time, it was not immediately clear to me who could have collected such information, or how, or why it would have been useful. The subject's workday was described, as well. As I found out, to my surprise, he himself was [redacted].

The drawer she had opened, I observed, seemed to have been a very long, deep file drawer, with probably hundreds or thousands of folders in it. And it is a very tall cabinet, as I said. All the way to the ceiling. I had only glimpsed a few pages from three of the folders. "Is that whole drawer dedicated to 243-66328?" I asked [Agent S]. And she responded, "This whole room is dedicated to 243-66328." She said, "243-66328 has been under investigation since [redacted], and he is still under investigation."

I don't know what I said. I think I expressed disbelief. It seemed more information than anyone could even read in a lifetime, much less compile, even given the resources of the Agency. I wondered out loud what 243-66328's suspected violation had been, that could justify such an investigation, and she said something sarcastic, to the effect of, "Why don't you browse through his files and find out? It's got to be in this room somewhere."

And then she said, as I recall: "He is not the only one. Every case is the same. Every single case." Then she took the remaining folder from my hands and climbed back up the ladder and replaced them all. I hadn't had a chance to really take a good look. She eventually came back down. By this point, I was very obviously concerned that this might not conform to regulations. This bothered me a great deal. There was no clear purpose for my seeing this information that I could cite to one of the regulations.

I told her, at that point, I think we should end this interaction. I did not physically remove myself, but I clearly stated to her something amounting to: "I shouldn't be here. We should leave."

She ignored me. She said, "We have a room like this on everyone in the City. We are filling a room like this on you."

I probably laughed. I said, "There is simply not enough room to store this much information on everyone who is subject to an investigation, much less everyone in the City. Much less me. There are not enough man-hours to compile it; the Agency does not have the resources."

And she asked, "How big is the City and its affiliated Territories? How much of that land do you think the Agency controls?" And the answer, of course, is all of it.

She was agitated. She did not seem herself. She continued talking: "Do you have any idea how many Agents there are? Let me put it another way: Do you know how many people are left at this point who are *not* a part of the Agency?"

I was dismayed. [Agent S] is my friend, as I said, and I had always looked up to her. She had always been polished, controlled, the very image of what an Agent should be, to my mind. So it was sad to see her in this state. It seemed clear that she was having another episode. The only thing that argued in her favor were the files I had seen with my own eyes, the files for 243-66328. But again, these were just a few pages that could easily have even been fabricated.

But despite her state, she still had her force of personality. She was speaking to me in a very persuasive manner. She had not stopped talking, because she saw that she was getting to me. I believe I had become visibly upset.

I said, at that point, "I think we should go. Please, let's go." I somehow convinced her to lead me out of there. And so, again, a very long walk. We did not speak much during that walk; she may have spoken, but I did not respond. And finally we returned to that part of the facility I am more familiar with. We parted ways—I don't know where she went, but I left her to complete my paperwork for the [redacted] investigation. And then I departed the [redacted]. I got in my phaeton to go home.

That is when I contacted [J]—after I got in the phaeton. I turned over the engine but before I began moving, I took out my Teletype.

I typed, "I have a lot to talk to you about when I get home," or something to that effect. I don't know what I meant, truly. I was upset. I did not specifically have any intention in mind. To be honest, it was not like our game or routine, that is, our "Guess what happened in the office" routine. I was just not even thinking that far ahead.

It was certainly imprudent. But as I stated, I had no plan yet in mind about what to tell him. So in my own conscience, I am clear that I had not formed the intention to reveal protected information. I can be sure of that because I know my thoughts. I believe I do. But to be perfect in my confession, it did cross my mind—the idea of revealing this information to him, revealing what I had observed that day—this did cross my mind. But crossing my mind (to my mind) is different from forming an intention, although it is on the same continuum. It was, I admit, a dangerous moment. It was a moment of weakness.

I would like to very clearly state: It was wrong.

[J] responded with something sympathetic or similar, curiously similar, like, "I know." As I mentioned before, we are both mutual friends of [Agent S] in our civilian life, as it were, although I am the only one who knows her as an Agent. He typed, "I know you have heard from [S]," or something like that. But she does leave messages for me at my home, in our capacity as personal friends, and so that didn't mean anything, necessarily. And he said, "Yes, we should talk." I don't know what he thought I was referring to, or what he was thinking; certainly at the time, I didn't.

At home, [J] had started fixing dinner. I went into the kitchen to help him, thinking that making myself useful might help me to relax. [J] did ask, "So what did you want to talk with me about? What happened today?" And I took a deep breath—I slipped right back into my training—and told him, "Oh, my day was kind of stressful, but really not that interesting." I was completely rededicated in my commitment. As startling as the afternoon might have been, it seemed clear that nothing [S] had said had been authenticated; certainly, nothing was worth compromising the integrity of the Agency, or my own integrity. I said, "That darn radio was acting up. I really need to replace the oscillator."

He looked at me very closely. I was chopping carrots to go with the roast. I was doing my level best, but frankly, my face may have betrayed something, because I was still somewhat upset; I was thinking about [S].

"Is that all that happened?" [J] asked. I couldn't bring myself to look at him. I kept my eyes focused on the chopping board.

These are, I must say, the difficult moments in the life of an Agent. Maybe you feel like you need to talk, but there is only so much that can be said, and only so many ways you can say it. I have encountered these moments many times, in my relationship with [J], and even previously, in a different way, with [N].

But I have improved, since my earliest days—I believe I have. And I accept that being an Agent entails some cost in terms of personal life. But that cost is worth it, because I believe in the goals of the Agency, to the extent that I know what they are.

And another saving grace that used to occur to me is that perhaps it does not matter that I cannot say a lot, because we should be able to glean enough, for our purposes, just from observing.

I said, "Unfortunately, that's all that happened. It felt important at the time. How about you? What did you want to talk about? What happened in your day?"

He turned around to put the roast in the oven to reheat it. He closed the oven and adjusted the knob and came back. "My day? You know how disorganized the shipping lines are. And the telegraph wires are always under repair. I spent all day just trying to reroute a shipment." Then he took a knife out of the drawer and began to help me with the chopping. "Same old story," he said. "Hardly left me time to get any real work done."

When the roast was warm, we ate dinner. It was a nice dinner—[J] always does a good job with the roast. We even opened a bottle of wine. In the end, it turned out to be a very relaxing evening.

7. CONCLUSION

I have read and verified the accuracy of this narrative. I freely acknowledge my wrongdoing pursuant to *Code of Agent Conduct* Ch. 25, §§ 201-212, to wit:

Unauthorized entry into restricted-access rooms at [redacted].

Failure immediately to report unauthorized entry.

Failure immediately to report violations committed by fellow Agent.

Receiving and reading protected information.

Unauthorized communication using Agency Teletype.

Entertaining a mental state conducive to forming an intention to disclose protected information.

I freely agree not to contest the outcome of any disciplinary proceedings initiated by the Agency. Pending the outcome of such proceedings, I request permission to remain fully instated in my current position.

Signature: [redacted]
Date: [redacted]
Document code: [redacted]

BIBHUTIBHUSHAN MALLIK'S
FINAL STORYBOARD

I

The filmmaker Jogesh Sen, preeminent art-house director of India, whose memorable first film, *Calcutta Nights,* earned the Palme d'Or at Cannes in 1975, will debut his twentieth film this evening on the opening night of the New York Film Festival. Accompanying him on Jet Airways to JFK are myself (Bibhutibhushan Mallik, his longtime production designer) along with the cinematographer and two stars of the film, plus Jogesh's wife, Nirmala Sen. It is only my second time in New York City; Jogesh has visited numerously. In the morning, Jogesh and actor Satyadev and cinematographer Anant attend without me the welcoming breakfast. ("Only three tickets, old chap," Jogesh tells me, by way of apology.) Later, Jogesh and Satyadev and Anant conduct some tedious interviews with American magazines. ("You never enjoy such things anyway, Chotu, eh?" Jogesh reassures me. "Dressing up, yakking, mugging for photographers.") Not missing the bore of an interview at all, Mrs. Nirmala Sen and I sit high atop the rooftop parapet of the double-decker sightseeing bus, cruising along First Avenue like a maharaja and maharani atop the royal elephant.

We pass by United Nations—location of such magnificent

scenes in *North by Northwest,* that triumph of production design: the smart suits, distinctive colors, and stylish sets. I imagine myself a Cary Grant, the bus in long shot; and next to me, my own double agent, older and achier than Eva Marie Saint, perhaps, but no less divine.

Mrs. Nirmala Sen and I have been lovers for the past nearly two years. We are old people, with saggy bellies and fat grandchildren. Our hair is less and our backs give enormous pain. It must go without saying that our love affair is not some hot-blooded whim or youthful indiscretion. It is a weighty matter, for it will surely mean not only the imminent destruction of our marriages but moreover a complete end to my thirty-five-year collaboration with Jogesh Sen, for whom I toil as exclusive production designer, art director, as well as storyboard artist. I create the entire visual concept for Jogesh's films; the public little suspects that by himself, great Jogesh cannot draw a human figure with pencil, nor propose a color palette, articulate a costume idea, nor properly frame the characters in the shots without consulting my storyboards.

But all that is nothing as to this: quiet, unassuming Nirmala Sen, in classic red sari and blue cardigan, plus a clear plastic poncho to protect against the spitty drizzle. She burrows her cold hand into the warming embrace of my own. With her sweet, sad face, Nirmala is looking down upon the pizza shops and sweet shops crowded like a family into narrow Bleecker Street, and she is sighing with a thoughtful and rueful detachment.

Mrs. Sen receives all the wondrous sights of New York City with the same deep sigh, a benign world-weariness, as if to say, what do these man-made things mean to me? These tall buildings and cones of colored gelato? Not that she is haughty, nor is she simply anxious about what we are about to do. Rather, Nirmala Sen possesses the profound knowledge that all monuments and pleasures in life are brief; she has the perspective, in other words, of a woman who has suffered.

This I am trying to learn from her. These last two years with Nirmala—coming toward the end of life—have been as the beginning of my life.

"Nirmala," I tell her after we return to the hotel in the early evening, "after his interviews, Jogesh is meeting with his distributor. It will take time. Why not you come in to my room?" In the solitude of the hotel hallway, I hook my finger inside of one of Nirmala's golden bangles.

Mrs. Sen grew up in a good and sophisticated family; she is well educated, has fine tastes and normal values. I find myself moved that such a woman would even dream of deviating from the regularities of married life for my sake. But some flicker of hesitation is there in her angel face. She looks down at her watch; she glances along the hallway. Like one of the lonely housewives so sensitively portrayed in several of Jogesh's early films, Mrs. Sen struggles daily with her unhappiness, although life is slowly coming around.

"That sounds lovely," Nirmala Sen finally sighs, as if I am the microphoned fellow at the front of the bus, urging her to get down and admire the view of some bridge or glassy building. She scrutinizes the wallpaper, while allowing her soft shoulder to lean against mine, and my heart explodes in bliss. Even after two years, I am overjoyed each and every time she accepts my embrace.

Only people the age of sixty-plus can properly enjoy love. This I have recently concluded. Fools in their twenties run behind firm little girls with no thoughts and no experiences, as foolish as I was myself, even paying good money to have my way with the poor prostitutes. My wife—yes, she was pretty, in the photograph, but we had no concept of how to please each other. We each grew accustomed to our mutual sourness—I even used to blame it on how old her flesh had become.

How wrong of me. Now see—I cannot resist Nirmala's drooping parts, the globular expanses and scored surfaces, the sinking into. Now see how I like to fall down with flesh my own age! I don't know why anybody wouldn't. Leave it for the youngsters the skinny and smooth and indistinct each-others.

With one necessary condition: if the old person is someone with whom I am soul-catchingly in love.

"In two days," I remind Nirmala, later in that evening. "In two days, we will not be required to hide and skulk."

Nirmala is hurriedly wrapping herself again in her red sari, carefully fastening her diamond earrings. She combs her thin white hair and ties it, then corrects her makeup in the mirror.

In two days I meet with Mr. Jefferson Bundy. Mr. Jefferson Bundy is a film producer working in Hollywood, California, and on Saturday he is flying across America to meet me. Quietly, over the last two years, I have written a screenplay, a true labor of love, which the wonderfully named Jefferson Bundy, it seems, has read and admired. I have wanted to write a screenplay for my whole life, but it has taken Nirmala to give the motivation and courage. It is a classic story: love triangle. Presuming I secure financing from Jefferson Bundy, I will no longer be beholden to Jogesh for my livelihood, and Nirmala and I can finally proclaim our love. I will become a filmmaker in my own right, here in the U.S., and all will be thanks to Mr. Jefferson Bundy. Mr. Jefferson Bundy: how I love repeating that hearty name; it may hold our future, our abundant American future.

Now Nirmala turns to me, a note of worry in her voice. "But who knows what he will say? He might have discouraging news."

"Please don't worry, Nirmala. All signs are pointing in the other direction."

I recline in the bed and flick the remote—it is Wyler's *The Little Foxes*: look at the funny shaving mirrors, the unusual, well-chosen props.

Before she steps out the door, Nirmala places her eye against the peephole and mutters a brief prayer.

"Simply come back to bed." I mute the television and flop onto my belly. "No need for prayers."

She turns, offering me a longing and a worried gaze—how she would love to return beneath the covers. "There is a need," Nirmala says softly. "Very big need." Then she slips quietly out the door and into the hallway.

2

That evening, Jogesh Sen's film is premiered. Before the screening, Jogesh's American publicist has arranged for all attending crew and cast to join together for a photo session outside of Lincoln Center. We stand in the stiff wind and grin and mug for some god-awful thirty minutes. Jogesh repeatedly rearranges his British houndstooth muffler, smoothes his oiled silver hair against his head.

"Damn wind, Chotu, eh? Isn't it bothering you?"

"Luckily, I don't have any hair for the wind to bother it."

"It must be cold for you poor bald men in this country. Look, you are getting goose pimples on your scalp."

In this way, we mock and banter, while in my stomach, I almost cannot stand it anymore. Like Jimmy Stewart to John Wayne in *Man Who Shot Liberty Valance*, why not tell Jogesh everything, plainspoken American, and simply have it out? *Dear Jogesh, I am in love with your wife. Plus I hope to quit you to stay in U.S. and make my own film, taking Nirmala with me. How do you like them mangoes, old friend?* But some element of Nirmalite prudence restrains me.

"Hey, Chotu," Jogesh continues, as the photographer replaces her lens. He presses his long fingers into my shoulder. "Thank you for keeping company to Nirmala these past two days. She would find it very difficult to see the city on her own. What a shame I don't have the time to enjoy it with her."

Jogesh has always called me Chotu, although I am six years his elder—it is because, at five feet and six inches, I am somewhat small.

"It is nothing to thank me, Jogesh," I assure him.

Now he leans to my ear. "Hey, Chotu. This afternoon, I asked the valet to deliver my new screenplay to your room. When you have extra time, can you please read it over and begin sketching up some storyboards? Some people here may be interested in it."

A new screenplay, so quickly? I am stunned, although by now I should be long accustomed. It has taken me two long years to craft the single screenplay of my life. It will probably be the last screenplay of my life, as I put all my available materials into it—a triumph, but a bloody difficult one. And meanwhile, fresh from his latest success, Jogesh is delivering to me the seventh screenplay of last four years—the twenty-oddth of his career—completed, it would seem, in the midst of his travels.

To calm myself, I fire a cigarette, causing fastidious Jogesh to take one step away from me. "Must you, Chotu?" he asks.

The publicist also chides me. "Sir, could you please put that out?"

"Just two puffs," I promise, rocking my head affably. "Please-please, continue photographing."

But the photographer has pulled her head away from the camera. Everyone is waiting for me, and Jogesh clucks his tongue impatiently.

"Oh, very well," I cry, stamping out the cigarette in the red carpet beneath my feet, and grinning as per the photographer's instructions.

There was a time when I was taken with him, just like everyone was. What, after all, was life before I met him? Hunched over my easel under the ceiling fans in the ad agency, at the old-already age of thirty, one of dozens among rows and rows sketching soda bottles and biscuit tins. Each of my concepts had to be redrawn one hundred times to answer the whims of this foolish client or that imbecile executive. Why should they respect my opinion? My parents had come to Kolkata straight from the village; I drank home brew at the dhaba, not G and Ts at the Tollygunge. To save myself, I removed my emotions from it, making the work mindless, so that the main challenge lay in calculating my movements to avoid any drop of forehead sweat or cigarette ash from falling on the drawing paper.

I would have liked nothing more than to be a Gauguin and say: To hell with society, I create only for myself. But I had to be practical: at night I went home to my wife and mother and younger sister, all of us living together in three rooms, all of us relying on my job. What a noisy flat that was! I didn't know yet what a life I was missing. Those three women were taste-less, tactless, strewing their knickknacks all about the house, kitten posters and stamp-pressed Ganeshas and little plastic boys whose penises spout water—mass-produced doodads as are found in city bazaars. "Don't remove them; it is our house, too," they would insist to me.

So, I was thirty when Jogesh joined, fresh from university, a young, handsome star of a copywriter from one of Kolkata's prominent families. He looked over my shoulder while I was sketching on the day we met. I was preparing a storyboard for a television ad: a family picnicking in a hill station, their clothes all brilliant white thanks to Rim! Brite-And-Clean clothes soap.

"Your composition reminds me of Jean Renoir's film *Partie de campagne*," the voice behind me said in tailored English. "Have you seen it?"

Who was this proper young sahib wandering the wrong departments? I wondered. His tall shadow obscured my easel; his European cologne invaded my nose. Was he trying to flatter or to mock me? One could never trust these privileged types.

"A lovely movie," I answered in a neutral tone, trying to fig-ure what the boy was up to. It is only incidental that I was lying.

Difficult to admit, but I had not yet even heard of Jean Renoir or *Partie de campagne*. How much I had been missing! Not speaking French, I even thought Jogesh might be referring to some Malayali film.

"One day I will make a film like that," he informed me, quite plainly. "It will be set in the Bengal countryside, using deep-focus shots as suggested in your beautiful storyboard. The story will revolve round a real Indian family, none of this popular humbug, and our local actors will act."

I turned and looked up at him: I could not help laughing at the boy's simple confidence and plain ambition, and Jogesh also laughed. Perhaps it was artful naïveté, but the impression he gave was of a talent so robust it could not be constrained by our normal, disingenuous Indian modesty. I was taken immediately by these qualities, even as I envied his lack of encumbrances, his youth and privilege, that allowed him to make such plans.

As for his own fondness for me, that is easily explained. He saw how I could sketch a scene even after five glasses of local brandy at our after-work dhaba, capturing every nuance of pertinent detail. He appreciated my thoroughness with an ad mockup, my considered choices for the props on shoots. He admired my aesthetic values.

He took me to all foreign film screenings, asking my opinions, in turn giving me such an education. (The Americans became my favorite: Ford; Hawks; Hitchcock; Nicholas Ray.) He wanted to prepare me because I had skills that would be necessary for him, and since our first film, he has relied entirely on me to create the visual scheme. It was I who urged him to shoot half of *Calcutta Nights* in black-and-white (village scenes) and half in color (city life). I sketched the costumes vivifying the family's progression up the social ladder. I carefully picked the furniture for the successive homes. And, of course, I drew up the storyboards that he was clutching in his hands as he instructed Anant on how to frame the shots. In effect, I created the visual world through which Jogesh's cinematographer moved the camera.

And Jogesh's skill? He was a manager and manipulator of people—a director, through and through. How he could talk! With such confidence, making each crew member feel they were the crucial link in a grand endeavor.

Jogesh quit his job in the ad agency to make that film. It was some two years after he had started at the agency. He simply walked up to my easel and bluntly he informed me: "I have submitted my notice, and so should you. Bibhutibhushan, I have secured financing. In twelve weeks' time, we will begin filming my screenplay."

I was speechless, exhilarated. Who else but Jogesh could make me even to think of quitting my cushy job, and facing the fury of my mother and young wife—both so quick with an insult.

"Bah bah! Where did you find the money, good friend?" I laughed.

He showed me then a small square photograph of a girl with huge eyes and creamy skin, staring into the camera with a wise and weary gaze even at her tender age.

"Our mothers play bridge on Sundays. Our horoscopes match perfectly. And her father—I am happy to inform you, Bibhutibhushan-brother—is unspeakably wealthy."

That Jogesh married for money was not the most shocking thing; in those days, very few of us married for love. What surprised me instead, in her quiet way, was Nirmala herself. At their winter wedding, as the priest babbled prayers and relatives anointed her, and later at the Tollygunge, as one by one the eminences of Kolkata society offered their empty blessings, this strange girl remained calm and apart, neither impressed nor intimidated, succumbing not at all to the whirl of pretension, rocking her head and smiling as needed. Her face was barely out of childhood, plump and sweet; but her eyes were like the eyes of 3-D Jesus glued to the dashboard of the car belonging to our soundman Mr. George—compassionate and knowing eyes, eyes aglow with the sad wisdom of two thousand years, mysteriously following you even if you move left, if you move right.

In the reception line, I made some swift, jovial little crack about all the overstuffed babus that even Jogesh didn't capture, nor my own wife. But a knowing smile flitted over Nirmala's mouth, a brief intimacy between us. At that moment, even through her silence, I became allied with her. I would not have been bold to have called it *love,* but in fact it was. And thereafter, at functions and parties, or visiting Jogesh's home office, I always went out of my way to attend to lonely Nirmala, to ask what magazine she was reading, and make some small joke and pull a smile from that face. She was so bored, with a mind like hers, in a house filled with servants and nothing to do. How could Jogesh be so preoccupied as to ignore this treasure? When she visited us on set, amid all those grave and intent persons, where everything was pukka tension, she in turn would seek me out, because I would always give her a little time, and we'd share some wry comments on the serious goings-on.

"Bibhuti-bhai, cheer me up. Tell one of your jokes," she used to beg of me, making my eager heart to melt. I would assume a voice or make a funny sketch: Nirmala's face on the body of a swan; Jogesh's sleek mug attached to a peacock or a wolf. It was the great pleasure of my day to elicit those satisfied giggles. She was my perfect audience.

Such diversions were entirely to Jogesh's satisfaction, for it took away some stressful burdens from him, freeing him to focus on his job—to focus, that is, on whichever beautiful and sophisticated actress happened to be on the set that day.

"What is he telling to her so earnestly?" Nirmala would ask me.

"Just directions, move this way, that way, speak more loudly and so on."

"Taking a long time for such simple directions, isn't he? Doesn't she know to move without his touching her like that?" Jogesh was bending over the actress, whispering animatedly, then pausing to listen. Taking her arms and moving them gently, like doll's arms.

"Indeed. We could all be eating dinner by now if he didn't take such a fuss over the actors. Vain creatures, actors; they will suck up all the time if you allow them. Look here: my own face on a swinging monkey!"

"What?"

"A monkey, swinging from a tree! Jumping into the water with the inscrutable swan."

"Looks nothing like a monkey."

"It does!"

"Chup. Enough nonsense," she said, smiling despite herself. "It's not amusing."

For all those years, we were not unfaithful. We were not malicious. At that time, nothing could have happened between someone such as Nirmala Swan and someone such as Bibhutibhushan Mallik, even had we met each other as unmarried persons. As our local films repeatedly remind us, this is the tragedy of our Indian system.

It would take more than thirty years. My sons would have grown, and through my connections, found jobs on Kolkata film sets: one a script supervisor; the other a cameraman. My own marriage would have further devolved into a graceless and purely practical arrangement, completely lacking sensuality. All of us would have grown into old people. And, while Jogesh was abroad and she was using the home computer, Nirmala would have stumbled into his open e-mail inbox, and read the fond and familiar message from the Mumbai Actress: final, irrefutable proof. And only then would she call me to her home and fall, weeping furiously, into my arms.

"Oh, God!" she cried, scratching her arms with her nails, pulling her own hair with her fist. "How could he have done this?"

"Ah-ooh-wa, careful, careful," I cooed, holding her arms gently to her sides and pulling her close against my breast—where she melted, where she melted.

"I want to kill him!" she wailed. "I want to cause him that much pain." Patiently, I flicked away her tears and kissed her on the hair—at first like a brother would kiss, and then . . . before our eyes our long-waiting love finally found its door and came into the beautiful open. Our children were grown; we were finally free to do as we pleased, society be damned.

Of course, we still kept it only between us, for how could I proclaim my love for Jogesh's wife while remaining dependent on Jogesh for my livelihood, while also living in small-minded and clannish Kolkata? We met monthly, weekly, whenever I found a stolen weekend, a private afternoon. Nirmala's fury at Jogesh had released a passion so intense, which she had never before acknowledged; while I myself discovered in her such universes of thoughtful tenderness. Nirmala would make me tea, would ask after my health, and then her watery wide eyes would drift, lost and anxious. That look, I learned, was the precursor to love. Until, mutually assuaged, we shyly wore our clothes again. She would offer me tea once more, also sweets. She would straighten my shirt and fold up the packet of sweets into my hand (for the long drive). She would walk me to the door and close it only after I had rounded the corner for the taxi.

3

That night, the premiere in Lincoln Center is a gala affair, drawing a full six hundred people to the auditorium. In the audience, I spy some American actors whose faces I have seen in cinema halls of childhood (look, there is Eli Wallach! And nobody recognizes him!), causing my stomach to revolve in giddy flops; even after so many films and so many festivals, the excitement of such moments never diminishes. As the film begins, my eyes gleam with satisfaction to see the results of my effort, the soundness of my design choices reflected in the rapt eyes of the audiences around me. When the credits roll, our film receives a deafening ovation.

During the Q-and-A afterward, one panting questioner begs, "Mr. Sen, how have you enjoyed New York?" Jogesh takes the microphone. "I wish I had more time to enjoy the city properly," he chuckles, in his finest imitation Oxbridge—the accent he always uses with Western audiences. "You see, New York is always so busy for me." I suspect he means this in more ways than one, because at the back of the auditorium I finally notice the Mumbai Actress. She is sitting, tall and fine-nosed, among a group of men in their neat stubble and linen scarves.

Eyeing the Mumbai Actress at the cocktail reception afterward, Nirmala asks me, twisting with both hands the corner of her dupatta, "Could it be that I was all along mistaken about the two of them? After all, she has come here only to promote her own film."

"Mistaken?" I ask. I hand to Nirmala one of the drinks I have waited in a long line to retrieve, gin with a splash of tonic, plus one big squeeze with my own fingers from a lime wedge. This question—this naïveté—somehow irritates me. "Come on, Nirmala. They are behaving innocently now, avoiding intimate conversations, but only because you are here, naturally."

"Oh, but she is beautiful!" cries Nirmala. And Nirmala's lovely face—crinkled with lines like a fine batik—tightens in distress.

"My darling, what difference does it make to us, anyway?" I whisper, moving my lips dangerously close to hers. "You are the real beauty in the room, and that dancing girl cannot take away one bit of happiness from us."

My words evidently reassure her. Nirmala rocks her head in agreement, blinking down her tears, and then (Deborah Kerr, *Affair to Remember*!) she takes one step away from me for our mutual protection.

"I want to get away from here," she whispers. Together, we step out coatless into the blustery wind of the vast Lincoln Center plaza. Its beautiful bright fountain towers grandly, spraying us with icy mist. Nirmala tightens her grip around my arm, and I pull her close.

"Over there," I say, pointing to the distant west. "That is where we will live when I am making my film. My cousin's condominium in Jersey City. He will loan it to me."

"Is it a nice place?"

"Beautiful, Nirmala. A full view of Manhattan." She leans eagerly to hear my description, so I continue. "It is on the thirtieth floor. You can see from the Statue of Liberty all the way up to Empire State Building. The whole city sparkles at night, brighter than stars. We can lie in bed and watch it."

"I hope there is room for Sharmila?"

Sharmila is her servant, her cook. I look at her a little confused—is she joking? "None of that in this country. At least not until we move to a bigger place."

"How about Chapati?"—her dog.

I shake my head sadly: "The building does not allow pets."

She stares at me a moment, on the verge of speaking, but then quickly looks away. She points up at the glassy Lincoln Center building. There are giant murals behind the enormous windows.

"Wonderful," she sighs.

"Marc Chagall."

In the paintings, some angels and villagers swirl into the air, unburdened of all heaviness, riding on birds toward the stars. "Like they are flying to a different part of the earth," I say.

"As if they don't wish to be tied to any earth at all," observes Nirmala.

4

After the grand success of *Calcutta Nights* all those years ago, life became a new thing for all of us. Jogesh's name was spoken with pride along names of great Bengali artists: Rabindranath,

Satyajit, Jogesh. Was it warranted? Never I minded: I was enjoying the fruits of it. "Even as we feel the international economy crowding us out, Mr. Sen gives us hope that India, specifically West Bengal, continues to offer something unique and invaluable to the world," wrote *Times of India*. Our Kolkata audiences filled theaters for months and months to see up on the screen a village like those their own parents had grown up in, brought to vivid cinematic life; a family struggling to make a living off the land, finally pulling up stakes and moving to the city, where they suffered and prospered, fell out of love and back in it, and raised children who turned into people just exactly like those sitting in the audience, staring up at the screen.

Our unknown lead actor Narayan delivered a stunning performance, going on to a wonderful career, and thus was established Jogesh's reputation as a star-maker. I was able to quit my job (for, despite Jogesh's entreaties, I had previously only taken sabbatical to work on *Calcutta Nights*). Jogesh easily secured funding for his next project, and next, and next, and gave me a salary such that I did not have to find work in advertising, or even with other directors for that matter, and could finally move my family to a proper house.

I didn't mistake Jogesh's generosity. Certainly I was grateful for the money, but he had no choice; he paid me so well because he needed me badly. His films could not achieve their beauty without me.

And in any case, he did not pay me so well I could put my wife in a separate flat, as she might have wanted. She watched *Calcutta Nights,* of course, and enjoyed it, but could not resist her little questions: "Why your film has too much of weeping? Why it only has one dance number?"

"Believe me, I asked Jogesh the same questions," I told her. "It is the modern style, that is all."

"Modern style is fine and all, but don't tease us with just one dance number. One dance number means neither coming nor going, neither sleeping nor waking, neither Puna nor Hyderabad. If you have one, then you must have several," she laughed at me.

Here was my one yearly respite: "I am going away for twelve weeks' shooting. Please look properly after the household and don't spend too much money. Call the boys over if you get lonely."

"Don't worry about me," she always replied. "I am quite satisfied with my own company."

Meanwhile, on the set of the films, Jogesh's behavior was different. He was no longer amiable Jogesh, available for Johnny Walkers by the poolside in the evenings as in days of yore. He was secretive, as if he were a famous movie actor, the pompous and princely side of him having come to flower.

"What is the problem, Jogesh?" I would ask, as I saw him berating the bellboy in the lobby. He would point to his perfectly fine garment bag.

"Absolutely crushed and ruined," he spoke in his quiet fury. "And I have a dinner appointment in fifteen minutes."

He began acting that way even to his crew—even to me. I remember the day when I could no longer walk in his office at will, but had to ask an appointment. Where once were equal partners in a grand endeavor, now were servants obeying the great maestro, who had his own private vision, his own private social schedule.

What was he up to? Even when at 3:00 a.m. we barged to his hotel room to see if he was free for cards? And there was nobody there?

I am implying nothing, and even at that time I was mum. Because that is the rule among our boys: What happens on the shooting stays on the shooting.

Okay, I will not lie: I knew about his affairs. I am breaking the rule, but: we all knew, even from the first day that first big actress came for her cameo (in two scenes she played—very improbably—a humble unmarried schoolteacher, for whom our hero is pining) and that night was eating private dinner with Jogesh, and by two weeks' time had no compunction to stand side by side with him, wearing her ostentatious blue jeans and all manner of diamonds, holding his hand and caressing his hair, even though she had no business anymore on the set. Jogesh and I talked freely of it—with our mutual understanding—about how smart she was, how well she spoke French, and so on. The crew and I actually admired him, our own little Jogesh making cha-cha with the famous actress; even as sometimes we wondered if we should instead be telling him: Shameful! Disgusting! Even as we suspected she was only using him so she could make her break into serious films. But I never chided Jogesh, and I never dreamed to mention it to Nirmala or anyone outside of our little circle.

But for this, am I guilty to Nirmala? Not even a choto bit. Jogesh's sin is Jogesh's sin is Jogesh's sin alone. Anyway, it has all worked out for the best.

5

Late at night, after Nirmala and I return unnoticed to the cocktail reception, we all retire to a celebratory dinner in some cavernous Manhattan restaurant. I see how Jogesh waves off the waiter who arrives to refill his wineglass, a gesture which I have never seen fit to imitate.

Jogesh is the only man in Kolkata with a private wine cellar, and yet he always stops after one glass. In some ways, success is entirely wasted on him.

It is difficult to watch him side by side with Nirmala. The Mumbai Actress is not invited, so all of false Jogesh's attention is to his wife. Although Nirmala's disdain for him is unmistakable, she makes an admirable effort at feigning amusement at his stories—look, she is tinkling with laughs at some long bore of a tall tale about meeting Fellini. ("Everything Federico did was with style, with passion," he is blathering.) Now Nirmala puts her hand on the back of his neck, demonstrating such admirably forged fondness that I am sweating through my shirt with unwonted pain and envy. For Jogesh's part, how he stands up when she leaves for the restroom, how he offers her the first bite of his food, how he whispers in her ear—forced and futile assertions of intimacy, pitiful, pitiful, which make me want to stand up and smack him.

I excuse myself frequently for cigarettes.

At 11:15 p.m. precisely, Jogesh rises from the table, taking Nirmala gently by the arm. He must always have his seven hours.

When he and Nirmala are gone, I beckon the waiter for more wine. "Fill it all the way, I say!" I bellow, irritated by the empty space in the top of my glass. And very early in the morning, thirsty and smoke-stenched, with full bladder, I barge into my hotel room to the sight of the manila envelope—Jogesh's new screenplay, which he had the valet deliver this evening. It is sitting fat and clean, like a smiling Buddha on my dressing table, with my room number penciled quietly on the front.

I go to sleep with dark dreams of stomach-churning catastrophe. Rain and tears, sounds on the window. A stairwell rising before me, tilting and warping every time I step on it. Outside the window, airplanes scream and plunge, while ahead of me on the stairs appears Nirmala in a trench coat and dark wig—or is it an impostor? I climb toward her but she outruns me; the walls shift, the stairs twist away beneath my feet. . . . Whirling Bernard Herrmann violin music and everything spinning like the tower scene in *Vertigo* . . .

It is only very late the next afternoon, after sufficient quantity from the pitcher of room service coffee, and four soft pancakes bubbling with blue-colored berries and good salty American bacon on the side, that I arrive soundly from the turbulence of the previous night, and can move myself to bend open the aluminium tabs and slide the contents from the manila envelope. I flip through the cleanly printed pages at an increasing pace. What polished dialogues! What unexpected turns of plot! What interesting characters!

It is a heavy screenplay. A screenplay which (as one A. O. Scott in the New York newspaper wrote of Jogesh's previous film) "looks into life and finds there the rocks, the boulders we have all been quietly hiding under, calling them the sky."

I feel my headache and stomach upset slowly returning. Half-way done and in despair, I turn the manuscript facedown. My own screenplay—how can it compare? I use my finger to wipe up the sugary dregs from the bottom of my coffee cup, and disconsolately I lick.

My screenplay took me two years—two years, after the thirty-three Nirmala and I had already suffered. It is the opus of my life, revolving around the giddy days of youth: A young man and creative soul with dreams of success; the bends in the road of life taking him this way and that. Also his close friend and bosom companion, a lofty and serious fellow. And the woman who comes between them.

Two years I struggled and wrote it. Slowly I sent it to foreign producers, only to face rejection upon rejection. I could not approach any Indian producers, because all of them were deferential to Jogesh. So I cast my line blindly into Hollywood ("Dear Sir, I admired your film such-and-such and believe you will be interested to read my . . .") until finally I received an e-mail, with the deceptively small-fonted subject line "i want to meet u!!!" from an independent film producer in California named Jefferson Bundy.

I think: Hal Pereira, Robert Boyle, Henry Bumstead. Who in the general public knows these names? They are Hitchcock's wonderful art directors, but for all their beautiful work, what acknowledgment? I am destined to be just as much forgotten, unless I make my own film. But as I read Jogesh's screenplay, such an endeavor is starting to feel entirely beyond me.

To calm myself, I take my sketch pad from my suitcase. I turn the screenplay open and begin drawing. I sketch quickly and with the usual satisfaction, envisioning the scenes instantly in moving frames, the sequences and characters in terms of color. As I draw, I fill the margins with costume notes, suggestions for which scenes must be shot on location, which can be economically built as sets.

Only when my stomach starts to grumble do I realize several hours have been passed in pleasant creation. I put down my pencil and stretch my back and legs. Still buoyed by a certain giddiness, I decide to go for a walk and search for some nice American clothes for my Saturday meeting. I leave my thus-far-completed storyboards at the desk for Jogesh to pick up later. Our last collaboration, I think happily, and not without a certain sweet rue.

I walk out into the cool sunny day. The pleasant weather lifts me further, makes my legs feel like skipping. At a small shop, I buy some slices of pizza and eat them outside, enjoying the breeze, the hot cheese scalding the roof of my mouth with nicely tangy pains. I am feeling elated to be among all the people walking madly just like in Kolkata, but wearing nice clothes on the clean sidewalks under the cool, clean-smelling sky! I wish only Nirmala were free to share the afternoon with me. Unfortunately, the poor thing has been forced by Jogesh to attend a boring luncheon; until our circumstances change, she feels compelled to go on being the dutiful wife.

Meanwhile, I am free to enjoy the city. I walk into Bergdorf Goodman, bah bah! It is so beautiful. The price is a little bit over my current head, but I fight down my frugal instincts (the production designer by nature hews to the budget) and fit myself out in a trim designer suit, a lovely silk tie. "Denzel's stylist was here last week," whispers the shamelessly flattering salesman, "and bought him the *same outfit*." Examining myself in the mirror, I momentarily indulge the delusion that Denzel couldn't look better in it than I do.

6

Interior, painting studio, daytime. A tall old man with silver hair and white stubble stands painting on a large canvas in his enormous studio. He holds his brush between long, bony fingers, slashing and stabbing the canvas with reds and yellows and blues. His focus is intense and violent. He wears a paint-spattered white kurta-pyjama and no chappals. Behind him, an old woman in a white sari—his wife—steps quietly inside the studio, sets down a tumbler of tea and plate of biscuits, then disappears again. The painter never registers her presence.

(What does Jogesh know about painting? Jogesh cannot even draw in a straight line. I suppose that is why he has written the painter as an abstract artist.)

Now the painter is visiting the renowned local arts college, talking to students and critiquing their work. With the self-assurance that comes with fame and great talent, he quietly and fearlessly shows the flaws in each student's painting, roughly dismissing the youngsters' questions, reducing them to awe, and in one case, to tears.

(What fantasies of self-importance Jogesh has! It is a well-written scene, however. The dialogues are crisp and essential, carrying electricity.)

One student challenges him. He quickly dismisses her challenge. But she repeats her point, drawing on examples from the painter's own work. Flattered, impressed, intrigued, even a little humbled, he turns and finally notices that the student—behind her glasses, smock, tied-back hair—is a very attractive young woman.

(Pure male fantasy! What is startling is that Jogesh, through his screenplay, inadvertently admits to so much.)

He invites her to his studio to continue their conversation. He hires her as his assistant, and inevitably, they start an affair.

(How embarrassing! What audacity! A twenty-year-old and a seventy-year-old. Vain Jogesh, imagining the whole world to have his own dispositions, that all men are eager for young flesh. But somehow he makes the improbable behaviors convincing, showing the vulnerabilities and pathos of both the old man and his lover. Even as I sketch and turn the pages, my stomach ties itself in anticipatory knots.)

Not plagued by conscience exactly, but constantly fretting, lest his patient and loving spouse should find out and be devastated—and also fearing that his young and energetic, independent lover will grow bored and leave him—the painter simply and with new vigor continues painting.

It reminds me of the time I couldn't find my reading glasses after paying a visit to Nirmala's house. This was most unusual, because I always placed them carefully inside my briefcase, which in turn I always kept leaning against the same chair in the hallway. How my wife berated me, immediately traveling to the glasses store to purchase me a new pair. Nirmala called me two days later.

"Jogesh found your glasses."

"Where were they?"

"In the bedroom. Just poking out from beneath the bed."

How could the glasses have gotten there? I wondered. My mind raced through all I did: a pleasurable reminiscence. Even with the teenage wildness of it all, the transfer of the reading glasses was difficult to explain. I considered that Jogesh had seen me many times wearing them, and was likely to have recognized them.

"Listen, Bibhuti. Was he behaving differently to you on the film set? Does he suspect something?"

"Not in the least. He has been perfectly normal, perfectly cool," I said, feeling a chill.

"Same in the home. He is absolutely impossible to flap. I don't understand it."

"How self-absorbed he is! What better proof of his vanity could there be? Anyway, let us not allow it to worry us. I am on page ninety-five already. Love triangle is being resolved."

"Sorry, Bibhuti. I can't think of your screenplay. I am upset."

"There is no need for upset, Nirmala. Whether he knows or doesn't know, who cares? Relax and feel happy. My film is the new beginning for us."

Walking down Fifth Avenue, in the bright sun and cool wind of New York, I feel it still: A new film, a new beginning. I remember a very similar feeling, in 1974, on *Calcutta Nights*.

We will make films about the people and the soil of Bengal, Jogesh said. It was a sort of manifesto. *We will write stories about our own land, and in the particular, we will reveal the universal.* After he became famous, in interviews with foreign magazines, he would say, in response to the inevitable questions about why he didn't use his fame to direct movies for a more lucrative foreign market: "I subscribe to Satyajit Ray's philosophy. Why would I make films about a culture I don't know? What would I have to say about it? On a practical level, how would I direct actors in a language that I did not grow up speaking?"

And so, for our first film, we found ourselves in a small village in the countryside, a dozen of farmers and children crowding us, eager to help. Anant had been hired because of his facility with a Leica, but what did he know about the 35mm motion picture camera we had managed to cadge from a commercial film studio only three days previously? Absolutely nothing, and as a consequence, the first five days' footage was underexposed and completely useless.

These were the sorts of problems we struggled with. Jogesh's father-in-law turned out to be a cautious man, so while our funds were sufficient to make a film, they were far from enough to import an experienced crew. Our soundman George, a transplant from Kerala, fancied himself a musician, composing melodramatic disco ballads of love in the style of the southern filmi musicians of the time. We hired him as soundman because he had access to some excellent microphones and mixing equipment. (Like my wife, he also chided Jogesh for putting only one full song in the film.) George took the job only because he thought it a stepping-stone to becoming a playback singer, and we did not disabuse him.

In this context, my own inefficiencies were relatively minor: showing up late and worse for the previous night's wear. But I was smart and skillful, and Jogesh and I needed to spend very little time in communicating. I knew his tastes and dislikes implicitly; he trusted my choices. I was the one he turned to, who had been there since he had voiced his first dreams of filmmaking, who understood his vision.

We had to cadge a shot of a pond on a particular farmer's land. The one stingy farmer in the whole village, he wouldn't let us approach it unless we paid him.

"Jogesh, I will knock on the front door and feign an epileptic fit, eh?" I told him. "This will draw the entire household to the front. Meanwhile, you and Anant carry the camera by hand and steal the shot."

When he realized I wasn't joking, he laughed and clapped me on the shoulder. "Now you are talking, my friend!" I did it shamelessly, vibrating on the ground and loudly gagging, drooling on my cheeks, eyes rolling up, for fully twelve, fifteen minutes! Which actor could have pulled it off better? Like that, we made it happen.

And every evening in the village dhaba, Jogesh and I would

plan the next day's shooting. He would have one cup of the local brew and take his leave, telling, "My friend, enjoy yourself, but I need you sharply by six o'clock a.m. tomorrow. I cannot make this film without your eye."

Finally it was my eye, my masterful and instinctive eye for visual detail—(How could I pick which rock was precisely the rock our hero should pluck from the path, and fling—shockingly—at his brother? It was moss-covered and dangerously angular, to be lifted with both hands. Simply I knew. How should I know which color to paint the walls of the home, so the figures would stand out distinctly in the wedding party scene? Not white! [Too bright.] But umber. Again, I just knew)—which gave the film the naturalism, the simple beauty, for which it was rightly lauded.

And lauded it was. Because, for all our inexperience, for all our foibles, we pulled off something rare. My God, everyone from the little village boy who happily ran our errands, and fell asleep one morning in the branches of a pipal tree, providing one of the film's memorable shots; to Anant's resourcefully tracking the camera on a bullock cart, with three farmers pulling—somehow, shot by shot, we made it, and it was a thing of great beauty. There was never another feeling like that first film, the joyful camaraderie and satisfaction of a job well done, the sense that we were inventing something new in our own lives while showing something new to India and the world.

I cannot sufficiently emphasize, it would have been a signal achievement even if it did not earn overwhelming domestic success, even if it did not win eleven festival gold medals, all of which it did, and our lives were never the same.

One was too happy to feel bad for Nirmala those days. She visited the set two, three different times, always with the same distant look in her eyes. Nothing could awe or impress her, and even when the film exploded, one sensed she might have been happier as the quietly wealthy wife of an advertising execu-

tive, rather than the publicly wealthy wife of an internation-
ally famous artist, because she had no part in it; it took place
entirely out of her ken, even as she had enabled it. And perhaps
even then she perceived—so rightly—that it would only succeed
in taking Jogesh further away from her.

7

When the morning of my meeting finally comes, it arrives with a
feeling of turbo-nausea, and a dry, anxious burning for a cigarette almost from the instant I awake, even before my morning
coffee. I smoke two of them greedily, sitting on the commode
top in the bathroom with the fan on, in blatant violation of the
room's little cardboard warnings. After flushing them, I spray
the room with my cologne, but the cigarette smell does not
perfectly disappear. At this point, I think better than to order
breakfast, for fear these healthy American room service waiters
will smell the lingering smoke and cause me trouble on my most
important day. I can postpone coffee until my breakfast meeting, regardless.

I take the taxi to Mr. Jefferson's hotel, arriving there some
twenty minutes early. The draperies in the lobby are very thick
and cream-colored, compared with my own hotel, and the sofas
more velvety, and the black marble of the floor feels somehow
butter-soft beneath my shoes. I am glad I am wearing my new
suit; otherwise this hotel might have intimidated me. I find the
restaurant and give my warm coat to a gentleman, and then a
beautiful lady with big brown eyes and a tiny nose listens to me
without smiling.

"You can wait for Mr. Bundy at the bar, if you'd like," she
says.

"What can I get you, sir?" the bartender asks me.

"I shall order when Mr. Jefferson Bundy arrives," I tell him,
forbearingly.

Forty minutes later, my head is about to crack for the lack of coffee. Busy Mr. Jefferson Bundy is running late indeed. I am about to put my manners aside and order the damned cup of coffee, when a high voice beckons me.

"Bibhuti."

"Yes?" I swivel in the stool and don't see him at first. Then I look down toward my feet. There is the littlest man I have ever seen in my life—and I am speaking to you as a small individual myself, but one who falls within the normal range.

"Mr. Jefferson Bundy?"

"Jeff," he replies up to me.

My heart starts pounding and my arms to tingle. It really is him. "Hello!" I jump from my stool, stumbling but catching myself, and extend down my suddenly quivering hand. "Hello, Mr. Jefferson Bundy!"

"It's Jeff," he only says more quickly, reaching my hand, then drawing me toward his table. It is hard to tell his age—perhaps thirty or younger—or is this an impression caused by his height?

"As for the screenplay," he says immediately, when we have sat down, "we really like what we see."

"Bhalo," I say, but I am not thinking. The buttons on his blazer are too shiny, causing my eyeballs to ache.

"It's gotta feel good to hear that, right?"

"Bhalo. Bhalo. Good."

I am aware that my upper lip is sweating. I lick off the salty drops. What does one do with one's hands at the breakfast table? I am asking myself. For suddenly I have forgotten. I fold them on the table, one over the other, but this looks lumpy and odd. I move them to my lap, but feel even stiffer. I take the sweating glass of water in one hand; the jangling tinkles of ice expose my nervous tremors—I am splashing water on the tablecloth—so I put it down again. With a wave of panic, I see that suddenly before Jefferson Bundy's eyes, despite my fashionable clothes, I am an old and frail and nervous man.

"We can talk about adding American characters. We can bring on writers to do that."

I try to consider this. Is this good or bad? My stomach is clenched and my head is cloudy, and I am quite sure I should have ordered the room service coffee come what may. Also my bowels are telling me that my morning cigarettes were a poor idea.

Suddenly, I remember something I have meant to say. "I printed a cleaner copy!" I inform Jefferson Bundy. Ever since reading Jogesh's new screenplay, printed in the hotel business lounge, I have been consumed with the onion-thin Indian paper I mailed Mr. Bundy.

Out from nowhere, a man in black passes by. "Coffee!" I cry, lunging my arm at him. Then I turn to Mr. Bundy, mortified at my sudden shout. "You also?" I ask meekly.

"He's not the waiter, he's the busboy," Jefferson Bundy calmly informs me.

"Oh."

"What is really holding us back," Jefferson continues, "what's really keeping us from closing the last thirty percent of funding," he says, "is the lack of experience at the helm."

I am struggling to follow. I am nodding madly. I wonder to myself, am I doing badly or well? This meeting is going on, but my body seems to have slipped somehow out of my control. Where is the damned waiter? "Coffee?" I ask even more mouse-like of another passing person, unsure of her status, but she walks quietly by.

"So we could increase your advance on the screenplay and talk about your share of the gross, if you'll step away from the reins and set up a meeting between us and your boss."

Still I nod and nod and bend my head to the table to slurp, without lifting the glass, from the arctically cold, too-iced water. The word echoes slowly in my thumping head. Slowly I hear what Jefferson Bundy has been telling me.

He says, "We'd do it ourselves but he doesn't return our phone calls. People tell us he won't shoot outside of Kolkata. But with you on board . . ."

"My *boss*?" I raise up my head.

"Just have him meet us for coffee. Just a drink."

My mind is slowly forming a focus, the words squeeze out in painful pairs. "For *coffee*? For *drink*?"

"I'm in town until Tuesday, so . . ."

"Mr. Jefferson Bundy?" I ask, a complete sentence finally congealing on my tongue. "Please tell me, is meeting Mr. *Sen* the reason you have traveled here to New York?"

"Well, it certainly makes things easier, when everyone's in the same city, and—"

"Mr. Jefferson Bundy. Mr. Jefferson Bundy." I realize I am rising from my seat, my legs holding. My headache is now something more like a rage which I can only dispel in shouting. "Mr. Jefferson Bundy, did I not already make it explicit and clear? Did you not express interest and confidence that I could serve in full capacity as—"

"Sure, Bibhuti, but considering the realities of financing the thing . . . And on your next project, with one writing credit already under your belt, we could certainly talk about—"

"Out of the question!" I realize with shame that tears are stinging my eyes, my voice rising to squeaky and unsteady peaks. "Out of the *question,* Jefferson Bundy! I will not set up a *meeting* with him. I will not enable you to have *coffee* with him, or any other sort of drink with him. I will not permit you to show my *screenplay* to him, and ask him to direct my screenplay, Mr. Jefferson Bundy. Mr. Jefferson Bundy!"

"Sit down. Please."

I see the whole of the restaurant looking at me. I feel sick and confused. The white drapes and snow-and-ice complexions of the black-shirted staff now make me queasy. I must get out of here, this meeting, what happened? I am walking out of the restaurant and into the lobby. Mr. Jefferson Bundy seems to have motioned to someone; some men in black suits are moving toward me.

"Sir. Slow down."

"Hold on, please," Jefferson Bundy is calling from behind.

The large men are blocking the doorway, my dream has dissolved, my life is vanishing, oh Nirmala, and I am pushing with my hands between their muttony shoulders.

"Listen, Bibhuti." Jefferson is pulling the back of my suit jacket. "Listen, turn around. Jesus H. One second."

In despair, I oblige him. Towering over him, I ask, "Yes, Mr. Jeff, Jefferson Bundy. In one second—what are you going to tell me in one second that you haven't told me already?"

"You can direct it."

I breathe for a moment.

"Okay? Okay? It's yours."

Dumbly, I stare down at him.

"Truly. See, I was brainstorming. I was just thinking out loud. Now I see how much it means to you. I see how driven you are, Jesus H. And that's the main thing I look for in a director. And that's all I was waiting to see."

"It is?"

"Absolutely. Okay? Relaxed?" He smoothes his shirt, trying to eke from me a smile. "Here's a Kleenex. Jesus H, you had me running. Let's go back to our table now." He tilts his chin toward the restaurant, raising his eyebrow invitingly. "Let's get you some coffee."

8

After I return to my own hotel, I see Nirmala in the lobby gift shop. I walk up behind her. "Dear Nirmala," I whisper. She is browsing men's wristwatches.

She turns to me with eager but contained surprise.

"You're back very quickly."

"It has all gone very well."

"Very well?" Her look—does it betray some disbelief?

"Yes, Nirmala!"

Slowly, her expression changes; she is on the verge of either laughter or weeping. She turns down, coolly caressing a silvery Cartier. Wary of spying eyes, she is trying to act like I am telling her nothing special. Now she motions to the sales assistant. "What is the cost, madam?" she asks her.

"You can tell him now. The deal is done." I wipe my cheeks, because some premature drops of joy have fallen already from my eyes.

"Ah, Bibhuti," Nirmala responds, finally turning partway in my direction. "Is it really so easy?"

"Just so. Now no one can keep us from enjoying, at long last, whatever time we have left."

Nirmala bends away again, still fondling the watch, her eyes glistening like Ingrid Bergman's, staring from the window with soulful passion (medium shot) as Cary Grant stands behind her, in *Notorious*.

"Why do things so abruptly?" she whispers. "Let me go back to India and tie things up. That way, the transition may be a bit smoother, don't you think?"

Of course she is cautious. But she is also hopeful; I trust her appraisal of the situation. "As you say, darling. If you think so."

"Sweet Bibhuti," she sighs. My camera-eye zooms to her hands. She slinks the silver watch from one palm into another, tilting it here and there to catch the light. Three-quarters shot: She blinks her eyes clear. "So beautiful, nah?"

"By the way, sweetheart, I don't wear wristwatches. They irritate me."

She shakes her head, then unsnaps her wallet.

"You and I will be so happy!" I murmur.

"Shhh," she admonishes, because now the saleslady is right

here. Nirmala signs the credit card receipt as the saleslady boxes up the watch. Camera goes high and wide (crane shot) as Nirmala walks with me out of the store, with the five-thousand-dollar timepiece weighing down her bag.

9

Sometimes life feels very long. What all I have come through! And other times, it seems as if it has all gone by too fast, and still I haven't learned, and still I haven't done anything. I feel strangely new to the world. When has one been alive long enough to draw some conclusions, to say anything intelligent about it?

In other words, what can I say about a culture that is not fully my own?

Every day, I am struggling to give the answer. Shooting is one horrendous ordeal. Being a director is not nearly as I had imagined, even having seen one hundred thousand film sets by this point in my life. Mr. Jefferson Bundy is far too intrusive, watching the dailies in the evening, then coming to the set groaning my name and shaking his head.

There are ninety-five headaches by 8:30 each morning, and another four hundred decisions to be made by teatime. (On my set, always we have ten minutes teatime.) The New York crew sometimes treats me like a bumpkin, as if they could make the film more quickly without me. In the night, I can hardly sleep for the pain in my neck and back and hips; I open my eyes every ten minutes with some newly remembered worry, another item to be scribbled urgently in my notebook.

But I am directing; I am plowing my own earth and seeing what springs up. The strange part is the loneliness of it. Every thirty minutes, the crew will dumbly stare at me, waiting for a decisive command—which they will then promptly dispute with a hundred contradictory opinions. Or they will simply hide on the edges, smoking and gossiping like hourly workers, like this is not someone's life's work. When I told Jogesh the news at the closing gala of the festival, the bastard was an absolute gentleman. "Congratulations, Bibhuti. I always hoped you would direct a film one day." He put his hand on my shoulder. "For a director, every day is a discovery. I wish you great success." He was so unperturbed that I wondered if someone had told him or he had all along suspected; if he was inwardly laughing at some cool comeuppance that was in store for me.

Mr. Jefferson Bundy has brought in as cofinancers Prakash and Akash, the Arora brothers from Mumbai, meaning I have come to America only to make a Bollywood picture in the end. So be it. My story, somewhat revised, revolves about young friends visiting New York, one of them serious, one of them happy-go-lucky, their bonds becoming tested over an American woman they both fall in love with. That woman lives in Manhattan; her parents are highly skeptical of the foreign suitors. In one grand scene, all three youths dance arm in arm through the Lincoln Center fountain—boy, what a hellish time it is shooting that, with the midnight gawkers and grumpy cops. My two lead actors, those big-headed, carefully coiffed Mumbai boys, sometimes become impatient; they try to cajole and move me, making up their own dialogues whenever fancy suits them. "This line isn't funny," "This scene isn't believable," they calmly inform me when I challenge them. "This costume isn't smart." Neither impressed nor intimidated, they pretend not to hear me for the din of traffic as I scream instructions through my radio; in effect they direct themselves. Later in the film (as the financers insisted), the friends get caught up in the web of post-9/11, and the suspicions, and finally in the question, Will they make a home here?

I know enough. Even for all the acclaim that Jogesh's first film earned, what did he really know about that village? He had grown up in a twelve-room house filled with books, and in his film were mainly thatch-roofed huts. But what a moving thing we made, perfect in every detail, even if some of those details were of our own invention.

We are just visitors. None of it is our own. What did Jogesh and I know about the human heart? And still, we showed it.

"We have to rewrite the ending!" Jefferson Bundy yells, after filming is over. "We have to reshoot the love scenes. We miscast the leads." And on and on.

Nirmala is slowly planning her move. When the servants answer the phone at her house, I use a clever pseudonym: "Mr. Shah from the grocers, regarding her order for Chinese apples."

"Soon," she says. "But Barun has had his second daughter. They need so much help around the house. I can't leave just right away."

"Soon," she says. "But I am hosting a fund-raiser in my home for the Satyajit Ray Memorial Scholarship. How can I leave everyone abandoned like that?"

"Soon," she says. "But . . . Jogesh is bringing me for two weeks to Paris. And then he has gone and hired me a third housekeeper, and somebody must stay here to train her."

Finally she tells me: "I confronted him, Bibhuti. I told him everything. He was furious for two weeks, and I was about to leave. But now he's contrite. He stays home on the weekends."

And then, when Mr. Shah calls, Mrs. Sen has gone for her tennis lesson; Mrs. Sen is taking tea with her grandchildren; Mrs. Sen conveys her regrets but would like to cancel her order for Chinese apples.

The footage is an alarmingly tangled mess. I sit in the shadowy editing suite with the taciturn editor that Jefferson Bundy has hired for me. In that pristine, computer-filled cave, I force myself to focus on the film, to fight the nausea I feel, to postpone all thoughts of Nirmala, and stop rehearsing in my mind our every moment together, every missed signal, my grand vision that lacked so much in the particulars. The impassive editor starts by shaving a moment here, a minute there; next, convinces me to drop entire scenes. I slowly realize I wasted whole days of shooting time; the editor discards them now with one awful click of the mouse. We examine dozens of takes of the same lines of dialogue, searching for hints of emotion, anything real or surprising; we order and reorder shots and sequences in end-less permutations, struggling to sift out any story or suspense, to bring this inert thing to life.

After each day's work concludes late in the night, I go walk-ing, becoming lost in the big life of concrete and people. I walk gingerly, feeling an odd lightness in my feet, as if at any moment I might slip and go flying; until the sidewalks grow vacant, the checkerboard eyes of the buildings blink closed one after another. And then I take the train to the silent condominium towers of New Jersey, hoping for a little sleep; but usually end up by standing on the balcony of my cousin's flat firing ciga-rettes, looking with queasy sadness out over the Manhattan skyline—straight-from-the-movies but somehow mysterious, this unreal view of the places I've just been.

Sitting on the train one morning, flipping through the *New York Times* for some distraction, I see a capsule review for a new film, Jogesh's latest. I truly don't have time for the two-and-a-half-hour movie; there are only precious days left in the editing room. Nevertheless, that evening I leave the editor with her takeout Thai dinner and go stand in line with the young stylish people outside of Film Forum and buy the twelve-dollar ticket. On a splurge, I purchase a cola and a chocolate brownie and popcorn, which I squirt with lime and cover with salt, and munching loudly, I watch.

Immediately from the opening title, I see that Jogesh has relied heavily on those storyboards I'd completed in the hotel room for the first half of the film (as I knew he might, for he sent me a check in compensation). The art direction is sloppy, and he has made some poor color choices. But after several minutes, I stop appraising the shots because so caught up am I with the story line. The aging Kolkata painter is played by one of our longtime local stars. He falls in love with his young, aloof student, played by a newcomer. A new storyboarder must have taken over at some point, but I forget to notice where. And what does it matter, honestly? Because the film is beautiful. The choices Jogesh has made are good enough. The dialogues are smart, the performances very precise, very lively. It is the work of a craftsman in its own way. I use my chocolate-and-butter-stained napkin to dab off my tears when the old painter returns all alone to his studio—wearing on his wrist the watch once gifted him by his outwardly passive wife—and despite the great mistakes and disappointments of his life, stoically picks up the brush, a slight tremble in his hand. The expression in the actor's face is remarkable—pained but dignified and unlike any performance this star has delivered in the past. I have a big realization at that time. Okay, there is framing the shots and fashioning the sets. There is editing and makeup and lighting and props, and there is even writing. But the greatest challenge always lies in how one handles the actors.

ELEPHANTS IN CAPTIVITY
(PART ONE)[1]

I don't have much time[2] so I must dispense with the obvious.[3]

---

1 My discovery of this document establishes, despite your most vehement protests, the existence of Englaphant, that strange tongue native to all places of elephant-human contact, which I understand now intuitively, having spent most waking hours for the past twenty-three years in conversation with elephants in captivity. My translation—of which eventually there will be thirty parts—is therefore precise, placing Shanti in a long line of great Englaphant writers, starting with the master Ganesha, who wrote the entire Ramayana in an Indo-European precursor of Englaphant, with the ink-dipped, broken-off tip of his right tusk.

2 Unless one is well grounded in Shanti's main tale, this bottom text might seem bumptious. I suggest you stop reading these footnotes, and instead give the above story a read, straight through. On your second run, allow yourself a lot of time. Better prepared to appreciate them, let your eyes wander down to these elucidating asides.

3 The obvious? We will never forget the images of the magnificent beast, seated on her haunches in the middle of our great park, her head bent intently down, seemingly oblivious to the commotion she was causing. In the middle of the park she sat! Nothing could have been more "obvious," or at the same time more incomprehensible. It is indeed the obvious that merits our most intense scrutiny. Shanti knew this, and so, despite this alarming disclaimer, she does not dispense with that which is most important to her narrative, which is to say that which is in the center, which is to

Helicopters clatter overhead, men with cameras[4] leaning from their open doorways. Their footage must be numbingly familiar to you, and might by now be all that remains of me. Please know that the contemporaneous accounts surely will be filled with distortions.[5] I write this in order to supply you with those crucial bits of history without which my story cannot be understood.

Before I begin, I want to make something clear: I am sorry for the expense and trouble I have caused. If I have hurt anyone, even unintentionally, then I can only hope for your forgiveness.[6] Many people have invested in my safety and comfort,[7] have felt that they've had my best interests at heart;[8] I have not intended to betray them.

---

say that which is right before our eyes and which yet we cannot see. And so at the outset already we know one thing which we saw and yet did not see, the answer to the question: What was Shanti doing there for so long, calmly, in the middle of a meadow meant for sheep, while all around the world people watched transfixed, while all around her crumbled a city she had inadvertently reduced to chaos? The authorities have been afraid to share it with us, this simple yet amazing truth: she was writing.

4 And guns, Shanti!

5 "Jumbo on the Run," quipped the *News*. "Rampage!" screamed the front page of the alarmist *Post*. "Had an elephant escaped?" worried the foolish Bengal Ming, remembering.

6 "Rampage!" screamed the *Post,* see footnote 5 *supra,* beneath a full-page picture of Shanti's enormous self. To capture his dramatic snap, the photographer from the *Post* dashed into Seventy-second Street just inches from her feet, looking up and clicking, clicking, clicking, clicking. Alas—that lump under your feet, Shanti, that squirming, screaming, unexpected, far-beneath-you thing—did you feel it? Reading this we have to assume, sweet unassuming creature, that you didn't.

7 It is hard to get comfortable, because my left foot always feels like it's asleep. Elephant tranquilizers are not to be trifled with.

8 I hope you hadn't forgotten, Shanti, the least of those people, who had observed you from the very beginning; who cared for you and loved you when you were at the most hopeless point on your hopeless journey. Why couldn't you have mentioned him here by name?

You must believe that I never sought to draw this kind of attention to myself. I am just one elephant, and I did not seek it, but I can sense it: my story is destined to be a part of this city's collective memory.[9] Perhaps, just perhaps, by the time you read this, my misadventure has inspired others to break free as I did.[10]

---

[9] But will her story be a singular and bizarre anomaly, a blip in the stream of popular culture, a moment of pure novelty? Or will her tale bear a meaning beyond its facts? Will it become a culture-shifting event, a watershed in the conjoined histories of our two species?

[10] "Break free" suggests incorrectly that freedom can be found simply by escaping captivity—Shanti sadly stands corrected. Neither is it true (as she also should have known) that all circus workers and zookeepers are intent on enslavement. There are some who work within that world in order only to subvert it. At any rate, have others "broken free"? The recent evidence:

- In Houston, this past October, a 700-pound Balinese wild boar unlatched the door of an improperly locked zoo vehicle with its tusk. It roamed the finer residential districts, entered a large, air-conditioned shopping mall, slid across the mall's indoor ice-skating rink (scattering skaters but harming no one), exited through the ladies' department at Saks, and disappeared for four days, until it was shot and killed while snacking on a stray dog behind a 7-Eleven.
- A gibbon in Cincinnati stole keys from its sleepy keeper, escaping its enclosure only to take up residence in the glass well of the popcorn maker at the zoo concession stand. It was captured and returned to its confines; the popcorn was discarded.
- An ostrich in San Diego disappeared without explanation; it was found three days later hiding in the back of an automotive store, having garlanded itself evidently in a stack of radials.
- A Galápagos-style Komodo dragon turned up in a swimming pool in Los Angeles. The owner of the pool failed to report the wonderful lizard, hoping to keep it as a pet. Sanitation workers discovered it in the trash weeks later. It had died of what was later determined to be a vitamin D deficiency attributable to the sudden absence of rodents from its diet. The owner of the pool had attempted to raise the dragon as a vegan.
- Recall, again, that infamous tiger, Ming, who terrorized another city for days. Man-eater and murderer, he ruled that city as his kind

Perhaps we live among you now as friends and neighbors.[11]

I have come far. This vast expanse ringed with trees recalls me to another green place.[12] My first memories are of green—the

---

> has always thought was its right, until he was, like all the others, tranquilized. He lay on the asphalt, tongue lolling, black lips pried back into a mock snarl for gums to be examined, the deadly ivory of his daggered teeth as vital now as unhammered nails, tapped and tugged by emboldened, human fingers; the very killing room of his mouth mute and empty, and violated by a plastic tongue depressor; his insensate, soggy mattress of a body, lifeless, unwieldy, shoveled finally onto a caged truck; and, dull eyes blinking, head pounding, awoke—sad groggy hungover Ming, erstwhile king—right back where you started, in the zoo again.

There is more anecdotal evidence (see Jason Hribal, *Fear of the Animal Planet: The Hidden History of Animal Resistance,* Counter Punch and AK Press, 2010). But did any of these animals, Shanti, achieve *freedom*? I have found not one example of an elephant escaping to live happily and with dignity in the city. Disregarding isolated instances, ill-conceived experiments, and unsubstantiated rumors, dear Shanti, your dream remains pending.

11 See above. What did you expect, Shanti? That people wouldn't bat an eye to see a tusker careening down Broadway? That the city would build elephant lanes on the West Side Highway, double-wide, for your slow-moving sisters? That your calves would study with our children side by side in the same schools, and play with them? That they would be popular in the playground, your elephant children, tossing balls with their trunks, spraying water of a summer's day at their bipedal friends? Did you ever fear, Shanti, that they would instead feel, for the first time, fat, naked, ugly, and odd? That they might fortify themselves in angry elephant enclaves? That they would stand in corners and cower, instead of flapping their ears against the city air and trumpeting out their freedom?

12 Elephants never forget. I'm sure you've heard this phrase. Here we see that, for good or ill, it's true. Everything Shanti has seen, heard, tasted, and smelled, she remembers. It is a burden. In this city, dogs wander the streets noting the smell of every beast who has been there before them, treading a landscape invisible to the rest of us, a landscape whose urine-marked rustle of green, its shift and sway, a thickness of thin blades that rise above my head—the grass we ate and lived in. Rushing through it, through the herd's feet, massive, thundering feet, which in the vision-clouding dust and seeming chaos, balletically precise, never miss their mark. My elders sense my clumsy, tottering body somewhere in the dust and grass far beneath them, and always step around me. So: in, under, around the massive god bodies of my elders, I rush forward. My trunk rises up, groping for the belly that bears the odor of my mother, Amuta, her trailing milky, musky scent. I find her, and she reaches down for just a moment, to smell my mouth, touch me on the head, to reassure me and confirm herself of my presence, and all the while we thunder forward.[13] Prior, primarily I remember: Green.

During the wet season, our old leader Ania would guide us out of our valley to graze among the upland bark and bush, to feed on the brief tender grass that sprang up along the monsoon rivers in the hills. In the dry season, she brought us back down again to the valley, where the earth's wetness contracted

---

boundaries we will never comprehend. Similarly, for Shanti every inch of life, every color or shape, bears a unique and pulsing resonance. Show her a face, say a name, make a sound, name a thing, and she could name you another that preceded it, whose memory rises unbidden in her mind, to press up against the present thing with its own painful force and reality. Every corner of the world she turns reveals to her a new vista haunted by an old one; every door opens into a new house whose furnishings seem stolen from a long-ago home. Elephants don't enjoy those simple Freudian-type luxuries humans take for granted: aphasia, repression, sublimation, omission. Memory for them is an edifice, a fixed and growing thing, enlarging itself brick by brick with each passing hour. It is a burden. In writing this, Shanti shares her burden, for a spell, with us.

13 Rushing underfoot, clumsy but eloquent in her own way, now straying from, now returning to the herd, in contrapuntal gallop with those above—an intuitive anticipation, dare we say, of her future editor's trotting underfootnotes?

to a small space of blue—our lake (I have never seen it, but I remember it)[14]—and where the grass was tough and tasteless but everpresent.

Life was full of change, but our home was neverchanging. Mother became our leader after old Ania died, a solitary grazer among hostile beasts. During our more difficult times, some would complain even about Mother's wise leadership, saying that if Ania were alive we would never have suffered as we did. (The elephants spoke, I say, but of course they didn't. Among ourselves, we elephants did not talk in words like those with which I now write this. We made noises, a broad range of them: grunts, whispers, low rumbles, ear-splitting trumpets, but we used them not as words. We made motions with our bodies as well—with our trunks, our ears, our legs, our eyes, with the angle of our heads—but these motions did not have distinct meanings. These gestures of body and sound were the stuff of our communication, yet they did not themselves constitute our speech. The source of our understanding, the substance of our message, lay in something broader and more round, a circle of intention that surrounded each of us and the herd. When we were together in the herd, we shared an understanding, concrete and actual; each of us felt with certainty what other individuals expressed to us, and moreover, we understood as a herd what the herd thought and felt.[15])

---

14 Hm!

15 The language of *words* would come only later—when she needed to communicate with humans. (Shanti's somewhat romantic faith in language—both elephant and Englaphant—must be distinguished from the attitudes of other literate beasts, particularly the German-speaking ape Red Peter [1883–1924], brutal truth-teller, joyless [though not humorless] genius, gifted imitator of humans, altogether remarkable creature, who started off his speaking career with a hoarse "Hallo!" not because of an idealistic desire for interprimate communication; not because, in conjoined existence with people, he perceived new possibilities of freedom [Red Peter

Ania left us during the long drought, when my aunts' skin hung loose on their jutting, angular hip bones, and the hard, ugly shapes of their skulls protruded from behind their kind faces. Ania always had faith in the old grazing fields. We all did. But one day she left us, and Mother remained the dominant female in the herd.[16]

---

mocked the idea of freedom]; but only and merely because, held captive by humans and at the end of his short rope, he needed "*einen Ausweg*" ["a way out"]. Language released him from a cage—nothing more.)

16 Elephants are a complex species. Their herding instincts are counterbalanced, if not contradicted, by the deep-running passions of their individual psychologies. For example, pachyderms may harbor personal grudges for years, remembering the beatings inflicted by a particular mahout, or the pokes and thrown pebbles of a mischievous young circus visitor; and on encountering the person by chance years, yea decades later, kill him.

A narrative, to be completely true, must plumb these dark depths. But keep in mind that Shanti, for all her perspicacity and eloquence, is at heart an innocent, as reluctant to suspect malice in her relatives as in the kindest of her captors. And she was short on time. Wouldn't she be regretful if the one person most intimate with her life and her tale, well studied in elephant culture and psychology, a writer not untalented in his own right, and who moreover enjoys exclusive access to her text, did not fill in for her those voices and details that she would have felt, on further and deeper reflection, were crucial? While the editor's job is normally to clarify, when duty calls, he must not shy from the role of a sort of *Shamspeare in love*. I humbly comply. Imagine, if you will, a scene, exterior, a jungle, daytime. Enter Shanti's mother, Amuta, a spry, keen-eyed young woman.

AMUTA: The herd trusts her implicitly, respects her fundamentally. But don't let misplaced respect and false sentiment cool your purpose. When the young among us are dying, there is no time to indulge fond old age.

Enter Ania, an old elephant, ears frayed from many battles, eyes rheumy with wisdom, kindness, or fatigue.

AMUTA: *(Aside)* Here she comes. Steady yourself. See how fat she is? For too long we have indulged her with portions of our grass while our own calves have gone hungry. If that ponderous cow had to seek her own food, she would starve. She lived her youth in fuller times, but since I was born we've had only lack. See her eyes? She was the sharpest among us once, the lithest and most fearsome. This is how we become when we live too much of our lives in prosperity, dull and clouded, susceptible (just watch!) to truism and flattery. How sad to see a bright star go dim. Better to put it out entirely. This morning I heard a tigress stalking a nearby valley. (Even the tigress has more logic than Ania—seeing the drought, she has left her home and invaded ours in search of meat.) I'll give Ania one more chance to change her mind and take the herd away from this dead land. If she stubbornly refuses (as I'm sure she will), then I'll lure her with this bit of fruit I found, buried in the den of a long-dead ape. I'll send Ania to pasture in the tigress's valley, and let her learn the jungle's logic. By herself, the fat old dam stands no chance. I'll flatter Ania and feed her. I'll play on her greed to seal her downfall!

ANIA: We are here. Why have you called us?

AMUTA: *(To Ania)* Have I made you walk far, Ania? I apologize. Rest under the shade of this tree. Here is some fruit I found and saved for you.

ANIA: Fruit? How rare, how delightful.

AMUTA: It's not so fresh.

ANIA: Don't be silly. These rotting bits might seem foul. These might be the undigested pieces picked from some far wandering monkey's shit. No matter. In times like this, such bits are as refreshing as heavy rain and a roll in the mud. We don't see fruit these days much anymore.

AMUTA: No, we don't. This season has been a poor one yet again. We have not had the rain we'd hoped for.

ANIA: Yes, but there is always next spring. We have lived through many more seasons than you, Amuta. Some are dry, but others are wet.

AMUTA: Your experience has made you wise. But surely this drought is unlike any you have seen before. Some in our position might consider seeking out a new grazing land.

ANIA: Leave? This is our home. There is no way to leave, no sense in the thought.

AMUTA: *(Aside)* That was your last chance, old dam. You've lived a full life, so there's nothing to regret. I'll not allow you to kill us out of respect for your empty years.

(To Ania) Your years have served you well, old Ania, and under your leadership we can only hope for fullness and increase. Have you enjoyed the fruit?

ANIA: Yes, young one. There is only one thing, they say, better than a bull on your back, and that's a banana in your mouth. You seem brighter than your cousins. We have enjoyed the fruit very much.

AMUTA: I know where you can find more of it.

ANIA: What?

AMUTA: Old Ania, I don't want to seem like I have kept hidden from the herd something which of right belongs to the herd. I only this morning discovered it and have eaten none of it myself.

ANIA: Either you are making a poor joke, Amuta, or you must tell us right now where you found it.

AMUTA: Old Ania, there is not enough for us all, and that is the only reason I didn't wish to disclose this in front of the herd. There is enough, I am afraid, only for you, and it is right that you alone should have it, because your survival is our survival. A body is nothing without its head.

ANIA: Don't worry about all that. Just tell us where you found it.

AMUTA: In the small valley nearby that was once shaded by evergreens. Some new type of tree has grown there, some windblown seed from elsewhere has sprung up a drought-loving tree that needs no water. It gives bananas much sweeter than what you've just tasted—in my rush, I picked only the rotting fruit that littered the ground beneath it. But it also gives mangoes and jackfruits and figs.

ANIA: All from one tree? It seems fantastic.

AMUTA: It must be a reward, old Ania, for your wisdom and patience. Soon many trees just like it will spring up, and all our worries will end. But now there is only one. Go and find it and eat your fill.

ANIA: This tree is too improbable, Amuta. It's a hunger-borne mirage. I'm sure you're mistaken.

AMUTA: I, too, thought so, until I touched the tree and smelled its fruit. Was that banana you just enjoyed a mirage, Ania?

ANIA: It was not. Then guide me to the tree. Right away, let's go.

AMUTA: No, Ania! The herd will grow confused and restless in your unexplained absence. I will go and feed them an excuse. You need only walk to the very center of the valley, raise up your trunk, and sniff the air. Try to detect a smell something like a tiger—one of the oddities of this wonderful tree is that it gives this most obnoxious scent. Be patient if you don't see it at first. Wait there patiently and surely you will find it.

ANIA: Very well. You are a bright young elephant and will go far. You have done a good thing. Be assured, you are acting on behalf of the herd.

Exit Ania.

AMUTA: Is it this easy? Has it always been this easy? With so little effort could I at any time have dispatched the unquestioned leader of our herd? Treachery in name alone is daunting. But her kind old eyes almost did make me doubt myself. Poor, befuddled cow! She is a slave to her stomach, and at her age she'd die if we didn't feed her first. But isn't this alone reason to replace her with a younger leader? Survival is not a gift for the frivolous or soft. I didn't invent this law, and bear no responsibility for it.

Now I hear the tigress growling. She must have spotted old Ania. Those snarls make even my strong bones shiver. God allows only such animals as this tigress to thrive in a time of drought: animals whose hunger makes them not weak, but more fearsome—animals for whom lack itself is fuel. Hear that? Ania is trying to fight the beast. Ha? Can that be Ania's war cry? Still so loud and violent, no fear in it? The tigress's blood will go cold at the sound. My plan will be ruined! But no, listen—Ania's cry is of no avail. The tigress also knows no fear, and she screams her attack. Ania is shouting for my help! Steady yourself and hold your ground. Don't let old instinct lead you to her aid. Hear the anguish in Ania's voice? Sounds of gnashing and of chewing, crunch of bone and gurgle of blood, unheard-of and unnatural elephant cries. Oh, close your ears! It is a gruesome, noisy death. But Ania's gathered a dying wind, and slurs out a scream. What? "Treachery!" does she yell? Does she yell "treachery"? Does she realize,

We had all seen our cousin herds stay in their old grazing fields and die, Mother reminded us. She convinced us to abandon our ancient land. She led us into distant unknown hills[17] where,

as she dies, that her death was by design? Oh, but why let it worry you, Amuta? What weight does an accusation carry that echoes in the empty air, and falls on the ear of no elephant but me? Now Ania's words are garbled, her moans weaken. There remains only the sound of that ravenous tigress glutting herself on the meat of an elephant, an elephant like me, one of our beloved. Why, what is it I have done? And having done it, can I still call myself elephant? Or does this act show that my veins run with the cold blood of some other creature? I am alone in this, and afraid, for this is treachery that goes against nature! But then, treachery always does. Every leader must act alone, challenging her very nature that her nature may be realized. Go on now, wipe the distress from your eyes. Walk proudly back to the herd. You have done well by them. When Ania's fate is found out, and her absence makes them feel the lack of strength and guidance that actually they lacked even in her presence, then they should look only to you for its fulfillment.

17 Shanti's precipitate excursion into our city occurred, of course, following her escape from the Silver Brothers Circus, the outfit which every year pitches its dirty tents in a distant borough of our city. The Silver Brothers Circus was founded in 1871 by Amar Selvaratnam, more commonly known as Amar Selva (or sometimes Silva or Selvar or Silvar), and even more popularly as Amos Silver. Selvaratnam/Selva/Silva/Selvar/Silvar/Silver was a dusky man of unknown origin, various versions of whose name began appearing in the inmate rolls of jails and prisons in cities as far-flung as San Francisco, California, and Chicago, Illinois, in the mid-1850s. From time to time, usually to escape creditors, Silver tried to pass himself off as his own twin brother, "Andy Silver" (thus, "Silver Brothers"). The existence of Andy Silver was never, of course, confirmed, and Andy was commonly assumed to be another one of Amos Silver's many frauds and hoaxes, until Amos's death in 1928. At that time, in a little-visited windowless car of the Silver Brothers' traveling conveyance, hidden among a family of cruel and filthy chimpanzees, was found a narrow cage holding a withered, naked, and equally aggressive old man. He bared his teeth and threw his shit like a chimp; he beat his chest like a gorilla; and he

with less competition for the bark of the baobab trees and the sparse, sweet grasses, she promised us, we would thrive.

Elephants died on this uncertain journey. My great-aunt Thoosha didn't survive the climb. She was ninety-four, and one morning along the long way, awake and lolling on her side, she calmly refused to stand up.[18] Manami's nameless, still-suckling

---

clutched with one hand a seemingly inexhaustible erection, like a gibbon. The chimp family among whom the naked man lived seemed to regard him, alternately, as God, fiend, whipping boy, pampered child, idiot— a source of irritation and awe and hilarious entertainment.

The discovery of this unidentified and unidentifiable man was heralded (by the circus's new management) as the discovery of the long-rumored "real" Andy, and he was quickly promoted as the star of the revamped and under-new-ownershiped circus. "Andy the Man Monkey" survived a scant fourteen months under the glare of the gas flares and flashbulbs, but it was a frenetic and productive fourteen months. He left behind a rumored legacy of twenty-seven children, all conceived during that hysterical time, born of various acrobats, contortionists, bearded ladies, soothsayers, midgets, and clowns, as well as (reportedly) the females of several nonhuman species (chimpanzee, yes; also giraffe, hippopotamus, alligator). These supposed, hybrid, half-human children would become, in turn, the stars of their own freak show attractions.

18 AMUTA: Thoosha, Great-Aunt, you are old, and may feel your age entitles you to some indulgence. But in fact it gives you greater responsibility. You have no right to delay the herd. Get up. Remember that I am leader now.

THOOSHA: Yes you are, Amuta. Therefore lead your herd ahead. New journeys are not for me. I am tired. If I find strength, I will go back home and rest among familiar trees, and let my bones dry among the bones of my mothers. The old life is all I know and want to know; one generation of hardship is not enough to make me abandon our memories.

But now I am tired. I will wait for sleep, and I will find my way alone.

AMUTA: Even if you make it back, Thoosha, three weeks' journey alone, as you say, it will only be to die. And in dying you will again have left. Why do you welcome that unknown journey, but fear this one?

son—he had been lively once, a rambunctious boy, but during the drought, when Manami's breasts grew shriveled and suckling became painful, when her milk dried up, this boy was the first among the children to slow his play, to reveal his weakness—he also didn't live to see the new hills. (Poor Manami struggled to bring him along. When the calf's pace slowed, Manami also slowed, the two of them trailing behind us a full day's journey. Mother did not stop the herd to wait for them, nor did Manami ask her to, and when Manami finally joined us again, she was alone. We touched her face with our trunks and rubbed our heads on her haunches, but Manami would not face our gaze or return our greeting. This happened before I was born, but I remember it clearly.[19])

In our new hills, striped with slow and steady mountain streams, we struggled and lived, but the memory of our old home lingered always in our bones like an ache. I was born in this new place, and lived here in these green hills until the age of eleven.[20] And although we were relieved here of the immediate

---

Now stop drawing attention to yourself and get up, old coward! We have no time for this. Baboon-livered mistake! Skinny, short-trunked, unlucky heap! I don't ask you anymore, I order you. The herd itself is your only home, Thoosha. You seem to forget that the old place was full of pain.

THOOSHA: It's not an unknown journey. I see the way clearly. It's a simple place, dark and cool. My body aches for it.

ELEPHANTS: Is it so, Thoosha? Can you see the new place also? Amuta tells us it will be cool and green, not dry. There will be water and sweet grass.

THOOSHA: Better than water and grass is absence of thirst and hunger. I'm headed for our only home. You'll join me there, one by one.

AMUTA: Leave her, elephants. If a lonely death is all she wants, she'll get it. Let's move.

19 What? See also footnote 14 *supra*.
20 Not long past the age of eleven, your humble editor was a student at

the Dolphin Cove Middle School, where he had certain experiences and conversations that may elucidate the claims made in footnote 17 *supra,* regarding the alleged hybrid progeny of "Andy Silver."

The history of animal-human love (let us avoid the anthropocentric term *bestiality,* and the politically fraught *miscegenation*) is clouded by popular misconception and mythology. For instance, among children at the Dolphin Cove Middle School, it was widely believed that chickens were the most easily accessible, manageable, and therefore personally satisfying of animals with which to copulate. Although cows were also desirable and abundant, they were rather large for our boys' frames, and known to kick at inopportune moments. Among the watery beasts, our mascot and namesake, the dolphin, was widely reputed to have the most human and snug-feeling of recesses, and moreover was considered so intelligent that you could maybe have a conversation with it afterward. But while there was much talk of arranging a nocturnal break-in at SeaWorld, the nearest one was six hundred miles away, and so, practically speaking, none of us knew how to get hold of the delightful fish. Little did we understand, reader, and less still could we have imagined.

Does such conversation disgust you? Keep in mind these were the lunchroom digressions of twelve-year-olds, and none of my acquaintances in that school ever actually copulated with any creature—chicken, cow, dolphin, or human—until several years later.

Which brings me to the subject of my penis—a subject, I daresay, similarly clouded by popular mythology and misconception. I still remember the first time I realized I was, shall we say, different—perhaps tragically, perhaps magically—different. As I stepped up to the urinal in the boys' room at our Dolphin Cove school, and my friend Brian—in truth, not a friend, but one of the boys known in our class for his uncensored mouth framed by shapely lips, his pretty hair, and his consequent popularity with the little ladies of our hallways—this bold Brian stepped up to the urinal next to mine, unzipped his pants, and began to guide his tiny dolphin out of its little cove. As he was doing so, Brian turned to glance at my own boy's bud. Then his eyes widened, his grin spread, and as I was about to set loose my stream, the shameless fellow grabbed me by the shoulder and swung me around to face him. "Your thing," he said. "It looks like an *elephant's trunk!*"

My face crimsoned. My ears pounded with the internal pulse of my own horrified heart. I then looked down at what I held in my hand and saw

that it, too, was beating with its own pulse, and, like the pouting, pointing prick of evil Andy Silver, it was unaccountably and uncontrollably
aroused.

And Brian was right. It looked like an elephant's trunk. Not that it was
especially large, but it had a particular cast and curl, wrinkled and narrow
and (having been spared the knife) flaring somewhat at the end—perfect,
you might think, for grasping a peanut.

But of course this message was obscured, and by the time I got to
high school, I was routinely greeted in the hallways with mocking elephant noises, and referred to as "Dumbo," the boy with the disgustingly
deformed appendage. I was called, also, various other sexually aggressive
epithets. I could never again piss, in that school, in peace. But perhaps this
is neither here nor there.

To return to our subject, I have found historical evidence for the early
and widespread occurrence, in our own country, of the love that dare
not moo or trumpet its name. *The Autobiography of William Blacktusk
Souldier, Esq., an Elephant Escaped from the American South, written by
Himself* (a text not yet fully translated, and available only to a small group
of scholars, namely myself) begins with an accounting of Blacktusk's own
heterogeneous parentage. Blacktusk makes the fantastic claim also that a
human boy on his plantation, who grew up to become one of the preeminent members of Southern Society, who even held a Seat in Congress, is
his own human Brother. William Blacktusk's autobiography begins thus:

> My father was a human. It was a truth never spoken but generally
> known. Indeed, one hardly had to be told of it to know it, with the
> evidence of my own countenance to betray me, my wide, light-colored
> eyes, my taste for curd rice and other human delicacies, my nearly
> inborn understanding of human language. My father was none other
> than the man who had taken my mother from the wild, years before I
> was born; who had locked her in his compound and used her to clear
> his fields and fell his trees, to drag his lumber. I was this man's own
> son, indisputably, and yet was allowed to live only half the life of his
> acknowledged, human child, the boy who sat inside the house under
> fans, in rooms built too small for elephants to even enter; that boy
> who had the privilege of study and of leisure, of working one day to
> build his own house, harvest his own feed, not someone else's. That
> lucky boy, my own brother, who in early days to pass the time would
> come to my newborn's corral and poke me with a stick; who would

threat posed by the lowland drought, the new land brought its own difficulties. There were hungry times here, too, but also new and unforeseen dangers.

Koni discovered the first disquieting sign. Koni was older than me by seven years, a teenager on the cusp of womanhood. My mother treated her almost like her own daughter, and for many years, in fact, I believed Koni was my true sister. I followed her in everything she did. When she waded in the lake and curved her trunk back over her body to spray herself, I did the same and choked as the water flowed back down my trunk into my throat. When we grazed, I would leave my mother's side only to follow behind Koni, to admire the deft way she handled the grasses with her trunk, nimble and precise; how she effortlessly held her own among the elders. Her eyes were larger than those of other elephants, depthless and black.[21]

---

ride me for sport when I was larger; to whom I was bound as play-mate and enforced companion while I was small enough to have no say in the matter, while I was innocent enough even to enjoy it—that lucky boy and I were brothers, and yet we were foreclosed from feeling for each other, as we grew, that natural love and respect, that mirrored feeling that finds in the other the reflection and complement of one's own virtues, that joys in the other's successes and struggles in his sorrows as if they were one's own, and even more so, which as brothers should have been our birthright. Conceived as brothers but raised as enemies were we: not Ram and Lakshmana, but Vali and Sugreeva, Cain and Abel.

21 The pachydermological distinction was not just in my nether regions. It was also in my face. My uncle Gustaf recognized the deformity in my features, and would come back from his travels with bags full of elephant-themed trinkets from Thailand, South Africa—wherever his work had taken him. He gifted me with articulated wooden elephants from Sweden, stuffed elephants from Vietnam, elephant-headed idols from India. These things amused me, I suppose, but no more so than animals did in general.

I always knew there was some concern for my well-being implicit in Uncle Gustaf's attention; and also, I suspected, some implicit association of the elephant's unwieldy, exaggerated features with my own odd countenance, some hope he hoped I would find in the elephant's ability to bear herself regally despite these apparent deformities.

Whence the real source of Uncle Gustaf's fascination with the fat beast, of course I had no idea at the time.

Uncle Gustaf was the brother of my mom, Katharina. They were German, the children, I believed, of Holocaust survivors; and my father, Burt, was a Chicago-born African American. My parents met—true story—when they both worked as stewards for American Airlines. Their romance therefore took place in airline bars and in curtained-off cabins high in the air, and also, I guess, in overnight airport hotels in various cities all around the world. They married in a small ceremony in Memphis and had their honeymoon the same day, then moved to a nearby state and settled down in the wishfully and weirdly named town of Dolphin Cove, and I arrived in 1978. And the first picture of the three of us together in front of the new house in Dolphin Cove is the happy picture that I keep, even today, so many years and so many rooms, apartments, and houses later, Scotch-taped above the table in the room in the northern city where now I sit, and outside which two drunks are currently having vociferous intercourse.

Here's a memory: Hovering over me to tuck me in at night, Katharina, my mother, stares into my face like she wants to cut me up in little stars. It is a look of sad affection. As I close my eyes and start to drift away, I cling to her hand to keep her from leaving.

She looks like she is about to cry, and all because of how ugly I am.

"What's wrong?" Burt asks her, peeking into the room as she sits there sniffling, thinking I'm asleep.

"His nose," she'd whisper. "His forehead. His whole face." It's hard, of course, to distinguish between real words and dreamworlds, but these were the conversations I thought I heard, as I drifted off to sleep.

"Nonsense," Burt would say. "Just wait till he grows into himself. You can never predict how handsome a boy's going to turn out to be."

If Uncle Gustaf were there, he might add, helpfully, "It looks like he has a little Chinese in him. Could he have any Chinese in him?"

"Let's go downstairs," Burt would say, cutting short the nonsense. "Katharina, Gustaf. Leave the boy alone." He'd lean over me and kiss me on the cheek, a smoky, whiskery, wonderful kiss. And then, lights out.

They were a nervous pair of siblings, Gustaf and Katharina (although they were perfectly mellow compared to their mother, the tragically, grotesquely and quite literally high-strung Nana Marina, who hanged herself

I did not know yet who Koni was. I could not have foretold the ways in which her actions would change my life.[22]

---

when I was fourteen, using the long cloth cord of the new electric iron my parents had gifted her on her seventieth birthday.)

Burt was always the calm one, but there was also poison in the well of his family. His brother Jerry jumped off the ——— Bridge one broke, drunk, frozen December, at the age of thirty-five, bursting through the mulchy ice into the black water.

And it used to occur to me, maybe that's what the whole family was searching for in my face so worriedly those evenings: some visible trace of the oblivion gene, the mark of future self-annihilation on "my nose, my forehead, my whole face."

And they were searching also (Burt and Katharina) in each other's faces. They carried a secret, the two of them—a secret, I often believed, that revolved around me. One could see it in their sad eyes, the way they looked at me, and then at each other, knowingly. And one could sense the vigilance with which they guarded each other, lest one of them slip away from the world and leave the other to bear the burden—of me, and of the secret—all alone.

There were many reasons for Uncle Gustaf's eventual falling-out with my parents. I got inklings from Katharina that Gustaf had been less than enthusiastic about my parents' marriage, and that while Burt had been willing to forgive and forget, Katharina held on to the prickly pear of pride (from a sense of fierce marital loyalty, and probably to balance out Burt's forgiving nature) and thenceforward was quick to find fault with her kid brother Gustaf.

"It's because he never was friends with a black man before in all his life," Katharina said once, a note of forgiveness in her voice, and that was good enough an explanation for me.

Burt and Katharina, my parents, died tragically five days before my twelfth birthday. It was a car accident: they parked their car in our closed garage and accidentally left the engine running (as they sat in the front seat clasping hands). And I was left in the hands, henceforward (until her own eventual demise), of Nana Marina.

22 *Exterior, jungle. Enter Amuta, now a strong, older elephant, followed by Koni. Jointly, they push down a large tree. It falls with a thunderous crash. They begin to strip it of leaf, branch, and bark.*

AMUTA: When Ania left us, and left you a motherless runt, Koni, we never thought you'd live to see maturity. But now look at you. Without your strong help, this herd would starve. We'd not have enough to feed our young ones. If only the others could be like you, eighteen years old, lithe and determined. You are brave. You are also foolhardy sometimes, and often you don't take the direction of your elders; but these unappealing traits will be tempered with age. Strength is everything for an elephant—it is all we can rely on—and this you have. If you learn to discipline your strength, Koni, there will be few beasts to match you.

KONI: Thank you, Amuta. If not for your kindness, I would have died an orphan, untouched and unfed. Your nurturing made me strong.

AMUTA: We are elephants, Koni, so we are all related. It was a duty, not a favor that we did for you, so you shouldn't thank us. We look forward to the day you find a mate and multiply yourself.

KONI: Men are strangers to me, Mother, and I'd like to keep it that way.

AMUTA: We'll see how long your shyness lasts. But if it lasts much longer, be warned, we'll tell the strongest, ugliest bull we can find to pin you down and pump you up with child. Your increase is in the herd's favor. Maidenly virtue is charming only in children. Womanly beasts must practice womanly virtues. Now strip the last of this bark, and I'll take these branches up to our camp.

Exit Amuta.

KONI: Why did she needlessly bring up my past? "When Ania left us," she said, "and left you a motherless runt." It's almost as if she takes pleasure in retelling it. She does it so often, although it pinks my ears with shame, and now I wonder if that is her very purpose. It still stings me, years later, the anguish of that time. My mother deserted this herd and died a mindless death. If it's a sin to curse your mother, then I am bound to hell. I wish that senile cow had never given birth to me, to make me bear the mark forever of her shame.

I have heard the stories—how my old mother was a kind and gentle leader who grew confused and weak and could manage only to fill her own belly; and how, finally, her hunger and senility led her alone into unsafe territory. She muttered aloud about magical trees and drought-loving fruit, and would not heed Amuta's entreaties. Instead of trees and fruit, my mother met the fangs of an outland tiger and died an absurd, unnecessary death. I went with the others to grieve what remained of her body. I smelled its decay from a distance and brayed and tried to flee, but my new mother pushed me forward. My mother's eyes had come unhinged and lay next to her body, staring upward in undiminished terror.

I have always strived to be as unlike the dimly remembered character of my mother as my muscles and mind would allow me. Everything I have done for sixteen years has been to separate myself from her image, and mirror myself to the image of my new mother. Amuta has been kind to me, favoring me sometimes equal with her own kin; and her favor has given me status among my peers. True, she always notes my past, never lets it slip far from view. But maybe she does it for my own edification. She has been a mother to me and more; she has instilled in me qualities to cherish. So why do I feel a lingering discontent? True, I could have been a princess, being born of a queen. But since that queen was no queen worthy of the name, I should count myself lucky to have been fostered instead by one who is.

Ho! But who moves there in the brush? Some predator or ape? Show yourself!

Enter Manami.

MANAMI: Forgive me, Koni, I was only grazing. I did not mean to intrude on your solitude.

KONI: Elephants don't enjoy solitude. We think as herd, move as herd. We don't know solitude.

MANAMI: Don't we, Koni? Forgive me, but I heard your lament. You're a young elephant, but like me, you have experienced the loss of that thing you loved most, and so you understand solitude. You were a child once, grieving for a mother, as I was a mother grieving for a child. Did the other elephants share in our grief, Koni? Did they understand it even distantly?

KONI: Any grief I felt, Manami, for the elephant I once called "Mother," was only the instinct of a child. We are grown elephants now, and although bound to remember our losses, must not linger over them. In these difficult times, many elephants know loss, not just us.

MANAMI: "We are grown elephants now," eh? How mature you've become. My boy, too, would have been almost your age. He would have begun to feel his manhood, and to think about seeking his living in the forest, alone. I know you remember how well the two of you used to play as children. You treated him like a little brother, pulling him along in everything that you did—I have never forgotten it. Many elephants know loss, Koni, but you and I share a special bond. Our losses were unnecessary and were caused by that elephant we both call our leader.

KONI: Manami, you are elder to me, so I speak with deference. But you, too, must be careful what you say: slander without substance is like burping on an empty stomach. It's true, the sayings: Rumors sprout most thickly where grass is sparse. And: Empty stomachs produce only fumes. These are old accusations you're making; like all elephants, you complain about Amuta every time our fortunes diminish. With respect, Manami, you still resent the choice we made, moving here from our old place. But finally, it was you who lost your child and not Amuta.

MANAMI: Of course these truths resurface when times are hard, because we are reminded again of our leader's poor judgment in bringing us here. But forget my case for a moment. Forget for a moment the tragic death, which was no fault of mine, of my innocent, toddling boy. Think only of the violence done to your own family.

KONI: Violence done by a tiger, Manami. You might as well blame the grass for being green.

MANAMI: The tiger was only the tool. I have never uttered word of this before, but I was there.

KONI: You lie.

MANAMI: It is true. I always used to follow Amuta in her grazing, discreetly, from a distance. She knew the best places for grass—she would find unfamiliar spots, and I would track her because I admired her and wanted to learn her techniques. And so it was that I heard Amuta luring old Ania into a dangerous valley, promising her a harvest of strange fruit. I heard your mother's cries of "Treachery! Treachery!" and saw Amuta ignore those cries. I myself fled to your mother's aid, but saw from a distance that I was too late.

KONI: How dare you put words into the mouths of the dead? And if it's true, you should be ashamed only of yourself, first of all for following after stronger elephants, to save yourself work and graze on their leavings; second for not going faster to my mother's aid. But I don't believe you. If you were there, you would have mentioned it sooner.

MANAMI: I didn't mention it because I admired Amuta. Forgive me, I thought she might have made a better leader than your mother, who was old and weak. When Amuta led us on this stupid quest, when in the process she killed my son, I realized what a misjudgment I had made. We were better off with old Ania.

Ever since that time I have waited. The herd thinks I am grief-stricken and bitter. They don't trust me and would never have believed me. So I have held close this bloody bit of knowledge. I have waited for you to grow mature and strong, for these facts concern you most of all. I knew that you alone would believe me and have the strength to act.

KONI: Elephant, what makes you think I also don't consider you bitter and mendacious? What makes you think that I alone am simple enough to believe such tales?

MANAMI: So don't believe me. Use your own common sense: Do you think it was a coincidence that Amuta was the last elephant to see your mother alive? That Ania would wander by herself through a deserted valley reeking of fresh tiger shit without being somehow deceived?

If we elephants were not so subservient, we would not stand for injustices such as this. We would not have clung to Amuta, ignoring the evidence of her guilt, simply because we believed she was the only one with the strength of will to show us what to do. I tell you, most elephants are born slaves. They never learn to think for themselves. They know only to listen to a leader. I include myself in this characterization—I will never do anything to avenge the death of my own child because I lack the power and the will, and because I know that my actions would not be respected by the herd. But remember, you are not like other elephants. You were born a princess. Therefore think with the mind of a princess and not of a slave.

KONI: Go on, Manami, you sad thing. If it were any other elephant listening to this treason, you'd be begging for forgiveness before Amuta herself right now. Go and finish your grazing. Stop wasting your breath on this pointless prattle.

MANAMI: You won't tell Amuta what I've said, I know. You wouldn't want her to stop me from telling you the truth. You know how to use your head, Koni, and when the time comes, you'll know how to use your tusks, too.

Exit Manami. Koni lifts onto her back a bundle of leaves and bark, and begins to wander back toward camp.

KONI: That cow gives me the creeps. She walks about so dourly, red-eyed and muttering to herself, as if trailed at all times by the ghost of her dead little boy. Poor insomniac wretch. Half the time she makes me want to cry for her misfortune, and half the time I want to scream at her, Get over it!

And yet I find it hard to deny her, everything she says pulls so hard at my soul. Determined to remember her loss, she does have a dignity and a power all her own. Perhaps it is only this that gives attraction to what she says.

Is an elephant capable of murder? Not a bull crazed by musth, but a normal cow, bound by all that is natural to the protection of her sisters? It shouldn't be possible. After all, what are our lives about? Grass, water, and sleep; and when these things are unavailable, the fretting over their absence. A constant seeking for safety and food, for time to enjoy the company of our sisters and our children. What could be more straightforward?

Yet how we complicate the seeking of our so-simple desires! I think it is because we are born into families, bound already at birth into a knot of disappointed affections, blood-strong desires. Our families breed in us our elephant and inelephant qualities both.

Look, there plays little Shanti, such a sweet calf. But a daughter already to Amuta, a cow so parsimonious in her affections, inspiring but also demanding, a leader battle-ready and hard. A beast capable of doing anything to protect her herd.

Look how affectionately and uncritically Shanti follows her mother. That affection is sure one day to be disappointed. Shanti's not the brightest calf but an earnest one, trying always to please. Other calves her age are embarrassed to be seen with their mothers, but not her. Look at them clinging close in the river, look at Shanti throwing mud at her mother's rump, the parts she cannot reach. The softening in her eyes when her mother touches her, that pure gaze of gratitude and joy. The motherly touch is a supersweet pleasure, an impossible bliss. All the sweeter when it comes from an elephant as usually hard as Amuta. For all the favor she has bestowed me, Amuta has never touched me in that way. The kindness she has bestowed on me, in fact, is only one tiny part of the kindness my own mother would have shown. Amuta has conferred me with status, but it is nothing like the status I would have enjoyed if my own mother were

Koni's confidence and tendency to solitude distinguished her from the other adolescents, especially when from time to time our group was joined by a clutch of noisy young bulls from the

---

queen. Why, I would have been the apparent heir, and not this clumsy infant Shanti, poor thing. I've played with her often, taught her to fell small trees. It's a joy to watch her grow, but she's no born ruler. She's a submissive calf, nothing like the little me. Yet she enjoys Amuta's truest love and is the favorite one day to lead our herd. It is a logic that makes no sense.

But what if it's true that Shanti's the daughter of a murderer, and I the daughter of a courageous queen? Then her qualities would be accountable, and mine as well. To rule would be my natural lot, and I have lived a life of unwarranted shame.

Only by bitter happenstance are we the children of our mothers, so how can I resent Shanti for it, that simple-minded, blameless calf? Yet our identities come from our mother's lives, either with them or against them we must be. We are implicated in our parents' choices regardless of our own choosing. Shanti's privilege is unearned. My sorrow is unearned. If we are to distance ourselves from our parents' evil and its effects, mustn't we also discount their good? Let Shanti renounce her mother and her right to the throne; let her fight me for it when she comes of age! Or, let her mother account to me for all she's done. Let her make amends by declaring me heir.

Deep down I know it's true: My mother's death was not her own doing. But to know this truth is far too painful. Everyone whom I have loved turns ugly in my eyes. Every clear elephant memory becomes questionable. Every close-held shame reveals its falsehood, yet makes me guilty for having held it. I see a world now where the young have no innocence, the old possess no necessary wisdom, our leaders merit no respect, belief in the herd is lost.

Such knowledge is a lonely-making thing. My own mother, Ania, how I miss you! I remember everything about you, every time you cradled my infant body in your trunk's embrace, and fed me food chewed in your own mouth. The memory of your scent makes me weak with longing. My own sweet mother, I'll never be forgiven for every time I've cursed your loving soul. I'll have to find a new way somehow, all on my own.

outlying jungles. These boys would camp a short distance from us and saunter into our herd by day, draping their trunks over their small tusks in feigned nonchalance, but quickly revealing themselves as overeager novices. Fancying themselves clever, they tried surreptitiously to sniff our undersides and taste our urine, to determine who among our older sisters were least likely to reject their rude attentions. When they approached an older elephant, one of our mothers, they would be greeted with a roar or a feinted lunge, to send them scurrying back to their cohorts. Our mothers had no time for these juveniles. But the adolescents and younger cows were curious about the newcomers, and some eager girls became positively giddy with excitement. The interest of men was still a novelty to them, and so, giggling and indiscriminate, one of my cousins might follow a boy elephant into the forest for days together.[23] Upon her return, her friends might surround her, cooing and fawning, eager to mark the ascension of one of their own into the ranks, they imagined, of womanhood.

Koni, I thought, was different from the other girls. Even when she reached maturity, she stayed aloof from the attentions of boys. She held close to the elders of our group, modeling her comportment on theirs. Some of the other elephants found such behavior haughty—a cow, they thought, should behave like a cow, but a calf like a calf. They felt Koni had not earned the right to carry herself as though she were superior to other elephants her age, to dominate and command those elephants.

---

23 How well do you remember your first time? I sat in an empty, late-night parking lot with a young woman I believed to be my friend, drinking shots of some purple-orange liquid she offered me. When we were both slump-eyed and slurring, she began to kiss me. And then, closing her eyes, and with a deep breath and a bitten lip, she popped open the buttons of my fly. Then she screamed. With her eyes still closed, with all her might she screamed. Then she fell asleep facedown on the pavement.

But to my child's eyes, Koni was not behaving as though she were superior to others her age. She simply *was* superior. It was abundantly clear.

But some months later Koni surprised us. We were grazing on trees on the grassless side of a hill, eating leaves, bark, and even the thin ends of branches, stripping down the trunks. In loose and fluid order we grazed, straying occasionally out of sight of each other, keeping our bearings by bellowing out loudly and then waiting to hear the rippling replies of our sisters. But then Koni called to us from somewhere distant, and the sound of her call was unformed and open, and we could not fathom its meaning. Her voice bellied out over the forest, an implacable ululation. Our stomachs dropped, our ears pricked out rigid and quivering with alarm, and we froze. Old Iala emptied her bladder in a rush of distress, then turned around as if to flee—we all saw her. But my mother sent forth a long, deep rumble that rolled over the forest floor, flattening grass: a reassurance, a reply to Koni, and an indisputable command to the rest of us. We rushed forward then, everyone, even flustered, shame-faced Iala, her ears flapping in agitation, with children like me struggling to stay close to the dust-clouded behinds of our mothers. And we rushed as elephants rush—splintering trees, obliterating the small, unfortunate mammals who people the forest floor—until we came across Koni in a forest clearing, standing watch over a gruesome sight, a massive and familiar carcass.[24]

---

24 Finding the massive and familiar carcass of my grandmother dangling by a cord from the lighting fixture in our own garage, was, I think, one of the events that precipitated my entry into manhood, and into the world, eventually, of elephants. Nana Marina was a severe caretaker to me, after my parents' untimely departure, and life was a bit of a living heck, broken by those brief respites when Uncle Gustaf came home from his overseas travel and temporarily took over the caretaking.

Nana Marina hated animals, and I had always suspected her of poison-

I knew the dead bull. Once a year he would visit our group, and I dreaded this visit in the pit of my stomach. His smell preceded him by an hour: a black, pungent odor that arrived not gradually but all at once, like a wet-season cloud. My aunts and cousins lifted their trunks to sniff the air and, receiving the smell, fell into an unseemly frenzy, braying at each other, urinating excitedly into the bush.

When he arrived, he broke through the surrounding trees without ceremony, his chin tucked in, his trunk extended, his eyes wild and intent. Black rheum ran down the sides of his face and along the insides of his thighs, and his penis hung low, enormous, dribbling some cloudy serum. Two massive tusks weighted his head, arcing down almost to the ground, the left one broken off and jagged at the tip.

The younger elephants who had reached maturity could not contain themselves; they bowed at him and shuffled with nervous, eager submission. Even Manami and Iala and my other usually dignified aunts excitedly circled this powerful bull, turning their backsides toward him in embarrassingly frank invitation. But he ignored them. His interest was already focused on a muscular cow, my mother, who stood some distance away, peeling the branches from trees, nonchalantly flapping her ears, turning only a casual glance at the visitor. The bull walked toward her, but my mother only walked away. He trotted faster, but my mother outpaced him, leading him deep into the trees. I watched the shivering of the treetops that marked their progress

---

ing the stray cat that I fed secretly on the back porch, and which I discovered one morning frozen in a pool of its own piss, its tongue stuck out in a perpetual postmortem raspberry. With Nana's passing, I felt free to leave home, travel to the city, and pursue my own passions.

Yes, I had always had a way with animals. Cats could understand me. Dogs respected me. But it was in the city that I discovered I could speak with elephants.

as they receded deeper into the cover of the forest. And then the forest was still.

About four days later my mother would return alone, weary and calm. She trotted directly to me, reassured herself of my well-being, offered me her breast, which I accepted, bewildered, but famished and grateful. My aunts reverted to their conditioned or inborn hierarchies, obeying Amuta's commands reflexively, none of them remarking on her absence. But if my aunts didn't resent him, I certainly did, this mysterious bull who was the only thing that could separate my mother from her daughter and her herd.

Now this same bull lay mangled on the forest floor, massive and bleeding.[25] Pink cavities marked the spots on his face where

---

25 On January 4, 1903, for the crime of trampling a succession of trainers, Topsy the Elephant was executed in spectacular fashion on the Coney Island boardwalk, wired to thousands of volts of alternating current—a spectacle devised by none other than Thomas Alva Edison. On September 13, 1916, for flinging a man against a building and then taking a stroll over his head, Mary the Elephant was hanged by the neck from a hundred-ton crane, before an enraptured crowd. (Hribal, footnote 10 *supra*.)

The roster of elephant executions is long; but few historians have been able to explain the murky death, on October 10, 1954, of the peace-loving elephant Clarabel, discovered in her corral in the Senaloca, Florida, winter quarters of Carlos Hermosilla's Authentic American Circus, strangled by a loose length of chain that had been crudely looped around her neck and hoisted over the ramparts. Her body was found—forelegs lifted into the air, asphyxiated—by the only night watchman on duty at the time, who was lame in one arm, but with twenty arms would still not have had the strength to hoist Clarabel's four tons of flesh. It must be noted that Clarabel had recently witnessed the tragic death of her own newborn calf and was moreover despondent from months of beatings by the circus's new trainer, a man known even to his friends as Angry Jim. Historians, biologists, veterinary psychologists, much less circus workers have been loath to draw the obvious conclusion regarding Clarabel's demise. Not even Hribal mentions it.

once his tusks grew, and his belly pulsed with the movement of maggots.

The sight of the carcass had an instantaneous effect on our herd. My aunts and cousins screamed in distress. They nudged the body with their feet, and when this did not wake it, they thrashed the ground with their trunks and threw dirt violently on their own backs. Some of the younger of us ran hysterically away from the site and back again, repeatedly, as if hoping each time to be greeted by some less terrible scene, while Koni, her breath gone, her screams reduced now to whimpers, shook her head with continued disbelief while her trunk evinced a growing acceptance, softly caressing the decayed body.

Amuta, my mother, stood at some distance from the others, and from this terrible elephant whom she had loved, absorbing the herd's dismay and Koni's familiar caresses. Finally she approached the body, nudging Koni aside. With her trunk, my mother probed gently the wounds in his belly, the bloody craters in his face, smelling and occasionally tasting his blood. She voiced no emotion, but these attentive explorations of her trunk, I see now, revealed her profound care and patient con-

---

Elephants are one of those rare species (along with humans and dolphins) known to recognize their reflections in mirrors *as* reflections. Self-consciously reflective (you might say), they see themselves as discrete individuals. Is it too far of a stretch to consider that they are also capable of *obliterating* themselves as discrete individuals? Of growing weary of the burdens of self-conscious existence and the heavy hopelessness of life in captivity? Of acting on that despair?

Consider the great elephant Jumbo, P. T. Barnum's star attraction. Despite the inconsistencies in the competing accounts of her death (see, again, Hribal), one thing is clear: after years of exhausting and mind-numbing work, Jumbo stepped forthrightly into the face of a speeding freight train.

Elephants (like the great bull of Shanti's tale) have long been subject to murder. It is a queer sort of vindication for me to point out that they are equally capable of suicide.

cern. When she had completed her investigations, my mother turned to the herd and spoke.

Now, when my mother "spoke," more often than not she articulated the intention of the herd, voiced our collective mind, crystallizing it, giving it form and direction. The herd had a mind and intention, true and plain, constituted by each of us, yet larger than our individual selves, and mother's voice would give body to this intention. And when she spoke thus, we understood her without effort, immediately. But this time, when my mother stepped Koni aside, we did not understand at first what she was trying to tell us.

This bull was not a member of our herd, Mother tried to convey, and so we needn't mourn him as if he were. She told us simply to return to our grazing.

Manami and the others pawed the ground uncomfortably, not knowing what to do. Our instinct, once we understood the new danger signified by this death, was first to mourn the bull, then to flee this country, to return at once to the relative safety of our old and original grazing land.

As the elephants moped in passive confusion, Koni responded aggressively. She did what not even the oldest and most revered of cows would think to do. She turned and trumpeted defiantly at my mother. Then she approached the bull and laid her trunk over him, taking mother's place, as it were. Koni would not leave without mourning this bull, for this bull, her actions clearly stated, had been her mate.[26]

---

26 KONI: You loved this man, yet you say his death is inconsequential? That we should blithely continue to graze in these foreign hills, not fearing the predator who killed him? But you aren't the only one who loved this bull. He was father to many of our children. He is father to the child whom I now carry. His blood runs in ours, and whatever killed him will be hungry for more. We must mourn him properly, and then we must leave this place.

Wrath rises in Amuta's eyes. But then Amuta's face calms; she seems cool, calculating.

Now Iala fluttered her ears and emitted a nervous whistle. The rest of the herd shifted their feet and lowered their heads as if to escape association with Koni's unprecedented insolence. And my mother, indeed, spread out her ears and widened her eyes in response to the insult implied by the younger cow.

It did not matter that Koni had only expressed the truth. My mother knew—they all knew—that a bull does not mate with only one cow. But to voice this one truth was to violate another: the necessary wisdom of my mother's leadership, the unquestioned and unquestionable unity that guaranteed our survival.

We waited to see if Amuta would reestablish her dominance, if Koni would suffer for her thoughtless impudence. Mother stepped toward Koni, and the younger elephant turned to face what she may have believed would be her bloodying.

But instead of charging Koni, my mother relaxed her posture. She paused and considered the younger elephant. Then she lifted her trunk to Koni, and we all drew our breath, fearing an attack. But Mother only made soft noises, flicking her ears, lifting up her feet and placing them back down softly, firmly.[27]

Mother spoke to Koni, but Koni didn't respond. She couldn't. I could see in her face the intensity of her emotion; her grief— and her anger at Amuta—was too much to bear. By her posture, it was apparent that Koni was still prepared to fight, eager to show her mettle, come what may; but Amuta refused to engage her in this way. Then my mother edged closer to Koni, touching her from the side, laying her head and neck against the smaller

---

[27] AMUTA: Koni, in your young life you've seen many elephants die. But this bull's death, like your mother's, is nothing to be frightened of. We're better off without this bull, just like we're better off without old Ania.

Rage rises up in Koni now; bitter tears sting her eyes. But she holds her tongue.

cow and draping her trunk over her back, and although Koni tried to move aside, bridling at my mother's caress, my mother would not let her go, until Koni finally calmed down.[28]

Then Amuta looked to see if any others wished to express themselves. No one did. And just like that, it was settled. Amuta began to walk back toward our grazing field, with Manami and Iala and all the others falling with easy obedience into line, Koni's small moment of rebellion forgotten, her very opinions seemingly altered by the redirected consensus of the herd. Koni's insurrection had not, in fact, been real. Mother had not allowed it to be.

And so we lived again content in our new hills. The rains that came thereafter were dense, cooling. In the mornings we fed on the new thriving of greenery, and in the afternoons we wallowed in mud, we sank under the shade of trees and slept. New bulls visited our camp, and my aunts played gladly with them, and there was no new sign of danger; and Koni never mentioned—nor even seemed to remember—the moment when she voiced an opinion different from Amuta's. That incident seemed, by the evidence of the herd's behavior, not an actual difference of opinion, but only and completely a misunderstanding—of each other, and of our own intentions. Those peaceful days were the last of my first green life.[29]

My second life began with a hole.[30] No, wrong, that's in retrospect. A lush expanse. Fallen branches and leaves, torn twigs. The ground it was. Just the ground under my feet. Then not.

---

28 Or seemed to!

29 Oh life, oh fate, oh Shanti! Would that you had died then, and not endured the hells to come!

30 Have you ever left home and moved to the city? How I longed for my Dolphin Cove, that ugly home I so often hated. What would I have done, alone in the city, if I had not discovered the zoo, that inexhaustible comfort

and solace? So many afternoons I stood outside the elephant enclosure in that vast, decrepit menagerie in that distant borough, eating someone else's discarded caramel corn, gazing into the elephant enclosure and watching, with keen eye, the flicks of tail and flops of ear, which, to the casual watcher, were simply random tics; listening to the hiccups, harrumphs, trumpets, and brays which I knew to be clear and intentional messages from the elephants to each other and (more pertinently) to me—the first buds of a blossoming Englaphant. For twenty years of invisibility, we slowly developed our inchoate language of mutual despair. It was my solace, my refuge, my real life beneath my "real" life. It was the zoo that saved me, in my deepest despair, from rendering my own self null and void, a fate which I often felt I couldn't avoid.

My unusual family history led me, recently, to do extensive research into the history of auto-oblivion. My findings with regard to elephants are alluded to in footnote 25 *supra*. But that history is nothing as to the rich chronicle of human suicides. I don't have space here to go into great detail, but allow me to summarize my findings:

A BRIEF HISTORY OF OBLIVION

Human suicide was invented in 1492 by Romeo Montague, with these words: "Here, here will I remain with worms that are thy chamber-maids; O, here will I set up my everlasting rest, and shake the yoke of inauspicious stars from this world-wearied flesh. Eyes, look your last! Arms, take your last embrace! and, lips, O you the doors of breath, seal with a righteous kiss a dateless bargain to engrossing death!"

Romeo's beautiful demise inspired countless generations of the world-weary and disaffected to slip their mortal coil, but none quite so beautifully. Not that they didn't try: After Romeo started it, across Italy there spread a cult of sorts, the Association of Beautiful Suicides, who tried to outdo each other in doing themselves in, with tales of pathos and of woe each more gorgeous than the last, as they slipped onto their bare bodkins, or dangled tragically by their gosling necks from the banisters of Florentine balconies. They killed themselves in the highly questionable hope that suicide could be more than an act of despair, or a coward's escape from an inhospitable world; that it could be a creative act, a gesture of life transcendent. The problem, however, was of genius and originality: After Romeo had done it best and first, everyone else came off as a pallid imitation. It was a secondary, creative death on top of the intended actual one.

As time went on, young men and women tried to surmount this problem by moving beyond mere verbal flourishes, to astonish and inspire with the means of death itself: thus, the five young men who swallowed lit fireworks—dazzling.

During his travels to the East, Marco Polo brought with him news of suicide, and it caught on like Venetian measles. In India, the mystics, ascetics and seers took up the challenge of the young Italian lovers, reaching sometimes new levels of the sublime. One woman skewered her tongue and tits with long needles, and spent sixteen months bleeding. A man covered himself with honey and sat silently on a bed of fire ants. It took sixteen hours, and he swelled up like a pumpkin squash. Another kneeled down before (yes) the temple elephant.

It became an annual event, a Maha Mela, the Festival of Beautiful Suicide. Men and women ate diamonds and shat blood; hired surgeons to thread their hearts with razor wire, one end of which they'd tie to the top of the temple gopuram before diving: "heart flossing"; they bought vicious dogs and pasted their bodies with chicken gizzards; they tied themselves to kites and lofted themselves over shark-filled oceans.

These suicide artists were ultimately stumped by the prime paradox of beautiful death: that is, its very creation was its destruction (or was its destruction its creation?). The subject of the act was the object of its obliteration. There was no way to improve a bad performance, and there were no second chances. In the end, what was so beautiful about death, anyway?

So the more far-thinking of them began to consider things more broadly. Could self-elimination be accomplished while still, at least technically, living?

The answer: sort of. The sage Babhuvallavar was the first to try it. He sat perfectly still for forty-four years—almost like dying, but more boring, frankly.

Taking the concept further, an offshoot of the Beautiful Suicides prescribed a yet more elaborate route to self-abnegation. "Imitation is suicide," said someone famous once, or was it me? Accordingly, the followers of this school set out, in a sense, to perfect and make intentional what the derivative Italians had stumbled upon unimaginatively. Recruited in their youth or early adulthood, they would each pattern their lives on another person's, studying the other's habits, adopting his behaviors, his clothes, his accent and manner of dress; then the imitator would go so far as to

I was nearly eleven now and fed on grass, not milk. I pulled my own food from the ground. I tussled with my cousins and siblings, and ran with the exuberance that we had during those full times. I ran to keep close to my fast-moving mother in the bright sun. And then there was pain and darkness.

I was in pain and felt the weight of something large upon me. It was dark and there was nothing I could see. I smelled my mother and there was another there, and the world was gone.

My mother stood up now, tall (and as she rose, I heard the cracking of bones—not hers but those of the body on which she was lying). I felt my way with my trunk, seeking to cower beneath her, but she swung her body in frantic movements

---

murder this other person, to clear the ground for the performance to begin (a difficult moment, as you can imagine—to eliminate the object of one's utmost attention and care). The suicider then became, as far as possible, the other person—taking his job, sleeping in his bed, answering to his name—so that the suicider himself was nowhere, any longer, to be found. This form of "suicide" in its purest form consumed decades of incredible effort, and still butted up most profoundly against a central irony: when it was successful, it became invisible. Other people wouldn't even know it was happening.

But it was seldom successful. In attempting this particular form of invisibility, the suicider achieved not exactly oblivion, but another kind of existence; by trying so minutely to inscribe his life upon another's, the practitioner of living suicide found that he inevitably and repeatedly deviated, and each deviation, however minor, signified the particular and unique life of the actor. The very thing which he had sought to render invisible became highlighted, offset, more pronounced. The act of self-annihilation became a (rather weird) act of self-creation. In other words, no one was fooled.

Incidentally, please do not mistake any of this for a defense of suicide. The preceding sentence, while sincere, is also a paraphrase of my dear Charles Kinbote, in whose footnotes my own footsteps suicidally follow. For while imitation might aim toward suicide, it often begins as love.

and did not recognize my form, and her seeming confusion terrified me.

As the light returned to my eyes, I saw that there were three of us here, myself, my mother, and my youngest brother (he lay still on the ground, his eyes rolled up in his head). My mother calmed down and recognized me now, and arched her trunk to sniff the air. The sky had risen high above us, a small blue circle in the middle of darkness.

We heard the rumble of the returning herd in the earth and blackness that surrounded us, coming toward us from all around.[31] And then we saw their faces in the space of sky above, looking down at us, bewildered. They kneeled on the ground and reached with their trunks but they could not nearly touch us. Iala wept and thrashed the ground. Others ran off to pull down branches and came back and held them down to us, hoping somehow to pull us up. And my mother pawed up the

---

31 When the menageries of the Silver Brothers Circus enter the city, the first thing you sense is the rumble—not the familiar rumble of motoring vehicles, but a vibration of a slower, more deliberate frequency—through the soles of your shoes, into your tarsals and up through your heel, tickling your humeruses, until it is somewhere inside you. Through the darkness of Lincoln's Tunnel, at the farthest end, there is a distant disk of light, a view, as it were, into another land. Suddenly, that light is blotted out, and one has only the sense that a large and inevitable blackness is approaching.

And then, when you have been lulled into a certain stupefied awe by this blackness and vibration, as if you had been tucked inside the world's own body, from out of the darkness burst forth the bright and dark visages of all the world's fauna. The tigers, ostriches, giraffes, and rhinoceri; the black bears and Koala bears and polar bears and grizzlies; the pronghorns and prairie dogs and parakeets and hawks on string; the snakes, turtles, crocodiles, and lizards; the orangutans and gorillas, the gibbons and monkeys (the tiniest of which were tethered to little chains, decorated with purple fedoras, and made to twirl and jump); and finally, bringing up the rear, what all deep-souled watchers were waiting for: the elephants on parade.

walls, unclimbably steep, only to slip back onto her haunches. One of my frantic little sisters tried to leap into the hole to join us, but another caught her by the tail, just barely.

I don't remember how long we stayed here, what other efforts the herd made in trying to rescue us.[32] After some time (hours? days?), all returned to quiet. I slept, and awoke in a delirium, hungry. In the circumscribed space of sky above us, my family members continued to gaze down, despairing.

And in the quiet, my mother spoke.

She gave the others an order. She told them to go away and leave us to our fate. She ordered them to leave.

The elephants responded by scratching the ground uncertainly. They looked about as if dumb, as if they hadn't heard; because what they heard would require them to do what could not be countenanced.

Go away without me, Mother told them again; you must survive now on your own. She knew that whoever set this trap would surely return. The only thing to do was to leave, and leave immediately. Mother was already as good as dead; and for the herd to remain with her to the end would mean the herd's end as well. To drive home her point, Mother rammed the side of the hole with her head, sending the ground above into shivers, bringing a shower of dirt on our own backs.

But the elephants only exchanged frightened glances. They looked down at us[33] and bellowed incoherently, and then looked to each other again. And still they did nothing.

---

32 "I don't remember," Shanti says, but surely what she means is that she remembers, instead, other things from that chaotic time. Whatever she doesn't remember, she didn't see in the first place. Cf. footnote 19 *supra*.

33 They came toward me, tail in trunk, tail in trunk, linked in that humiliating way circus elephants are always linked, each one moreover individually hobbled by a heavy chain leading from rear left to front right ankle. And I saw something distinct in the eyes of each one. Not just the watery sadness one finds in the eyes of all elephants in captivity, but something more specific, more familiar. And when she approached, I knew immedi-

Perhaps they did not know how to move, how to translate even the simple command from head to legs, to turn around and walk away, without Amuta physically there to guide them. Their confused faces ringed the circle of blue. My cousins, playful youngsters and graceful young women; my stately aunts, strong and imposing, reduced now to an extreme of helplessness and agitation; my younger brothers and sisters pawed the ground madly and shook their heads, calling out to us, tears streaking their faces.[34]

My mother was resolute. She understood the situation perfectly. She bellowed to them and spoke clearly, she tried to persuade them in a hundred ways, but they would not listen.[35] For Mother *was* the herd. Without her, they could not function.

Did they finally leave? I didn't know. Their sad, beautiful faces receded from view, away from the circle. I was thirsty. My brother, my unnamed infant brother, lay still, barely breathing.

---

ately that we, too, were linked; that somehow, across space and across time, my trunk was curled round her tail; that somewhere else, wherever I really came from, we had been kin. Once I saw her, I could not part myself from her, each year that the circus was in our city. How could I allow her to live in captivity? Her large ears flapped open, as if to say, *Speak to me!* Her truthful eyes spoke more directly, begging for *a way out*, yes, but more than that, for *freedom*.

34 Whose face is not seen, whose name is not mentioned? Which elephant was smart enough and had every motivation to lead Shanti and Amuta into this trap, to collaborate, as it were, with whomever dug this hole? Which elephant? Shanti doesn't tell us, but we know.

35 AMUTA: *(Aside)* I must loosen momentarily the ties of loyalty that keep these idiots from leaving.

(To the herd) Fools! Imbeciles! Think of yourselves, and flee! Don't just stand there! Morons! Iala—you suckled me as a child, but I am not a child anymore, so don't stand there cowering! Weak old woman, a burden to this herd. No man wants you so you wish to bring the herd to the grave along with you? You would allow them to die as you let your own children once starve?

My mother sat on her haunches in the darkness as the quiet of night set upon us.

We would never see the herd together, alive, again.

In the final stillness, Mother was quiet, making noises only on occasion. It was a hopeless time, and Mother, so powerless, could only try to comfort me.[36] She believed we would all die; she no longer resisted it. Her despair had become quieter but also more total. Our chance for choice was over, our fates clear, our actions fit for judgment; and it was obvious to her that she had failed. I feared her hopelessness more than I feared my own personal doom; I feared her grief, her final, unassailable sorrow, palpable even in its silence, in the darkness of that hole during those last hours.[37]

---

36 *It is the "final stillness." Amuta speaks quietly, coldly.*

AMUTA: Why do you run close to me, Shanti? Hm? *(pause)* Why do you cling to me as if you were a baby? *(Amuta's quiet rage is unmistakable.)* If you were not so attached to me, if you ran freely with the other elephants of your age, you would have been safe now.

(Shanti shakes her head. Tears stream from her eyes.)

AMUTA: You are a coward and an infant, and so we will die together.

37 In the dark, quiet corral of the Silver Brothers Circus, a frequent visitor, enthusiastic volunteer, accused impostor peeks from behind a pile of hay: It is deep night; the circus murmurs only with the occasional snoring hippopotamus, or drunken midget weeping softly over an old loss. In the shadows, the visitor senses the rustle of the greatest of beasts, chained in their sleeping quarters, doubly chained by the fatigue of the day. Slowly, he makes out the quivering silhouette of one particular elephant, not asleep but swaying from side to side, tail twitching from anxious loneliness.

In the interloper's backpack is a giant bottle of Gitranquizol ("elephant keeper's friend") pilfered from the house veterinarian's poorly padlocked cabinet. The mysterious fellow mixes half of the powerful tranquilizer into a bottle of orange soda he has brought with him for this purpose. He edges toward the elephant, sits down near to her.

Shanti extends her trunk to sniff at his strange concoction.

Would you like some too? he asks. *It is a way out.*

But she withdraws her trunk, detecting the drug's unpleasant odor.

The man quaffs the bottle, emptying it entirely, and burps. Then he curls up at Shanti's feet, awaiting the inevitable.

The man notices his toes and fingers begin to numb (indeed, his left foot will never again recover full feeling). His eyelids quiver. The ground feels cold; his tongue grows stiff; the world is filling with beautiful lights, a side effect of the medicine.

But just as his vision begins sprouting with impossible patterns, the precursor to death, he feels a nimble trunk opening his mouth, a stiff scrap of hay inserted into the back of his throat, tickling him there, until he is vomiting uncontrollably. And then the gentle press of an elephant's foot upon his breast, massaging his heart back to action.

In the clouded midnight of my near death, she bends her face close to mine, pinches me awake with her trunk. I cough and splutter, returning to the world of living animals.

When I am finally able to speak, I ask her: *Why have you done this? Why have you brought me back to life?*

In response, she speaks her first fully formed words of fluent Englaphant: *Why should you die alone on the ground,* she asks, *when you may die through me?*

Then her trunk finds its way into my knapsack and discovers there an extra, untainted bottle of orange soda; tucking it into her mouth, she crushes it until it bursts, then flings the empty broken plastic onto the ground. *Orange is my favorite,* she adds—pausing to belch in stentorious elephant fashion. The man's ears quiver, elephant-like, in surprise; his eyes widen in wonder at his understanding, before narrowing again with cunning.

That moment of mutual recognition puts me in mind of another such instance, again from the memoir of William Blacktusk, the famous (or soon to be) birth scene:

> From the moment I spilled onto the blood sotted ground of this dimly lit world, I wanted only to crawl back inside the endless warmth I had left behind—the loving soft source of infinite benignity, the single memory of which today is all that remains to me of Mother. I tried to stand and fell; tried and fell. (And still do we try and fall.) There on

The light came in the morning, and the sounds were like the morning sounds. And as we did in the morning, I emptied my bladder, moved my bowels, there on the ground where we stood, on the body even of my dying brother. I could not help myself. The cries of alarm came first, then the pounding of our sisters' feet vibrating through the earth. These sounds told us they had not traveled far during the night, had not really traveled at all.

---

the periphery, two individuals stood distinct even to my newborn's eyes: one human figure casually stern, granted deferential berth by all those assembled; and on his shoulders a bouncing, excited, and awe-struck toddler, whose face would become so familiar to me. These two stared with mute regard at the bloody wonders of nature, but would not touch me: I was wonderful but too grotesque. (Did they believe I had naught to do with them? Or did they recoil because they knew my wrinkled massive lump was flesh of their flesh?) But now comes the gnarled mahout, someone who in his old age had evidently earned my mother's trust, and was allowed to touch and to bathe me, spilling cold waters into my mucus-clotted ears, my sticky eyes. I coughed and spat and out came the tube of soft white mess glutting my throat, and now I mewed and cried and heard my own voice call-ing. (The cold shock of that mahout's brusque efficiencies notwith-standing, the sureness of his human touch was somehow fortifying, and my instinct tells me retrospectively that this was a man whose place of trust was well earned; but after that night, the silent old man disappeared as suddenly and irrevocably as my mother, whom he served.)

And long will I remember the little looking boy's final exclamation. He had sat a long time in speechless wonder, straddling the strong shoulders of his father, staring in witness of the moving spectacle of my elephant birth, when finally the powerful emotions building up in him those silent minutes broke forth. His small face screwed up like a knot in a tree, and bursting into sobs, he squealed, "I love him! I do, I do!" Then he buried his face in the neck of the human who held him, his alarmed confession bringing a disquieting smile to the lips of this man, and sending a bristle of unease through all the elephants assembled round me.

Confused, chaotic gallops. And then came the screams. From a distance and close by: terrified, pained screams. We could not, of course, see what was happening, what the danger was, who was dying. We could only imagine.

For seeming hours it lasted, their horrible, helpless cries. These were the most terrifying moments of my life; I was more frightened than I am even now. Mother stared down, her eyes bearing a terrible intensity, fully attuned to the destruction of her herd and her own inability to stop it.

When the screams finally quieted, we heard indecipherable noises, footsteps of elephants or of other animals, calls and cries of beasts unknown to us.

Rough vines were thrown down into our hole, maneuvered with sticks around my body and my mother's. The vines were hoisted about us and pulled tight, cutting sharply into our hides, and we were lifted bodily upward until we rested on our hind legs alone, our front feet dangling helplessly. Then a rain of dirt came down on us, great heapfuls, from all directions, on us and around us, covering my brother's body even as he slept. For hours the dirt fell until the ground filled up to the level of our feet, and we were able to stand squarely again. And then the vines again were tightened, and again we were lifted painfully up, and again the dirt began to fall.

For days this process repeated itself, until the dirt in our hole had filled up nearly level with the ground. I was famished and delirious, almost too exhausted to be afraid, to be curious any longer about what was happening and who was doing this. But when we could glimpse finally over the lip of our hole, I was excited and comforted to see that the world was filled again with elephants. Not our family, no one we could recognize. Elephants fitted out in strange coverings, pulling at the vines that lifted us, accompanied by strange gibbering animals. But the world was filled again with elephants.

ON THE BANKS OF TABLE RIVER (PLANET LUCINA, ANDROMEDA GALAXY, AD 2319)

THE BODY IN QUESTION WAS IMPALED on the branches of a calthus tree, where uncleared jungle abuts the grassy track of the via. The time was earliest morning, not yet third dawn. The lights of my hovering hearse illuminated the unfortunate scene: torn wings, sprawling feelers, several legs at impossible angles. The body had belonged to Eth, an acquaintance of mine, a janitor at the Heavenly Paradise Resort, whose son had been one year behind my daughter in academy.

Down below, on the flat track of the via, walked our human constable, Inspector Barhoeven, with his nervous underling Palmena, sullenly striping the vines and thickets edging the roadway with the bright beams of their lamps, bending to retrieve bits of plastic and chips of paint from the hundreds of scraps always caught on the floor of the via. The investigation, I felt sure, was largely a formality. A drunken hit-and-run, casualty one local resort worker, is considered less a crime here than a necessary collateral of life. Sure enough, as I exited my craft and flew down to him, the good inspector immediately began making his case.

"Sorry to call at such an odd hour, Thoren."

"Not at all."

Barhoeven swept his five-fingered hand upward, the badges looped to his neck clanking against his bony chest.

"Isn't it a crying shame?" Barhoeven's face had a stricken, pleading look, as if searching for divine explanation, as if he didn't see such corpses along the via at the rate of one per month. "Oughtn't she to have known better?"

"Sorry?"

"Flying in the middle of the via! I thought Eth was a smarter being than that."

A smile came to me, but I stopped it from reaching my lips. Clever Inspector Barhoeven—blaming poor Eth peremptorily, thus saving himself the time and trouble of tracking down witnesses, of embarrassing our planet's guests, of starting down that long and troublesome road.

"You see, Thoren, I calculated the speed and distance she was thrown based on the angle and extent of penetration of the bough through her back and abdomen. The craft must have been proceeding at a moderate speed, when she passed directly across its path."

Was he sincere? I have never known how to understand humans such as Barhoeven, so earnestly analytical, so confident of themselves at close of day. Perhaps he really was the planet's most ingenious detective. "She should have bought a craft," he muttered now, rubbing his tiny eyes. "She's too old to be flying by her own wings." In the dim light, I was surprised to see liquid beginning to streak Barhoeven's cheeks.

"Eth took the safety of our planet for granted, Inspector."

"So it would seem. We live in a city, Thoren. Not the damn countryside."

I fluttered back up to give Barhoeven time to gather himself, and to give myself the opportunity to appraise the work ahead. Eth's head was swollen to the proportions of a misshapen charlie fruit; her skull, a palpation suggested, was shattered into half a dozen pieces; her proboscis was torn, her incisors scattered into the grass or lost down her throat. And now it fell to me to take Eth's battered body, drain it, cake it, plump it, paint it, prepare it for funeral; build it back more beautiful than it was in life. The people of my planet expected nothing less of me than miracles.

Later that morning, in the basement workshop at my burrow, I began to remove the fragments of wood from the terrible hole in Eth's abdomen. Palmena and I had had quite a job of disentangling the body from the tree and transferring her into my craft, as Barhoeven intermittently wept and called directions from the ground. The inspector had been sent here by the Government of Earth nearly fifteen years ago, as an adviser to our nascent police force. He fell in love with a local being—a brave thing to do, at that time—and together they adopted an orphan larva, who entered the Special Learning Academy just this year: a new kind of family, two parents of different species, both of whom live past mating. But Barhoeven's female died of sugar fungus two years ago, leaving him increasingly strange, unpredictably emotional.

Through the mud ceiling of my workshop, I heard my child clattering out of her room. How good that she had woken before first noon. I rely on her help very much; she has a gift for the work, her efficiency and craftsmanship far exceeding mine. I crawled up to the kitchen to greet her. She was beginning to take her breakfast. From the glowing sheen of her face, I could see that she had slept—this relieved me. Last night, I'd been woken by her agitated footsteps clomping about at strange hours. She has only recently begun to manifest as female, and the change seems to have disrupted her sleep and darkened her moods.

"You are just in time, Nippima. We have a job today."

Nippima bent down to sip nectar straight from the pot I had cooked and left on the hot plate; then she imbibed from a bowl of aphid porridge that I had masticated for her and placed in a covered dish on the floor. She ate so quickly and thoughtlessly that I wondered: Does she realize that someone has prepared her breakfast and kept it specially; that someone has thought of her, that someone is always thinking of her?

She looked up at me. "Ka, I don't have time to help you."

"Why? You have big plans for the day?"

Now she twitched her feelers indifferently—an irritating gesture.

"Speak up."

"I'm going to the river," she mumbled over her porridge. Her abdomen full, she shoved the dirty dishes into the corner, stood upright, and walked toward the portal.

Nippima is a beautiful, fine-featured female, considerably taller than I am; her segmented abdomen swirls with the rich reds, oranges, and aquamarines of youth. Her wings are taut, iridescent, and her features remind me so much of my mate's: her dark, straight proboscis, perfectly round eyes, and long feelers. Moreover, Nippima is a true artisan—unlike myself, whose clumsy feelers would have been better suited to a hundred professions less exacting than the one I was born into. But perhaps all this is parental pride speaking.

At the portal, she condescended at last to look at me, giving me just a hint of her beguiling smile. "I've got clients," she said.

Of late, Nippima has begun to neglect her calling, taking it into her head to attempt a side business of her own, serving as a tour guide for the Earthlings. She hangs about the riverside resorts and cafés until she finds some gullible youth who will allow himself to be tied to her abdomen. Then she flies out over the river, into the jungle, down the vast purple gorge, until she and her passenger are both quite breathless. These "clients" pay Nippima with scraps of foil; they buy her a cheap meal and some nectar back at the resort. She talks about all this very seriously, as if she were the planet's great business tycoon, burrowing away large piles of foil for future investments. But I see that it is all a pretext for consorting with males. I suspect

Nippima already has some particular friend she hasn't told me about—isn't it inevitable? Yet no prospect worries me more profoundly.

"I would appreciate your assistance today, Nippima. Poor Eth died this morning, struck by a craft. Do you recall: her son Orlip was behind you in academy?"

She paused near the portal, remembering.

"Orlip always used to admire you. You tutored him in English and he invited you to his molting ceremony, but you didn't attend. You remember, right?"

She flipped one of her feelers up to indicate, *Yes. Of course, yes.*

"You might also recall, then, that the poor boy's mother was enormous. My back has been giving me trouble, and you are much stronger than I am. Not to mention that the corpse is terrifically mangled; your skills may be required."

She seemed to shudder and looked away from me, feelers folded, eyes vibrating with disgust. Then she picked up her strapped sunglasses from the floor and slid them into the pocket of her absurd, Earth-style miniskirt, cut wide for her bottom six legs. She was wearing colored anklets above her feet; her right feeler was constricted by a tight, ornamental ring.

"Sorry, Ka. I said I can't."

"Of course you can. What are you going to do, wasting your time at the resorts?"

She shrugged her feelers again and began walking away.

"You lazy being. Stay!" I wrapped my feeler around one of her legs, my frustration getting the better of me, but she easily pulled free of my grip.

"Jesus, Ka!"

Jesus?

Then she stepped out of the portal, kicking it closed behind her with a snap. I heard her wings flapping as she floated off into the green.

· · ·

I have taken a long time to learn to be a parent to Nippima, and I fear that she has not had the easiest time under my care. When she was young I spoiled her, and now I struggle to find the balance between softness and sternness. We beings don't like to differentiate between male and female parents, yet I sometimes wish for Nippima that my mate had lived, for she might have understood our child in ways that are foreclosed to me. But fate has taken its own route, and we must do our best with what we are given.

Late that afternoon, Eth's child Orlip called on me to discuss arrangements. After squeezing his huge body through my portal, he clasped my feelers and awkwardly bowed.

I have found that some family members treat me with exaggerated respect in times of grief, as if I were a healer or a priest— and perhaps in a manner I am a little of both. I am in any case intimate witness to their last act of care for the loved one, and so they may feel compelled to convince me of their sorrow and rectitude.

"I am so sorry, Orlip. It was an unfortunate accident."

Orlip unburdened his body to the floor and nodded abjectly, his proboscis dripping saline. I outlined to him his options for the arrangements. When he asked me, I explained the costs. When he heard the figures, he didn't flinch or question me, but instead simply seemed to stop breathing for a moment, his feelers drooping to the ground.

"I know it seems a lot, Orlip. But unfortunately, in this case a great deal of work will be required if the display is to be a dignified one." Orlip dabbed his saline from the floor with a feeler, then twined the feeler snugly around the end of his proboscis to stem the flow—a child's gesture in a grown being's body. I saw in his anxious countenance that he would like to pay, but was frightened of the expense.

Orlip works at the Heavenly Paradise, as his parent had. He, too, is a janitor there. It is hard work; I wonder if this is what Eth had hoped for her children when she brought them all those years ago from the jungle's interior, as my parent once did. In the interior, life also would have been hard, but Orlip at least would have had elders nearby. They would have advised him in such tasks as arranging this funeral, calling on a preparer like myself only for the final touches. Those days are far in the past, for better or for worse, and Orlip is on his own, with only siblings to help him.

After we finished our discussion, I guided the youth to the portal and unsnapped it. As he made his way out and lofted his broad body into the air, I saw Nippima's tall form approaching just below the canopy, returning from her day's activities. The two young beings stopped in midair and hovered near to each other. I could not hear the words that passed between them, these childhood friends grown distant. Nippima has long stopped spending time with her classmates from academy, hardworking, sincere beings like Orlip. She is a willful creature, nothing like I was at her age. These days, Earthlings are the ones who seem to catch her eye.

After a brief moment, Orlip flapped slowly away, naked to the world. And Nippima, my child, alighted near the portal, shaking the dust and pollen from her wings.

"Did you offer your condolences to poor Orlip?" I asked.

She looked at me with a hard glitter in her eyes—to indicate how stupidly condescending my question was? Or to show how little she thought of condolences, how poorly she rated the gravity of a young being's losing a parent?

My suspicions regarding Nippima were confirmed, indeed, the very next day. I had flown my craft into town to transact for ice. More and more, I rely on my craft for such small errands. My wings are not what they used to be, or perhaps I have simply grown lazy in late middle age, unwilling to endure the heat of the suns.

When I first moved here, the commercial center consisted of just a few treetop stalls along the river bend, but the Earthlings relocated these businesses to a cleared area along an inlet, now congested with translucent pods in which are hawked every variety of goods. The pods are thronged with Earthlings during high tourist season. The riverbank, in turn, has been reserved for a growing number of resorts, some dug into the soil in grand imitation of our own burrows, others rising up in undulating waves of latticework steel. Meanwhile, farther downstream, away from this picturesque bend in the river, the Earthlings have installed their mineral extraction operations.

I hovered my craft in the parking-sky over the commercial center and descended. By the time I'd finished transacting and had loaded the ice into my craft, I was exhausted and badly in need of a nectar. Unwilling to wait until I returned home, I resigned myself to visiting an overpriced café at one of the resorts.

I settled on the Lodge Grand Royale, a relatively modest glass-and-adobe structure. Leaving my craft with the valet, I descended to the human concierge, who walked me through the main building toward the café. I stepped carefully to avoid leaving sticky footmarks on the floor's polished terra cotta. At the café, the female offered me a nice table on a balcony overlooking the river, pulling back a chair for me to sit in. A chair! I glanced about to see that the two or three other local beings were also sitting in chairs like Earthlings, so I, too, forced myself awkwardly backward into the angular wooden contraption.

From the balcony, I looked out at the wide, glassy river: the suns were at their fierce peak. Few swimmers had braved the heat, if even for a dip, and the water's edge was quiet. As I sipped my nectar, I opened a book I had brought with me—I have been making a study of the classics of human-English literature: Conrad; the Bible; Amy Tan. When I looked up from my reading, I saw walking through the café's entrance a very striking couple: a young, broad-shouldered alien male in cloth pants and shirt, sunglasses. He had not bothered with a bubble helmet or bodysuit, which could have meant he had been here long enough to have developed resistances, or merely that he possessed the eager fearlessness of the young. The local female accompanying him wore a light flowing skirt. As poorly suited as clothes are for our bodies (I myself felt a buffoon in my six-legged pants, reserved exclusively for these outings into town), looking at this tall local female, for a moment, I understood their appeal. I admired the way the white skirt set off crisply the red-orange-blue of her abdomen, the captivating flutter of the soft fabric among her several limbs, how it veiled and revealed the form of her long legs. I admired her as any aging being enjoys an image of distant youth. The young female was staring away from me; she seemed to be laughing and chatting amiably with the handsome alien, the two of them thoroughly carefree.

I wondered, when I was young, why did I not take nectar with such females? Why was I never at my ease? Why didn't I dress in a bold manner and enjoy life at expensive alien hotels? It would have been nearly unthinkable at that time, yet I regret it. Instead, I stayed dutifully in my burrow, helping my parent to prepare corpses, until I met my mate, who would be my first and only female.

It was several moments before the young being near the entrance turned three-quarters in my direction, and I realized that I was staring with longing at my own Nippima! How disconcerting for a parent, when he begins to see his child as a stranger. I observed the couple quietly for a moment, now with a parent's pride and a parent's panic, to see his beloved as she is seen by others, as just another being in the world. I was gratified to note at least that Nippima was comporting herself as a decent young being, standing her ground impressively among the Earthlings. Still, I was anxious that she should not make any mistakes. I noted her every move almost as if it were myself there, my presence in her body.

Nippima and the Earthling were waiting to be seated. Now she turned in my direction; our eyes met; her smiling, happy face went slack, her feelers unfurled to the ground, her mouth fell open in utter dismay. Allow me to say, it is *not* a nice feeling to be greeted by one's child with such a look. In any case, I raised my feeler in greeting, but she shook her head to discourage me from communicating further.

I realized that I had been mistaken: she was not charming and confident and at her ease. Instead, she was hanging on by the barest of threads, just maintaining the plausible appearance of comfortable dignity in front of the handsome Earthling. But now the human himself had also turned and detected the transaction of glances between my daughter and myself. Some whispered words passed between them, and then his own mouth fell open, widening to a grin. Meanwhile, Nippima's behavior had altered so completely; she could not meet the eyes of the boy with whom she had just now been having free conversation.

"Mr. Thoren!" called the human.

I smiled, nodded in modest acknowledgment. He took Nippima's feeler and guided her in my direction. I rose in welcome. When they drew close, I touched them both, effortfully maintaining a warm smile.

"Mr. Thoren, it's so nice to finally meet you. Nippima keeps mentioning you. I'm Alessandro Peng."

"Ah, yes," I said, pretending to recognize the name. When he removed his sunglasses, there were bright white patches of skin around his little egglike eyes, where the lenses had saved him from the intensity of the suns. "How nice to meet you."

He showed me a row of broad white teeth, edged with brown-pink mouth flesh. Just as the image of my daughter was deflated moments ago, something about this young human up close seemed suddenly distasteful to me.

I thought, Ah, the little Alessandros of our planet, with their weird eyes and doughy skin, their blunted features, full-grown but unformed as maggots, attractive in that strangely queasy-making way. The Alessandros running about in boisterous packs during the tourist season, with skin of mud and cream and ochre, beating each other's backs and guffawing in their broad accents, chasing after their balloon-breasted Jennifers and Prageethas, loudly calling to each other, stripping off their protective suits and roasting themselves like barbecued jungle-weasels along the river. Slumping drunkenly onto each other's shoulders in the taxis that buzz about our town after dark, just for them, just for all these little Alessandros. My daughter is affectionate for an Alessandro.

I had hardly opportunity to ask, "Why don't you sit?" when the boy glanced to Nippima for permission—but my poor child was staring at her feet, about to die. So Alessandro forthrightly seated himself, and Nippima followed suit. What blithe and carefree creatures these aliens are!

"Are you here on spring holiday with your friends?" I asked him.

"Oh, no. I'm here by myself, on a research fellowship. I'm earning a degree in entomology."

"How wonderful."

"Back home I did a thesis on the digestive systems of larval hunting wasps. Here, I'm developing a research project at the Higher Academy, on the chemical transmitters that supplement verbal communication among beings, and how it compares with Earth's insects."

"Earth's *insects*? I should hope the comparison works to our favor!"

"Oh definitely, yeah. In some ways. I'm looking at sort of the intersection of behavioral entomology and biochemistry and linguistics."

"My, my."

I found it a relief at least that the boy talked so much without any prompting, sparing me from having to demonstrate my awkward conversing skills. Aliens often make me nervous.

"I like to climb, though. I met Nippima on my day off, hanging out at the gorge. Right, Nip?" He grinned again, in that fearsome human way, at my nonresponsive child. "Hanging out. Ha. I was suspended from a rappelling line, and she landed on the cliff wall next to me."

The more and more he talked, I found—to my surprise—I was beginning to see something endearing in his liveliness, his easy familiarity. For all his Earthling obliviousness, there was a distinctive quality to this Alessandro, earnest and quickly delighted, some hapless charm. Perhaps my suspicion of him was just a protective burst of xenophobia. I must acknowledge that he was quite a handsome alien, taller than most, with hair of wavy copper, wearing a string of brown river beads around his ruddy neck. I felt—what I felt was surprise, and a touch of pride, that my daughter had done so well as to befriend such a cheerful, good-looking human.

"Well, how wonderful."

He reached over and held Nippima by the feeler, right in front of me—what local male would be so bold? And as I observed his five-pronged claw gripping my child's elegant limb, I began to feel something vaguely shameful—I began to feel relief. A human: Was this the creature who would finally protect Nippima when she was no longer in the shelter of my burrow, who would shower her with resources, whose nature would never cause harm to her? There was something reassuring in his boldness, in the strength of his grip. I noticed now, peeking above the cloth of his shirt was some coloring he had dabbed on his chest. He had painted his skin pink, yellow, green—I've noticed it in more than one tourist at the resorts—in imitation of our own abdomens. The server finally returned, and I requested two more nectars.

"But I've been *dying* to talk to you," said Alessandro. Oh, no. "Nippima has told me all about what you do."

I turned, surprised, to Nippima, who was staring at the table in sheerest agony. "She has?"

"Yeah, I sometimes think being a doctor—or, I mean, a healer—must be more gratifying than pure research."

I stared again at my child, who was studying the table's ceramic pot of mammal milk with increasing focus. She turned to offer me the briefest of pained glances. Oh, Nippima! I was moved beyond words with hurt, with pity for my child, so eager in life, so desperate to move beyond herself. I would do literally anything to see her advance, but naturally it distressed me deeply that she was so ashamed of our profession that she had lied about it.

But I would rather die a thousand deaths myself than hurt her. So I straightened in my chair and conceded to the humiliating lie: "It is a fascinating profession. Very gratifying."

The human's face lit up. I did not know how much more to say, for fear of contradicting something Nippima had already told him.

"What kind of patients do you treat?"

Now here was an uncomfortable silence. I would have to venture over the brink.

"Well, at the moment I am treating a middle-aged being. Suffered terribly in a craft collision. But we are using some, ah, traditional measures. And we hope to make her reasonably whole."

"Oh. Oh, I see," he responded with grave interest, struggling to make sense of my words. "That's so fascinating."

I feared that I had said something wrong, because Nippima wouldn't look at either of us. Her feelers were winding around each other with increasing constriction, and I was keen to put her out of her misery as soon as possible.

I turned to my child and rubbed her abdomen affectionately

with my feeler, only to see her flinch. "But with that, Alessandro, I am afraid I must be going. Duty calls. Enjoy your nectar." I got up abruptly, leaving a large piece of foil on the table, over the youth's protests. As I rose, at last Nippima looked up at me with an anxious smile, embarrassed, apologetic, but still grateful for my departure.

That evening, Nippima and I at first made no mention of the afternoon's awkward encounter. Together, we tidied the kitchen in a strange silence. Then my imager lit up: it was Orlip. He was weeping saline furiously. "I have no foil to pay for a display," he wailed. In a long, tortured soliloquy, he confessed to me—as if seeking my forgiveness—that he had surreptitiously squandered his parent's savings on games of chance at the resorts.

I tried to reassure him. "I am sorry about your savings, Orlip. But try not to worry about the leave-taking. Simple funerals are increasingly popular these days. They can be equally beautiful."

"How will you do it?" he begged me. "How will you conduct the leave-taking, if not a display?"

"We can cover her with a coffin."

"A what?"

"A box of calthus wood."

"A box!" Orlip howled in horror. "My ka, covered in a box."

"It is perfectly dignified." I struggled to calm him. "It is what the humans use. It is not bad at all, really. A very pleasing arrangement." I didn't dare repeat the word that had so upset him. "I could inlay a little foil at no extra charge."

After the call was over, I turned to Nippima. "Lost his parent's savings on games of chance! Can you believe it?"

"Of course I can believe it," she answered.

"Why do you say that? Do *you* play games of chance?"

She became suddenly preoccupied in assembling the dishes against the wall and did not respond.

"It is too bad. I would have liked to do a display for Eth, but the strings and the armatures and so on are so expensive. Not to mention the time involved. In any case, a coffin will be fine."

She remained silent.

"By the way," I said—now that I was talking, I decided to continue on to the subject that was sure to make us both uncomfortable. "I enjoyed the company of that Earthling. Of course, it bothered me that you lied to him about us. You ought to take pride in our work."

"Sorry, Ka."

"But he seems a good human."

She shrugged her feelers.

"I wouldn't mind if you mated with one of them."

"Ka, for crying out loud!"

"I suppose it is safer, in many ways, than with a local being," I called to her, as she scuttled off, embarrassed, into her room. What should I have said? It occurred to me once again that my mate might have been better equipped for such conversations, would have more fruitfully been able to talk with our child.

I worry so much about Nippima. Young beings like her and Orlip are adrift in this new world of ours. I feel I have done my best to guide her, but we grown beings scarcely know the way ourselves. Each month in the city passes like a year in the interior—so fast are we leaving behind our old ways. Perhaps even my own profession will soon become obsolete; we will begin stuffing our dead into ovens, compressing the ashes into vacuum-packed tubes, as so many Earthlings choose to do.

The fact that there would be no display for Eth would save me a great deal of labor, but there was still much work ahead. The next day I rode to the commercial center to transact for the wood to use on Eth's coffin. On my way home, the suns were low and warm in my face through the windows of my craft. Where the via runs flush with the river, I looked out across the flawless pink water, studded with small black figures—swimmers and air-surfers—dark, sun-sharpened silhouettes. The air was still; they floated and bobbed on the water, the suns setting behind them, clinging to their turbined contraptions. Occasionally, one of the surfers would catch a slight breeze and skim along, tickling the blushing glass of the surface.

Was my child there? At this distance, I could scarcely distinguish the aliens from the beings. Was Nippima one of the swimmers? I hoped not. In fact, I worried for all these youths in the water, their bodies rising and falling with the gradual swell, subjecting themselves to the whims of the current. Which of them were neophytes, not conditioned for the hard work of staying afloat in the deceptively thick, mineral-rich water; who would sputter and slip and need to be rescued by someone more skilled than they? Who would be pulled down by one of the suction tides, and wear themselves out by trying to swim up against it, instead of abiding the surge, and swimming transversely? I thought of the bodies who come back from drowning, blue and wave-battered, rock-bruised, saturated. The suction tides are unsparing, and so many are lost.

Nippima had a romance once—a very innocent romance—before the Earthling. This youth was a being, a poor swimmer. They were eating and drinking on the grassy portion of the riverbank late one night, virtually alone at that hour. I have always told her not to stay out late, but my advice is frequently unheeded. The male insisted on going into the water, although she warned him not to, and he disappeared beneath the surface. Nippima swam after him, going down and down for an hour, endangering herself. Finally she caught hold of him, swam him to shore. It was nearly dawn when she brought him home to me directly, having flown with him over her back, all the way down the via. I told her she should have left him at the beach, called the authorities. That poor, distraught, confused child.

I dressed the poor being myself; I did not ask my child to help me. It was a terrible thing. My poor Nippima—she has not had an easy life.

Beneath my craft, a few barefoot aliens were walking along the bottom of the via—the thrifty ones, backpackers, who economize by renting simple burrows away from the city center, by not bothering with craft. They neglect to wear protective suits, and dine on aphids and weasels to save foil. Predictably, they are frequently laid low with dysentery.

All these inexperienced, vulnerable youth living on our planet, and we must look after them. Level with my vehicle, some local beings flapped by their own wings along the trees that border the via. I passed by them one by one, their softly floating forms, until I came to see one long, familiar body: it was Nippima, on her way back to the burrow. I was so pleased to see her. She was flying slowly, by herself.

I snapped open my window and called to her, smiling. She didn't hear me, so I sounded my alert, leaned out of the window. I was upon her now; but still she did not turn to face me.

"Hey, Nippima!"

Now, finally, she looked at me. Her eyes were huge and burning orange, her proboscis pouring forth saline.

"What happened, Nippima? My child! Are you okay?"

She shook her head.

"Get in the craft." I was hovering now. A large cargo craft waited patiently behind me.

"Go away," she spat.

"Something is wrong. Get in the craft."

The cargo vehicle sounded its alert. Several more craft hovered behind it.

"Please," I pleaded. She was making me impatient, drawing a scene. But I forced myself to talk gently. Nippima is a stubborn being, but she has taught me to be the same. My advantage over her is that I am not susceptible to shame, as she is. The alerts behind us multiplied. I crept forward just enough to stay abreast of the child, until finally she turned and in a sort of fury opened the craft's portal while it was still moving, and flew inside, slamming the portal behind her.

I gazed toward her now, as I pulled forcefully on the accelerator. She was panting and heaving, her face twisted into a rage, getting saline all over the craft. Whence this anger? I had not done anything to her. She seemed to me confused and seething, somehow monstrous. There are moments when my child becomes so unfathomable; I cannot imagine a creature more alien to me.

"Is it the Earthling?" I asked. "Tell your ka what happened."

She looked at me with rage in her eyes. "I hate you," she barked. "I *hate* Earthlings!"

Her face broke into an agony of weeping. It was nearly unbearable to witness the wretchedness of her expression. How I wish I could insulate my child from the disappointments of life!

I felt I had to say something, and there were several things that burned inside me, that she did not seem to have understood: "I liked that alien well enough. I don't mean to talk badly about him. But I do not like that you felt you had to lie to him. Is anyone worth that kind of dishonor?"

She did not respond.

"Our profession is a dignified one. We have done it going back at least four generations. If these Earthlings don't like it, then—as you like to say—they can go to hell. Must we live only by their model? Must we forget the old stories, give up every last remnant of our culture? Aren't we as good as they are?" Still she said nothing; she had quieted her sobbing. To my surprise, she seemed to be listening. And finally she spoke.

"You don't get it," she said. "I told him the truth. I told him what we really do. And guess what? He wasn't disturbed at all. Oh, no. It was exactly as I feared: he was *fascinated*. He wanted me to tell him every detail—if I'd been willing. He thinks we're freaks, Ka. He only spent time with me because he wanted to study me."

I looked down at her, noticing then that her feelers were spotted with dirt and dried blood.

"What happened?" I reached toward her.

She pulled her feelers back, braiding them tightly, and tucked them to her side. "I just got scratched up on the cliffs."

Then she turned away, to hide from me the distress in her face. I spoke: "I wish I could take your pain away from you, absorb it into my own body. I suppose it is no comfort for you to consider that this is often the way with young love; it is not meant to last."

"What would you know about it?" she whispered.

"I have lived longer than you."

She responded just as softly: "I wish I had a mother."

My child—she has a tender way of gutting me. Slumping low in the craft, she let her gaze wander out over the recently cleared jungle, the rows and rows of hastily dug burrows. "She would know what I should do. I wish she was here, Ka. I wish that you had never killed her."

An alien concept, "mother." Beings are raised by only one parent, a ka, whether male or female. Nippima's mother and I met when our families first moved to the city from the interior. We were nearly children ourselves, having just reached manifestation. Her parent and mine had dug burrows near to each other, close to where I live today, when this area was still dense with vegetation, considered the farthest outskirts. This was well with me, as I preferred to live in uncleared jungle; the idea of the city still terrified me.

The two of us would fly together collecting fiber, wood, and leaves for our families. We filled gunnysacks with aphids and weevils; we worked in concert to flush out and capture rodents.

She was a wise, imperturbable being. While I still missed my native place in the interior, she seemed curious about new things. She could understand and assimilate change with equanimity. My love and I were together the first time we saw an Earthling. The human had come near to our burrows to register our names on behalf of the Interim Authority. My reaction had been one of instantaneous panic: I flew into the air, beating my wings as loudly as I could and arching my abdomen to intimidate the alien. I was a fool. Meanwhile, my mate calmly let the female Earthling approach; she sniffed the human, appraised her with the end of one feeler, and then looked up at me with a reassuring smile.

A beautiful presence. Her parent and siblings disliked me because of my family's profession, which they considered unclean. But their superstitious attitude only bespoke their own backwardness, for they were common laborers. The main concern of both families, however, was that we were too young—they did not trust us to delay consummation. This was a matter of great anxiety for my ka. She worked herself into fountains of saline every time I left the burrow. "It is nothing against the being," my parent insisted to me. "I like her. I love you both too much. But please listen to someone with experience in life. You are young. Enjoy yourself for some more time."

We should not have needed our parents to tell us; we were old enough to know. Yet at that age, a being believes one's own love is unique, that it can overcome all of nature, and the normal rules don't apply. In any case, we were held back by my own nervousness, my dull and dutiful nature. How many times, in retrospect do I see, I missed very obvious hints and flirtations. Although the same age, she was more sophisticated than I was. And so we did wait; nothing happened for more than a year. Until finally, one long summer twilight, at the end of a day spent exploring the edges of the gorge, the attraction became overwhelming. We had spent our afternoon among boughs of red flowers, staring down at the breathtaking purple abyss. On our journey home, we found some excuse to stop in the jungle, sit and rest for a time. She leaned against me, raised her eyes to mine, slanted her face into my neck. I savored the warm felt of her face and proboscis, her feelers encompassing my head. We breathed each other's air, felt each other's bodies, slowly becoming more sure of ourselves, our desire gradually growing urgent, until it began to feel as if any price would be worth it. There was no discussion—as one, we rose up.

I remember the clacking partition of her legs, the give of her abdomen, as I pressed myself upon her, arching into her. The fall and surge, each unbearably pleasurable movement inside of her, and then a moment suspended: the delicate interval poised between touch and release, the pressure just so. The final scream from her mouth and mine, gut-rending, sublime agony. I withdrew, pulled my abdomen away, clacked my rear legs backward, but kept my face pressed to the flushed felt of her own, her feelers still entwined about my head. We wanted to treasure the last few tender moments, beginning to fear—but not yet understanding—what was to follow.

We burrowed into each other's neck, rubbing our cheeks together, purring softly for a moment. But then she unwound her feelers from my head and pushed me away. Her abdomen writhed and pinched; she arched her back and tucked her lower abdomen down to the ground, groaning and wincing, her stomach rippling and undulating, twisted with pain; until finally the fertilized egg slipped out and fell softly to the dirt. We both looked at it: one egg, no more—a small, inexplicable feeling of disappointment. We scuttled toward it, her legs still unsteady from the birth. Together we smelled it, walked around it, examined it from every angle. Already, my emotions were transforming, the urgency of my desire for her draining into a peaceful emptiness; that emptiness gradually shaping itself into lack, into aching concern for the descending egg. Now the egg was present, our egg, our child, and that feeling intensified again into an even fiercer love—I would call it a madness—for that slime-covered soft white oblong.

Soon it would be hungry. These next few minutes were crucial to its survival—we immediately knew it. My mate walked protectively in front of the egg, stepping her feelers up. I did not like to have my vision of the child blocked; it caused me panic. I tried to walk around her, but she edged me away. I raised my feelers to move her, and that is when the fight began.

We each spread our wings wide and pushed against each other, our feelers entwined, grappling. We were conscious still of avoiding harm to the egg, and scuttled mutually away from it. Once we were in the clear, she flapped her shoulder into me and knocked me flat. She used her legs to stay down my feelers and legs, freeing her own feelers to wrap themselves around my neck.

She stared into my eyes then, her face the very emblem of fury and regret. I scarcely recognized her. I could not believe the suddenness of our transformation, our powerlessness in the face of it. In her expression, I saw reflected my own sad shock; it was all unfolding exactly as my parent had warned me, exactly as it had happened for every being before us to the beginning of time. We were no different. Moreover, we had no desire to be different, because it was now entirely clear that this was the only course, the best hope for the survival of our child. Still, we attempted to draw some last drop of affection from each other's eyes; it was of little use. The instinct to fight was too strong. I could not think or care about who would be winner or loser of this fight; I wanted only to fight, to save our egg and draw to a close this drama initiated by our own impatient love. I tried to push her off me, but she was too large. I resisted with all my force. She bent open her mouth and lowered it to me, but I thrashed and squirmed, avoiding her. Then she looked up into the trees and arched herself beautifully backward, pulling her feelers so unbearably taut around my neck that they began to tear into the felt. My proboscis stretched up, retching in vain for any particle of air. My mouth widened into a soundless scream.

As my body began to shudder, the muscles of each of my legs jerked up against her unbearable resistance. Then two of them found leverage in the dirt, just enough to tilt my body to the side. I had the angle now. I lurched my head toward her, with incredible effort raised my neck up, until my lips were flush against the side of her warm head. She pushed and thrashed in surprise, pulling her neck away, but she was too late. I had worked my incisors into the soft spot behind her ear, and released the paralyzing toxin, a single dose from our lifetime's allotment.

I waited with desperate hope until her legs one by one slacked and buckled, and I was able to free my feelers and unwind hers from my neck. I pushed her off and sat heaving by myself, recovering my breath, probing the wound on my neck. But I gave myself only the briefest moment to recover, then turned again toward my mate. She had fallen onto her back, her legs bent into the air, her proboscis lifting and falling slightly with each breath. I sniffed her and touched her to make sure she was paralyzed. I did not look into her eyes; it would have been too painful, and at this point, a sentimental indulgence that might have weakened my resolve for what I quickly had to do. I focused on her beautiful, bright abdomen. With my incisors, I began biting away a spot of hard flesh until I reached the pulpy underbelly beneath. My jaws would never again know this strength, would never again experience this taste—or at least lack of revulsion—for the flesh of another being.

Finished, I turned urgently to our child. To my enormous relief, it was still alive, the eyes and striations already appearing in the fast-growing egg. I gently wrapped my feelers around it to lift it. Its round, just-opened maw was expanding and contracting, chewing the air, pulsing with hunger. I held her so she could not bite me, and walked her carefully over, placing the babe in the small hole I had dug out of my love's abdomen, where immediately it began to eat.

My mate would draw breath for another three weeks; by that time, my child would have eaten her way deep into the soft tissue, growing large and strong on that warm, living sustenance—flesh which in a dead being would have rotted by that time. Finally, it was Nippima—not I—who killed her mother. Because of what the Earthlings now tell us, I can infer that my mate would have felt unimaginable pain before breathing her last, that the toxin affected her motor centers but not her senses. But even if this is true, I know she would have been willing to bear that cost for our child, because I know that I also would have been.

As Nippima began her long first meal, I commenced digging into the jungle floor around them, creating a burrow for them to sink into. This burrow would become, after numerous enlargements and clearings, the same burrow where we now live. Nippima has been raised here from a larva.

There was no leave-taking ceremony for my mate, because finally there was very little body. We mourn for the dead who live past it, but for those who die in mating, there is no funeral. Their ending is more tragic but more noble; no ceremony could add to it. But when Nippima pupated, my mate's family would enjoy pride of place in the celebration; their daughter's praises would be sung. Perhaps it was small comfort to them, but all could see that in our child, my mate lived again.

For so many years, the Earthlings were preoccupied with the "brutality" of our mating—some of us began to believe it. They insisted that what we regard as natural is only a choice. That there was another way—the way the humans do it. But our way has nothing to do with brutality. It is the furthest thing from murder. I see clearly that it is for the propagation of our species. Life feeds other life: it is equal with the act of love, another facet of love.

But in recent years, the Earthlings seem to have understood. They scarcely mention it anymore, or if they do, they excuse it as "instinct." They have forsaken their prudish sanctimony—or perhaps it is only their desire to do business here. They may have noticed that, outside of mating, our incidence of violence and murder is actually somewhat lower than that of purely human societies. And as more and more Earthlings have themselves mated with locals, they have learned that although the mechanics of love may be roughly the same, the need and impulse for the drama that follows never arises, because no eggs are formed.

But I've always wondered if Barhoeven's mate, Sroot, had ever had the urge, while Barhoeven was sleeping, to sink her teeth beneath the base of his skull, to chew a small home in the flat of his stomach and press her larva inside. Without this, did their love feel properly consummated? They raised their adopted child in an incubator on protein mush for its first month—could this be the reason the poor being must now attend the Special Learning Academy? That strange couple—did they do right by each other in the end? Did I do right by my own family? Perhaps we all take too much for granted, human and being alike, going along too thoughtlessly with what has happened before.

For two days after I found her on the via, Nippima was very subdued. She did not visit the resorts as usual, but spent much of her time sulking in her room, escaping only in the evenings for some hours of flight. On the third day, Inspector Barhoeven knocked at my portal. I touched him and invited him inside.

"What can I do for you, Barhoeven? Has there finally been progress in finding the driver of the craft that hit Eth? Would you like to reexamine her body?"

"That case has been closed," replied Barhoeven, his tan, wrinkled face blushing red. "I wondered, actually, if I might talk to Nippima."

"But she is still asleep. What is it regarding?"

He began pacing about the burrow, examining the dirt walls—unfortunately, I have no chairs at hand for human callers. He said: "It seems a visiting student went missing from the Higher Academy three days ago."

"But what should Nippima know about that?"

He parsed his words carefully. "Apparently she took him for a flight a number of times. I just wanted to ask if she knew anything."

"She takes many people for flights, Barhoeven. They are her clients."

Of course, I feared I knew to whom he was referring—there are not very many visiting students, and my Nippima knows fewer. I thought of her unpleasant state three days ago, the dried blood from climbing, when I discovered her along the via. It was an unhappy coincidence. The bug of anxiety entered my abdomen. Immediately, my parental instincts told me that Barhoeven had better not know about it, at least not until I had talked it over with Nippima.

"She's still asleep, I'm afraid."

He finally ceased meandering about the burrow and stood in front of me. "Thoren, I wouldn't bother you if I didn't have to. Probably he just went camping in the gorge and didn't tell his roommates, but he was here on a Government of Earth scholarship. His parents said he usually calls twice a day. A lot of people are already breathing down my neck about it."

But Nippima was just a child, no less vulnerable than the missing human, and I must protect her.

"I'm so sorry, Barhoeven. Please come back another time."

Now I saw Barhoeven's pearly eyes flicker with frustration. He could have chosen to be more forceful with me, could have threatened to invoke the compulsion of law. But he considered my unperturbed face and decided not to press forward at the present moment.

Instead he changed direction.

"Why don't *you* talk to me, then, Thoren? I understand the three of you enjoyed a meal together at the Grand Royale?"

Now *my* feelers were the ones to twitch—it is disconcerting to realize the extent to which one is observed in the course of a seemingly private day—but I quickly regained my composure.

"*That* boy is the one who went missing? Oh, dear. But it was just a nectar, not a whole meal," I said, for I did not see any purpose in denying it. Barhoeven had begun walking again, and was bending now toward the entrance to my basement, inhaling the air from there. "A perfectly civil cup of nectar. It was nothing dastardly. Do you think I am keeping him bound in my workshop, Barhoeven?"

Inspector Barhoeven turned to face me and started to laugh, and so I laughed, too. For a long moment, we stood there laughing.

I found it hard to appraise Barhoeven's mood. He had become emotionally unsteady since the death of his mate, whose body Nippima herself prepared for funeral. That is a trauma we local beings are thankfully spared—to lose a mate after many years of matrimony. I believe Nippima did a good job for Barhoeven, that he was comforted by the ceremony. Her craftsmanship was beyond surpass: she smoothed away Sroot's fungal scars, filled up and painted the abdomen in vibrant, youthful hues, made a garland of the organs. And yet one is always concerned about aliens. Will they understand our rituals? Will they find them grotesque? Will they feel included? Sroot was Barhoeven's mate, after all, and he could have chosen to conduct the leave-taking in Earthling style. But he has shown little interest in clinging to the ways of his home planet. I asked him at the funeral—because I had always wondered—"Barhoeven, do you miss Earth?" He answered: "I have nobody there anymore." But here he stood having lost his closest local relation. Who was left for him here? He had not convinced me that his journey had been worthwhile.

At any rate, I described to Barhoeven my meeting with the Earthling; he explained to me the circumstances under which the boy had gone missing; and then he left, promising to come back for a visit with Nippima.

When my child finally emerged from her room, I confronted her. "What exactly happened between you and the Earthling?" She stood at the edge of the kitchen, abjectly dabbing at the porridge I had cooked for her. "Inspector Barhoeven came here. He said the boy has gone missing."

Her mouth opened, and she let out a short moan.

"Do you know anything about it? Have you been in touch? They are searching all over. They may start scanning the riverbed. The Earthlings have even requested permission to send a vehicle to the bottom of the gorge. Do you know anything that could help them to find him?"

"I don't know anything, Ka," she told me—to my enormous relief. Of course, I did not suspect her of anything; but one does not want to become even peripherally entangled in such situations involving Earthlings. "We decided not to see each other, and that's the last I spoke to him."

Having eaten a bit of the porridge, she was sliding her sunglasses into her pocket again. She was in a hurry to leave. "Where are you going now?" I asked.

"Out."

"Out?"

And with that, she opened the portal.

A child does not tell a parent everything. It has never happened and it never will. And even if they were to tell us, would we understand what they had to say? Nippima is a being of uncommon intelligence and talent, beyond even my ability to comprehend. That much is clear. I sometimes feel that I myself had only the slightest involvement in the process. I impregnated my mate and out came a small white egg, who grew into this remarkable creature. I created something bound to exceed me—I have known her from birth, yet I have no idea of what she is capable—and something bound to frustrate me, for no other being can cause me so much worry and pain.

I thought, All that has happened is that a youth has gone missing. Either he would return, or he would be transformed—those were the options, as I saw them. It has never been different. We can only try to take good care of them, help them become wise and strong enough to understand their world—or what lies beyond their world, as the case may be.

"They have retrieved his wallet, his clothes," I called to Nippima. "Several humans have told the Inspector they'd seen you together."

I don't know if she heard me. She rose into the trees, her purple iridescence flickering softly against the dark calthus leaves of the jungle, disappearing.

The next day would be Eth's leave-taking, and so I had work to do. I descended to my workshop. It was very cool there, but I had placed the body on ice for good measure. It was therefore still well preserved. I had cleaned Eth and minimally composed her, but she was sadly the same mangled corpse that was found at the side of the via five days ago.

It took me most of the afternoon to assemble the coffin. I left off the lid and postponed transferring the body inside until I could ask Nippima's assistance, later in the day or the next morning.

But Nippima did not come home that afternoon. I sat in the kitchen, reading and waiting for her. At some point in the evening, I fell asleep on the floor of the kitchen. In the earliest predawn, I suddenly woke to the sound of some being clattering about downstairs in my workshop. It must have been Nippima. What could she be doing down there on her own? It was most curious. I listened through the floor for some time, wondering if I should go to check on her. But I was nervous to intrude, and decided finally not to disturb her, to go to my room and take a few hours' sleep.

I woke the next morning, the morning of Eth's leave-taking, to silence. Crawling down to my workshop to complete my preparations, I cautiously peered inside. Nippima was not there. I was surprised to see that Eth's body was not there either, but that the coffin was completely built, its cover closed.

How strange. It was a lot of work for Nippima to have done by herself. I approached the box, ran my feeler along the joints and seams; it was beautifully constructed. I pried my feeler beneath the edge; I supposed I could open it and see inside, appraise the condition of Eth's body, how Nippima had managed to place her. But may I confess a foolish thing? I felt frightened to look. Possibly because of my poor sleep, some strange thoughts passed through my head.

I decided to wait for Nippima to wake and come out from her room. I ascended to the kitchen to find that Orlip and his two siblings had already arrived and were waiting patiently outside my burrow. I invited them inside. Now there was no more time—the ceremony should soon begin. I went to the portal of Nippima's room; from inside, I heard the sounds of her hoarse slumber. But I could not wait for her to wake and prepare herself. I asked Orlip and his siblings to help me load the coffin into the craft.

It was enormously heavy; I had not recalled Eth being so massive. But we managed to move it, sliding it snugly into the back of my hearse. And together we drove off, the four of us, toward the gorge's edge.

I am not a religious being. The last time I visited a temple was when my parent still lived. I don't know what happens after a person dies; I suppose I don't really care. But I know the body. The body does everything wisely: growth, healing from injury. Even decay is a sort of intelligence. Even disease; even death.

Die that you may live: I believe that Jesus taught this. When we look at a corpse, we see all that the person was; but there is no person anymore. It is a mystery inside of a fact. We see what it was: an elaborate and subtle mechanism; something entirely contingent and slight, part of some wider logic which it can no longer even glimpse; a manifestation and a dupe of nature. We see nothing.

Bodies do not disappear; they are only transformed. I was here in this city when a being was known to beat his children, to beat them mercilessly. Why does a creature do that to those whom he loves most? I abhor violence. I have tried to teach this to Nippima. And one of those poor children bought a concentrated gun from the Earthlings and shot his parent dead. How can a child gather the will to do that to the being who gave him life? And then that child turned the weapon on his sibling, and then on himself. When it was all done, they brought the bodies to me. Did I understand better what had happened; did those bodies explain a thing to me? The living beings had been unhappy, confused, hurt, rageful, entirely unfulfilled. These silent bodies were content. They were complete. That is what I understood.

I thought of my own mate's body, at the end of three weeks: a crumbling hull of abdomen, a rustle of cartilage beneath loose felt, a sightless face. Parts of her must still be there, beneath the floor of our burrow. Perhaps there are other ways of living; perhaps there is love without such pain—the humans would like to teach us this. Or perhaps we should accept the strange wisdom of the body.

We arrived at the lip of the gorge; I hovered my craft the merest inch above a grassy clearing. I saw that Orlip had grown emotional during the ride here, and as we slid out the coffin, his feelers were shaking. We set the box on the grass, and the poor child shook his head and beat one of his feelers upon the wood. He was most upset.

"I want to see her," he said. "Uncover her."

"Orlip, that would not be a very good idea."

It appeared a group of humans had wandered out from the whispering trees a few yards from where we stood. They wore bubble helmets and bright orange bodysuits. They held a basket with bottles of vine rum, and a blanket. They saw us; they saw the casket. They were terribly intrigued. They settled down in the grass and pretended not to watch us.

Now Orlip was prying up the lid of the coffin with his strong feelers. I was horrified.

"It was a bad accident, Orlip. It would not be well for you to see her."

But he ignored me. I tried to physically restrain him—his siblings staring in dismay—but Orlip was too strong. I looked at his twisted face: he had none of his parent's orderliness, her finesse. Children are monsters, strange versions of ourselves, and we love them as fiercely as they grieve us with fear. The plank finally broke open with a resounding snap. And we both stared inside:

Eth had been restored. The hole in her torso was no longer there. Her abdomen was full, enormous as it had been in life, more so. And brighter, all its faded color returned. Her proboscis was as if healed, her face clean and beautiful, covered with thick felt, the glorious round golden eyes open, staring at us, each cell individually lacquered as if lit from within. All her teeth were somehow intact, and she was smiling enigmatically—a trick of imperceptible threads.

In her left feeler, she grasped her own blue heart. In her right feeler, she held the necklace of her intestine: a body that had triumphed over the body, a being beyond fear and death. Nippima had done this, using her own resources.

Orlip looked at me, his mouth hanging open.

"Thank you. You gave her a display."

We are just a small planet, and we must all look out for one another, beings and aliens, parents and children, and the children for the parents no less.

"So it appears, Orlip."

We agreed now to do away with the excess of the coffin, and even of the craft. We slid her out onto the grass, and conducted the simplest of ceremonies. Orlip poured a drop of nectar into his parent's mouth, and I sang a brief elegy, something generic in the old tongue, which Orlip and his siblings perhaps didn't even understand. Looking at their rapt, youthful faces, I considered that while change is inevitable, the old ways still have some logic, and we do well to pass them on, in some degree, to our children. It gratified me that Nippima seemed to have understood this. And then the four of us put our shoulders into her and hoisted her up. Her weight was incredible; thank goodness Orlip and his siblings were nearly as big as Eth was. We flapped as hard as we were able, until we took flight.

Think of life as a story. Each one must come to an end, for it to have form and meaning. What gives life to the stories are the bodies at the end of them.

Together, we lurched out over the wide purple gash, farther than we should have dared, and let her drop. Our bodies flew up with the loss of that weight, and we stayed there hovering. I thought of Nippima, in her room, sleeping. Let her enjoy her sleep. She had done fine work, for Eth looked content as she floated softly toward the flowering vines and thickets of the purple valley below.

ACKNOWLEDGMENTS

I am deeply grateful to Jake Donham, Beth Ford, and Carrie Messenger, unstinting friends and brilliant readers who have improved all my stories; to Nicole Aragi, my agent, for always holding a true compass; and to Robin Desser, living proof that real editors exist. Heartfelt thanks also to Jordan Bass, Dev Benegal, Chitra Banerjee Divakaruni, Christie Hauser, Michele Kong, Jennifer Kurdyla, Nitin Mukul, Meera Nair, Krupa Parikh, James Pate, Sarah Rothbard, Arun Venugopal, Anita Wadhwa, and others who have supported this book; as well as to the MacDowell Colony, the Ucross Foundation, the Corporation of Yaddo, and the Stadler Center for Poetry at Bucknell University.

This collection is dedicated with love to my first authors, Lakshmy Parameswaran and P. G. Parameswaran, whose imagination and faith have been my good fortune; and to my brother, Ashok of the gracious heart.